THE VIOLIN AND CANDLESTICK

THE VIOLIN AND CANDLESTICK

MIKE KINGDOM THRILLERS
BOOK 3

DAVID JARVIS

This edition produced in Great Britain in 2024

by Hobeck Books Limited, Unit 14, Sugnall Business Centre, Sugnall, Stafford, Staffordshire, ST21 6NF

www.hobeck.net

A CIP catalogue for this book is available from the British Library.

ISBN 978-1-915-817-58-7 (pbk)

ISBN 978-1-915-817-57-0 (ebook)

Cover design by Jem Butcher

www.jembutcherdesign.co.uk

Printed and bound in Great Britain by Clays Ltd, Elcograf S.p.A.

ARE YOU A THRILLER SEEKER?

Hobeck Books is an independent publisher of crime, thrillers and suspense fiction and we have one aim – to bring you the books you want to read.

For more details about our books, our authors and our plans, plus the chance to download free novellas, sign up for our newsletter at **www.hobeck.net**.

You can also find us on Twitter/X **@hobeckbooks** or on Facebook **www.facebook.com/hobeckbooks10**.

CHAPTER ONE

Leonard de Vries fell out of the taxi onto the gravel of the pub car park.

This was all the more embarrassing as he was arriving for lunch, not leaving. Fortunately for him, he suffered no real injury apart from a slight graze to his nose. In fact, the act of standing up posed a greater problem, and he arrived at the door of The Greedy Pelican out of breath and licking the blood from his podgy finger, which he had been using to test his face for any damage. The taxi driver pulled over to a shady corner under some trees to eat. He was thinking that, if some punter wanted to pay him to sit and wait while he ate his sandwiches, he was more than happy to comply.

The only other person who saw this dramatic entrance was Leonard's ex-employee, Michaela Kingdom, who was sitting inside and looking out through a grubby window. Mike, as she was known, was almost embarrassed at the pleasure she was deriving from watching the short, overweight man attempt a forward roll across the gravel. She had never forgotten him telling her that he had the mind of an athlete.

"No chauffeur to open your door today?" she asked as he

approached her table; the pub was virtually empty at midday on a Tuesday.

"No, this is unofficial. That's why I chose here," he replied, explaining why he had come in a taxi from Chiswick to some godforsaken eatery near the reservoirs under the flight path to London Heathrow. He seemed disorientated and, after looking around, said, "I thought that this was just called The Pelican?"

"You mean you've been here before and still decided to come back?"

"It's handy, and they used to do big rib-eye steaks, if I remember correctly."

"Well, it was The Pelican, but now it's part of a chain and has been rebranded. I had to google it. If you're interested, that carved beam up there is from HMS *Pelican*, one of Drake's ships that went around the world in 1577. I'm guessing that any other link to Sir Francis is pretty much lost. It now does 'a mixture of Indian and Chinese', or 'fusion' as they call it. It's basically anything with rice. It's ironic that Drake brought the humble potato to England from Virginia. I hope you aren't hungry?"

Immediately, she regretted saying this as his face displayed just how hungry he was; this being nothing new. He wore his dark-green tie loose at the collar, in the style of Sir Les Patterson, more because the knot had tightened to a small lump over the years from his greasy fingers trying to adjust it.

"Sir Francis must be spinning in his grave," he said.

"He was buried at sea."

When she'd arrived, Mike had no idea if Leonard had actually booked, so she asked the manager to turn around the reservations diary so she could read the names. There she spotted Sir Donald Reeve. "That's him," she said as the manager, who had been born locally in Poyle, gave her an old-fashioned look. Mike was getting accustomed to Leonard using anagrams of his name specifically to irritate her and to test her decoding skills. Continuing professional development, he called it. She had another phrase in mind.

Carlos, the manager – and indeed people within a radius of several miles – would never have guessed that Leonard, under any of his aliases, was actually the CIA director in London and head of Five Eyes, an intelligence-sharing mechanism between the USA, Canada, UK, Australia and New Zealand that was based in Chiswick. Any subterfuge was really unnecessary: nobody even vaguely took a bit of notice.

Mike and Leonard agreed that, before getting down to business, they would order food and drinks. This didn't take long.

"Right, let's lay down some rules. You aren't going to ask me to do any fieldwork, are you?" Mike asked after twenty minutes of small talk. The previous three times he had sent her into the field, it hadn't gone well. This shouldn't have been surprising as she had been a CIA analyst and not trained to leave the office.

"No, I swear on my mother's grave. This is desk-based analysis." His soft Alabaman accent made this sound almost believable, although his mother – who was just having breakfast in the suburbs of Montgomery, the state capital – may have had something to say about that.

Mike was wearing her jet-black Cleopatra wig and motorcycle leathers. She looked at him with her very-dark-brown eyes, but she said nothing.

"What?" he asked, holding out his arms, his palms upwards. "I really need a freelancer for a small task. It will suit you down to the ground. I can't use my team. You'll understand why when I explain."

She stretched out her damaged left leg under the table, unfolded a napkin and placed it on her lap. "The second I think it might lead to fieldwork, I'm right out of here."

"I get that." He was at his most appeasing. "I know you're

an analyst, which is why I've lined up an operative you can call on if it ever becomes necessary – which it won't," he added quickly. "We call him Crip."

"Leonard!" She put her head in her hands. "Leonard, you're so un-PC. You cannot call someone that." She contemplated this for a few seconds, then said, "He doesn't actually sound that suited to fieldwork. I mean, really?"

"It's short for Crippen. Chris Crippen. He worked for me, like you. He's now a freelancer, like you," he emphasised. "We'll make a great team."

"Oh, sorry." Mike was so used to Leonard having a casual disregard for rules, manners, political correctness and just about everything that she had jumped to her own conclusion.

The waiter turned up with a basket of bread and some butter. Leonard picked up a roll with a crust so hard and thin that it shattered into pieces across the table as he tried to break it. He brushed his palms against each other and took a folded piece of card from his jacket pocket. On it was a series of telephone numbers, codes, names and addresses. He handed it to her and explained some of them before getting down to the real reason for the lunch.

"You know that the coordinating role in Five Eyes rotates every two years. You may not have realised that my term has just ended, and now it's the turn of Barbara Aumonier from Canada. I can't stand the woman, but that's probably not important; she doesn't like me either. It is important, however, because the USA thinks someone in one of the five agencies has been compromised and is selling the family silver. Finding this person is going to be difficult because we're searching among friends. The team in the Counterintelligence Department at Langley is checking as discreetly as possible, but they have to be careful not to leave a trail. Heck, let's be straight: they're just pussyfooting around." He stopped as the waiter approached with a large, well-done steak, some rice and a jug of an odd-smelling Asian sauce. Leonard waited until Carlos had served Mike her plaice with capers and retreated out of earshot.

His plate was very hot, and the steak was almost stuck to it. "So, this is what they mean by fusion, is it?" he said before tucking into the meat with a wooden-handled steak knife.

"How can I help? You know I no longer have access to the five countries' systems, and I'm more likely to leave a trail or tip off anyone interested." Mike looked at the small fork and fish knife she had been given. "Unless you can get me some access?"

"That won't be possible."

"Why?"

"Because I'm currently behind the eight ball. This week, I'll probably be suspended and sent back to head office. If I'm lucky, I might get the job of ordering light bulbs. If I'm unlucky, I might be in a cell staring up at one."

Mike looked at her old boss with genuine surprise. "Really? What have you done?"

"Jeez, you know I don't always follow the rules, but I get enough results that no one cares. Now they've started digging and are wondering if it's me."

"And you have no idea who it might be?"

"Personally, no ... but they think it must be someone with my level of access. It's some of my files that have mysteriously turned up in the wrong hands."

"How do I contact you?"

"All the numbers and codes are on that card. I didn't want anything on the system connected to you. Crip's details are on there too, but you won't need him. I may not be able to contact you, so I wanted you both to have each other's details. Nobody else knows, and please don't tell anyone. There's one more thing: this came in the post the day before yesterday." He took out of his pocket a brass key with the word 'DUPLICATE' written on the attached tag and handed it to her.

"What's this and who sent it?"

"I've no idea. There was a piece of paper that said it was for safekeeping and that he would call very soon to meet up. There was no name."

"What am I meant to do with it?"

"Keep it safe in case I'm suspended. I don't want it in our office, especially if we've been compromised."

"Where do I start? What do you want me to do?" She was suddenly excited but, at the same time, overwhelmed with the magnitude of the task.

"Before they began to suspect me, they told me they were looking at a senior Australian agency director who might have got involved in some construction fraud. His name's on the card. You could start with him."

"Leonard, we've had our differences, but I'm sorry – really sorry. I'll do my best."

"And I'll try to let you know if I'm suspended. Are you leaving that rice?"

———

She watched him leave before putting on her helmet and setting off around the M25 and up the M40 to her home in the woods of Oxfordshire. It gave her time to think. She felt sorry for Leonard, given his predicament and his grazed nose, but she had been fooled by him too many times. Despite this, however much she held him guilty for the ambush in Holland that killed her beloved Dylan and wrecked her own health, she knew Leonard was no traitor.

As the Italian motorbike – her pride and joy – bucked over the hardened mud of the track to her cabin, she looked forward to playing on her computer. There was nobody better at searching databases, and although she had never looked for a traitor before, it couldn't be that different from tracking down the Colombian and Mexican drug cartels on which she had worked for years in Seattle, Langley and London. The bedsit studio in which she lived above a forester's garage came into view, and she parked the bike next to a tractor and trailer. She pulled herself up the outside steps to her front door and entered her cabin. Well, she thought of it as a cabin, but it was actually a pine-panelled single room with a large gable window looking on to the forest edge.

The first thing she did was to take off her wig and rub her bald scalp. The relief was beyond words. She placed the black wig on its polystyrene head with the name Lachesis written in bold felt-tip pen. Next to this were two others bearing matching bright blonde and red wigs, named Clotho and Atropos, respectively. These were the three Fates of Greek mythology, and they resonated with Mike. She opened her fridge, took out a Peroni beer, knocked its top off, and searched for some peanuts. This was the best time of the day, when the afternoon sun streamed into her room.

She pulled out some of her electronic gizmos from their hiding places, connected them together and powered up her computer system. She was ready.

———

At that precise moment, an Emirates Boeing 787 Dreamliner landed at Dubai International Airport and began to taxi to its stand. It was early evening, and the dust in the atmosphere had begun to produce a warm, orange glow as the sun lowered to the west. A young man with short, ginger hair who had been travelling in first class put on the white linen jacket of his suit and pulled out his cabin bag. The luggage label would have told anyone interested that his name was Callum Murchison.

Thirty-five minutes later, he was lifting two silvery, rectangular metal suitcases from the carousel. Then, after avoiding a gaggle of golf professionals and their caddies, who were blocking his way, he headed out of building and got into a very large, black Mercedes. As the door clicked shut, the external noise disappeared, and he settled back into the luxury of the cool, scented interior. It was a two-hour drive north-east to his destination.

The road surface was so smooth and the car was so comfortable that he hadn't even reached the next emirate, Sharjah, before he was asleep.

In time, the sinuous motorway began to approach the mountains in the emirates of Ras Al Khaimah and Fujairah. Not that this troubled Callum Murchison, who had woken to find that it was a cloudy night and all he could see was the road illuminated by the headlights. The driver turned off onto a small road that wound its way upwards with only a crash barrier between it and the perilous drop down into a rocky valley. As the car passed around the shoulder of a particularly steep mountainside, views far down to an industrial port opened up. Next to this, two cement works were also visible, their lights sparkling in the desert air.

The view was abruptly blocked by a long, man-made bank that was under construction using waste and soil from the quarry beyond it. It was meant to screen the extraction activity and rock faces from the south, but it tended to draw the eye with its unnatural silhouette. On the other side of this bund, the enormous quarry – which provided the limestone aggregate and cement raw materials for much of the Middle East and the countries around the Indian Ocean – stepped down to the sea in a series of thirty benches, like a giant's staircase.

Fifteen minutes later, the Mercedes passed through a gate and was driven up the private approach road to an imposing villa. The passenger was now in a political no-man's land. This mountain retreat was perched high above the Strait of Hormuz, with Iran twenty-five miles across the water. The villa was in Oman, although on the border with the United Arab Emirates (UAE), but no one here cared. It appeared ahead, lit up like the White House, which it oddly resembled.

Harper, who was thirty and two years older than Callum, came down the steps escorted by two houseboys. Jay, the chauffeur, didn't get out of the car, but he released the boot from inside. The servants extracted Callum's two suitcases and carried them into the villa, and Harper opened the back door and slid in to sit with his brother. They fist bumped but said little. The car was driven off, partially retracing the route, but this time dropping down towards the coast. It seemed to take a long time, and after countless hairpins, the tyres were squealing and the brakes were hot.

At sea level, they entered the gates of one of the cement works, avoiding the queue of lorries waiting to be loaded. As it navigated its way through the towering structures, the Mercedes was throwing up clouds of grey-green cement dust, which were illuminated by the floodlights. Finally, it slowed and continued out of a perimeter gate and along the seashore for a mile; there was no other way to gain access to this narrow area of flat land that bordered the Persian Gulf. The car's progress had been monitored since they had originally entered the cement facility, as this second location was strictly off limits to the public.

The track came to an end, blocked by a large, rocky outcrop. In this idyllic location by the sea, backed by lofty limestone mountains was a single, large industrial shed clad in pale-grey sheeting. It wouldn't have looked out of place in any distribution park on the outskirts of any European city. The car halted, and the two men got out and walked into an air-conditioned office located at one corner. Callum lifted his black laptop case onto a desk and began to unzip it.

CHAPTER TWO

Mike Kingdom was drinking her second bottle of beer. She had made only limited progress. *I may well need a third*, she thought to herself.

The name of the senior Australian agent under investigation was Andrew Woodhouse. Unfortunately, this wasn't looking like a promising lead. From a link to a file marked "Confidential" that had been provided to her by Leonard, Woodhouse appeared to have been suspected of providing an Australian property company with intelligence on its European competitors. The companies were all trying to buy a collection of British shopping centres and a football stadium. The Australians had been successful, and although he denied it, Woodhouse appeared to have been paid handsomely for his trouble via a Singaporean bank account. From the initial CIA investigation, it looked likely that he may have needed the money to pay off some eye-watering debts that his son had allowed to spiral out of control.

Even if the accusations were true, his misdemeanours were commercial espionage. There was no evidence of any other wrongdoing. This confused Mike. Clearly, Andrew Woodhouse's career was unlikely to progress much further, and the Australian criminal justice system would take over as necessary, but how was this continuing to compromise the CIA or the rest of Five Eyes? Wasn't this an end to the matter? Why would the CIA still be interested in Leonard or any other person?

No, something isn't right, she thought; it was time for that third beer.

A military plane from RAF Brize Norton flew over her cabin. It always distracted her as it was the only sound of human activity that she heard, if you discounted the forester, who used the tractor and trailer beneath her about twenty times a year.

After fetching that beer, she sat back down and lifted her left leg onto an upturned wooden box; this gave her a few minutes' relief by moving the ache from one part of her calf to another.

Then it was back to the beginning. Always go back to the beginning.

"This is Leonard we're dealing with. What did he really mean?" she said out loud to the three impassive, but neatly coiffured Greek sisters lined up on the shelf. Her eyes fell on the blonde-haired Clotho – who represented birth, the spinning of the thread and the beginning. "OK, Clotho, out with it. Where do I start? Give me the end of the thread."

Leonard. Leonard is the start. Mike knew that so much of her life over the last five years or so had started (and nearly ended) with Leonard de Vries.

She thought about what he had said at The Greedy Pelican: one of the five agencies was possibly compromised; an Australian was under suspicion; he, Leonard, was likely to be suspended; and someone called Chris Crippen, an ex-operative, was the only person she could talk to.

Of the four things he had said, two were pretty much

beyond her scope and analysis: the compromising of one of the Five Eyes' agencies and the fact that Leonard may be suspended. What was she meant to do? The Australian she had checked, and the various relevant authorities seemed to have this under control. Certainly, she had found nothing new. This left Chris Crippen, the so-called 'operative' who was there in the unlikely event that Mike needed a field worker. Leonard knew she wasn't an operative, and he had said this job wouldn't need fieldwork, but *in the unlikely event this was needed*, Chris was available. He had also been briefed by Leonard, and this might mean he had been given more information.

She swallowed the last mouthful of warm beer. It was time to make contact with Chris Crippen.

Yes, she could telephone him, but their conversation would be heavily constrained. She had no idea what encryption was available to them both. In fact, she had no idea where he was or what his role had been in the secret-squirrel world. She did some checking. There were over 2,000 Crippens in the USA, and none of those called Christopher appeared to fit the bill. Of course, he might have British nationality. She checked and there were only fifty listed, and they, too, were irrelevant on the surface of it. As an ex-agent, she thought about this and concluded that, perhaps, it was a code name? After a few minutes of delving further, she decided to give up and send him a harmless message asking him where he was based.

"Loughborough" came the reply. "Where are you?"

"Oxfordshire."

However, before she could check the distance to Lough-borough, he had replied with "I could call in tomorrow on my way to London, say 11.30am?"

She sent him the postcode and some instructions. There was no further communication; everything could wait until tomorrow.

———

It was late afternoon on Tuesday when Barbara Aumonier walked into her new office in Chiswick. It didn't match what she had enjoyed in the 'Wedge', the HQ building of the Canadian Security Intelligence Service (CSIS) in Ottawa. That building had been the centre of her life for twelve years until her first major posting to Riyadh – a complete baptism of fire. Not that there was much baptism as she couldn't find a church. There weren't any. All her waking life she had gone to church, beginning in Fort-de-France in Martinique and then in Ottawa after her parents had emigrated, encouraged by Canadian missionaries. Black, Christian and a woman weren't the automatic characteristics anyone would choose for a foreign diplomat in Saudi Arabia.

She was the assistant to the commercial attaché at a time when many Canadian companies were trying to win business in Saudi Arabia. Barbara proved adept at navigating ways through the interminable red tape, the cultural minefields, the logistics, the submission deadlines and the whole issue of bribes. She had strong morals and was a stickler for rules. While this went down well in the diplomatic community in Riyadh, it would lead to disagreements with Leonard de Vries in London years later. He regarded rules rather like slalom poles: things to be swerved generally or flattened if all else fails.

After a period back in Ottawa while a problem with her thyroid was treated, she was sent back to the Middle East as the commercial attaché in Qatar. Three years later, she was in London, and two years after that, the post of Director at Five Eyes passed to Canada and to her.

In London, her base was still at the High Commission of Canada in Canada House on Trafalgar Square, but for the next two years, she had inherited a desk vacated by Leonard de Vries in the Five Eyes office six miles to the west in Chiswick.

It was a rather empty room with walls that were pale grey apart from some unseemly stains where her predecessor had used the wastepaper bin against a wall as basketball practice for any food waste, not that this was a frequent occurrence – the food waste, that is.

"Come in," she said in response to a timid knock.

Tom, who had served as Leonard's assistant, entered the room. He had a slight stammer, especially when nervous. Sitting at the desk was a woman of roughly the same shape as Leonard but different in just about every other regard. She looked up at Tom with her slightly protruding but kindly brown eyes.

"You must be Tom?" she asked.

"Y-yes. Is there anything you need? I'm just down the corridor. P-Please press 104."

"Tom, it's good to meet you, and, yes, I'll call you if I have any questions. Actually, to start with, what's that yellow stain on the wall?"

"T-That's where L-Leonard de—"

Tom never had a chance to explain, as Barbara Aumonier put up her hand in disgust. She did *not* want to visualise what Leonard de Vries might do against a wall.

"I'll talk to Building Maintenance," Tom said.

"I start officially tomorrow when I would like to gather the staff at 10.00am and introduce myself. Today is just a quick look around, and I wanted to put some things in the safe. Is it you who'll explain access to the computer network here?"

"Yes, whenever you like."

"And I understand that you're aware of Project Ortolan, which is one of the main things I want to make progress on." Occasionally, her accent came to the fore, especially on French words such as '*ortolan*'.

"Yes, I've been c-collating data from all of the Five Eyes. Do you want access now?"

"Tomorrow morning, please, after the team introductions."

Tom was almost embarrassed. He had grown used to Leonard, and the word 'please' hadn't featured prominently. His new director was surely going to be easier to work for than her predecessor.

————

Mike didn't have visitors. She didn't count the two times that Leonard had turned up unannounced – particularly the latest occasion about eighteen months earlier. Even though he had been chauffeur-driven and deposited at the bottom of the external stairs, he had been out of breath by the time he had reached her door at the top. Now, oddly nervous, she put on her black wig and checked herself in the bathroom mirror. This wasn't something she usually did. She was happy that she didn't look too threatening in her white blouse and dark-blue jeans. What about her baseball bat by the door? Would it freak him out? No, he would understand; he was an operative.

Six minutes before the appointment, she heard a car pull up. An inordinately long period of time passed, and no one had tapped on the door. What was he doing? Curious, she walked across and opened it to find a good-looking man with wide shoulders and bulging forearms pulling himself up the stairs using the handrail.

At the top, he looked around at the view, turned back to face Mike and offered his right hand. "Hi, I'm Crip. Nice place you have here."

Mike was at a loss for words, but she managed, "Hi, yes, it works for me. Come inside."

Crip, wearing a pale-grey tracksuit with the Olympic logo on the sleeve, walked unsteadily into the room. He was six feet tall and olive-skinned with black hair; his beaming smile never appeared to vary.

"Cool place. Have you lived here long?" he asked in a mild mid-Atlantic accent.

"A few years." She paused. "I've rented it since what Leonard's insists on calling my 'accident'."

"Leonard told me about that; I was sorry to hear about what happened to you and your husband."

"Another time I would love to know what Leonard actually told you. Take a seat. Would you like something to drink?"

"Water, please. I'm in training. Leonard probably told you?"

"Ah, no. He told me nothing. Absolutely nothing. What are you training for?"

"Well, ultimately, the Olympics. In Paris. In 2024." He had a habit of speaking in a slightly staccato way.

"Oh, that's impressive," she said as she was walking across to her refrigerator. "For your information, Leonard told me your name, your nickname and that you used to be an operative. That was all apart from your phone number."

He walked over, sat on a kitchen chair and rested his arm on the table. "Why did he think you might need me?" he asked, watching her return with two glasses of water.

"Leonard didn't tell you what he wants me to do?" She was trying to establish some sort of common starting point.

"No."

"Talk about divide and rule. I have no idea why I might need you, but he seems to think I do. He's asked me to find a bad apple in Five Eyes or one of the agencies." She took a sip. "This is meant to be desk-based, so I have no idea why I might need feet on the ground."

"Good job ... I don't have any."

She looked at him, frowning as it sank in.

He pointed down. "I have prosthetics below the knee on both legs."

"Great, so we have one good leg between us." She shook her head. "I have so many questions."

"I have plenty of time. I'm not running off." A smile spread across his face.

"Leonard ... I could kill him. Was it him who started calling you Crip?"

"Yes, but my teammates all do as well. If your name's Crippen and you're in a wheelchair, what do you expect?"

"When did you lose your legs?"

"It was on a job ... for Leonard, four years ago."

"I ... I ... I really am going to kill him. What does he think we are? Cannon fodder?"

"It wasn't his fault."

"Well, I still blame him for my damaged leg and this." She pointed at her wig, but her visitor had assumed it was her real hair and didn't get the full implications; his was the same glossy black.

Without asking, she got up, found a tin of biscuits and put them on the small table between them.

"He must have given you a brief?" Crip was intrigued, but he was beginning to wonder what the point of all this was.

"Yes, but only to find someone in one of the five agencies who is compromising everyone and is a liability. That's it. He gave me a name that Langley is pursuing, but from a quick look, it seems like an open-and-shut case. I'm not sure what else I, or you, can do."

"Do you think it has something to do with you or me or us? Why put us together? I don't get it. Neither of us work directly for the Agency any more." Neither of them referred to it as the CIA.

"Do you mean it might be related to something you or I have been involved in years ago?" she asked.

"Or a combination of skills that you and I have? I'm clutching at straws unless the person we're looking for plays basketball."

"Leonard loves basketball. He has a framed shirt on his wall in Chiswick."

"I know. It was the main topic of conversation whenever we met."

"Cr— Chris – sorry, I can't call you Crip – this can't be about basketball or sport in general. This must be about something big – a major world power or issue."

"Perhaps we should spend a few minutes telling each other about our backgrounds. It might reveal some overlap or trigger an idea?"

"Why not? Shall I start?" she began, "I was born just outside of Portland in Oregon. My parents are Czech immigrants, both involved in music. Surprisingly, I'm not musical. I like mathematical patterns. I have ADHD. I don't suffer fools gladly, though somehow Leonard seems to have flown in under the radar. I was" – she corrected herself – "am, a research analyst. I specialised in Colombian and Mexican drug cartels and their outreach into Europe. I ended up under Leonard at Five Eyes in Chiswick. After that it went horribly—"

Her phone pinged, and she checked her messages. "It's from Leonard. He's been sent back to the US."

CHAPTER THREE

Barbara Aumonier was standing at the front of a crowded room. It was 10.00am on Wednesday.

She was about to introduce herself to the twenty-seven individuals who comprised the bulk of the Executive Secretariat of Five Eyes. Although the vast majority of the espionage work was undertaken by the individual national agencies, there was still an important collation, distribution, policing and administrative role to be undertaken.

"As some of you know, I had a meeting at the US Embassy yesterday with the directors of the other agencies at which they formally handed over the chair of Five Eyes to Canada, now their term has finished. I intend to be here at least three days a week for the next two years, with the rest of my time spent at Canada House." She paused and adjusted her black-framed glasses. "I'm grateful to Leonard de Vries for his help in making the transfer so seamless. I understand he's going back to the USA for a well-earned rest."

Almost everyone knew the real truth about Leonard and Barbara's relationship, and they didn't believe a word of what she was saying.

She carried on: "As with Leonard, Sandra will be my PA and Tom my principal researcher. Please direct everything through them." As she spoke, she indicated a blonde woman in her forties, who was wearing a peach-coloured bouclé suit, and Tom, a man in a checked shirt whose nervous energy was barely under control.

Barbara continued speaking for about ten minutes and then allowed everyone to get back to their desks. She asked Tom to stay behind and explain the computer system to her – this took another twenty minutes until she felt comfortable. "Thanks, Tom. Now would you call up the files for Project Ortolan from all five sources and draw up a list in date order."

"I-I've done that," he said as he tapped in a few commands. The full schedule appeared, colour-coded by the originating country and in chronological order.

"Have these all been distributed fully?"

"Yes, all except those m-marked with a yellow flag."

"Thanks, Tom, I'll call you in if I need you. I want to look over the files and, particularly, the sequence in which they were produced." She bent down and took a folder from a box file next to her and placed it on the desk. "I also want to check if anything needs redacting."

Why would you want to do that? Tom wondered. *If a country releases a file to Five Eyes, it's expecting it to be circulated. Any redaction to protect its own interests will have already been done.*

"Was Leonard interested in Project Ortolan?" she asked.

Tom felt a certain loyalty to his previous boss, despite having been expected to put up with his idiosyncrasies. "He was m-monitoring the situation, b-but nothing new had come in for a few weeks." The truth was that it had been almost impossible to know what Leonard was interested in – apart from food and drink.

"OK, Tom, I'll look these over."

———

"It's got something to do with you, I'm sure." Mike was leaning against her kitchen cupboards, her legs crossed at the ankle. "Why would Leonard pick you?"

"Because I'm good-looking?" Chris was still beaming.

She gave him her 'yeah, right' smile. Mike did admit to herself that he was easy on the eye, with an infectious smile; he would be even more attractive to her if he relaxed his face once in a while.

"It's Leonard we're talking about. He doesn't think like the rest of the population. Why you?" She paused. "Tell me about you. I can see you're missing some limbs and play wheelchair basketball, but that can't be it, surely?"

"Well, my pop's a third-generation American and my mom's from a Jordanian family who moved to Tucson in the 1980s. I speak Arabic and did international studies at university. I joined the Agency and, after some time at Langley, was sent to London, where I was mostly tracking individuals in the Middle East. I've been here eight years."

"Tell me about your accident, if it's not too painful?"

"Bomb in Iraq. Wrong place, wrong time," was all he said.

"Leonard sent you?"

"Yes, I was following an Iraqi who lived in London. He was the target and was killed. I was just far enough behind him to survive."

"Why do you think Leonard put us together?"

He leant back in his chair. "Apart from speaking Arabic and a bit of French, I don't think I'm different from any other operative ... ex-operative." His smile faded for the first time, but only for a few seconds.

"Do you think any case you were working on is relevant?"

"I can't think of anything. Remember, I've been recovering

for over three years. I've done a few things for Leonard since the bomb, but most of my cases are now old."

"Well, we can't ask Leonard now he's been suspended, I presume. That would compromise him and us."

———

In the Middle East, after a good night's sleep, the two brothers were back at the isolated building on the shoreline of the Persian Gulf. Callum Murchison had finished his coffee; this, he had made himself as there were no Sri Lankan tea boys waiting to serve him refreshments like in so many offices and factories in the UAE. He was ready to walk around the building with Harper and undertake some more adjustments. At a secure pair of double doors at the back of the small office area, they tapped in a passcode, went through and entered the vaulted main space. It was one very large, windowless room. They were faced by rows of shelving on which sat computers – all the same size and type. There were no keyboards or monitors or printers, just row upon row of dark-grey tower cases on two levels. Above each one was a fan dispersing the heat and circulating the cool air from the industrial-scale galvanised ducting that was part of a state-of-the-art system with the sole function of maintaining the temperature at twenty degrees Celsius. The room was kept at this constant temperature twenty-four seven for 365 days a year. There was minimal lighting, as this would generate even more heat, and there was a loud buzz from the 500 fans. The facility wasn't labour-intensive. It only required eight permanent staff to be on-site at any one time, and four of these were providing security.

The new software Callum had brought with him the previous day, which Harper had installed, was so valuable and so secret that sending it via any phone line, cable or satellite link was too risky; it had to be delivered and installed by hand.

Time had flown by, and without windows to the outside world, the two men had lost track of it. They were pleased with progress, and their work had broadly been successful. Callum thanked the duty manager, and they headed for the exit. It was getting dark outside, and the ring of security lights was already illuminated.

On their way home, the Mercedes retraced its route parallel to the rocky shore, through the cement works and along the main road until it turned back uphill, traversing dozens of hairpin bends, each illuminated by a back-and-forth sweep of the headlights. It was a dizzying combination that induced feelings of car sickness and vertigo combined. At the crest, the chauffeur drove through a notch in the skyline and rejoined the road that led back to the villa.

In front of the building, the two men exited the car and walked up the steps and through the thirty-foot-high, white pillars to the front doors inlaid with gold and, oddly, without any visible means of opening. As the brothers stepped across the marble tiles, the double doors opened silently, and the men entered the atrium with its gravity-defying crystal chandelier. Harper led the way down a corridor in search of the study where their father would be sitting as usual; he wanted to tell his father what he and Callum had done.

A servant was carrying a tray of *karkade*, a refreshing drink made from hibiscus petals. With the silver tray held high with his right hand, he opened the study door with his left. Harper and Callum walked into a room that managed to be both large and intimate – full of valuable paintings and statues, yet still cosy. Their father was asleep – as was so often the case – sitting in an armchair upholstered in a gold fabric, his hand hanging down, pointing at a book on the floor. He was staring towards a thin, bronze Giacometti sculpture that was about three feet high and stood near to him on the floor; it was called *The Running Man*. The eyes of the bronze striding male were firmly focused on somewhere in the future – and so were those of their father. He was dead.

———

Tom was in his office, eating a tuna-and-sweetcorn sandwich for lunch. Something about the way that Barbara had asked him about Project Ortolan, which was concerned with Iranian influence in the Middle East, had unsettled him. He decided to check what she had done over the last hour and began to explore. If she had accessed a file, altered it or redacted any part of it, it would be logged and immediately obvious. A model of Woody, the *Toy Story* character, looked back at him from a position next to the two screens – a Secret Santa gift from a work colleague. Everyone thought Tom resembled the tall, thin cowboy, right down to the checked shirts.

She had accessed many of the files, but she hadn't altered a single one. Perhaps she had genuinely been reading about an active case and his suspicions were unfounded. His opinion of her may have been tainted by Leonard's dislike of 'Barbie', as he called her. *A quite mild nickname by Leonard's usual standards,* Tom had thought, *but then again, given the sexist and racist overtones, perhaps not.*

However, there was something else. Tom couldn't put his finger on it, but it made him continue in his idle search. Then he saw it or, more accurately, then he didn't see it. A comparison with a copy backed up on his computer showed that two files had been deleted. He called them up and saw that they each had a yellow flag, so they had never been circulated to any of the agencies. Why would his new boss want them removed? He quickly cast his eyes over the two files and couldn't see anything unusual, controversial or related to anything he thought might warrant deletion. Tom checked, and the only name common to the two files was 'Murchison'. He could only vaguely remember seeing the name mentioned before.

The traffic flowing in and out of London on the elevated M4 motorway, as viewed through his sixth-floor window, temporarily distracted him, and he finished the sandwich. As he screwed up the wrapper into a ball, he was reminded of Leonard, who would have launched it at the wall, trying to get it to bounce down into a wastepaper basket. What would Leonard have done about Barbara Aumonier? For the first time since Leonard's suspension, Tom truly missed his old boss. *Always better the devil you know.*

He picked up his jacket and made for the corridor and the lifts. After passing through various security doors and barriers, he found himself outside under threatening rainclouds. He wandered off. New graffiti had appeared on the underpass since he last walked through it, but he paid it little attention. At a bench outside a boarded-up shop, he stopped and pulled out his phone. He searched for a number and pressed the green icon.

———

Chris had been rolling up the bottoms of his tracksuit trousers to show Mike his prosthetic limbs. The technological advances were beyond her comprehension. He was pulling up the final zip when her phone rang.

"Hi, Tom," Mike said as she answered it and sat back down on a kitchen chair.

"Mike, I p-probably shouldn't" – he hesitated – "I p-probably shouldn't be ringing you. I don't know who to p-phone. Leonard's gone b-back to the USA ... I think you know?"

"It's fine. Tell me what's bothering you." He had been the liaison between Leonard and Mike on two previous cases, and they had worked together very efficiently.

"Well, it could be nothing, but I'm a b-bit worried about my new b-boss. You know who I'm talking about?"

"Yes."

"The first thing she did this m-morning was to delete two files just before they were about to be circulated. They're the only files that m-mention someone Leonard was interested in."

"Who was that?

"M-Murchison. He's an Omani and owns a company in the M-Middle East. It's involved in quarrying, cement, construction ... that sort of thing."

"Why was Leonard interested in him, Tom?"

"I checked b-back, and in the only reference I can find, Leonard had called him a 'carpetbagger'. I don't know why."

"I'll look into it. What are people in the office saying about Leonard?"

"Actually, they m-miss him. Nobody can understand why he's been suspended and sent b-back to Langley apart from—"

Mike interrupted him: "His management style?"

"Y-yes."

"Is this the best number to get you on?"

"P-Probably, but let me give you my sister's number. She'll p-pass on any m-message to me. That might be b-better." When he had read out the number, he ended the call.

"Is that Tom from Five Eyes?" Chris asked. "I think he had just started there when I had my accident."

"Yes, he's worried about this Canadian woman who's taken over. It seems she's been deleting files, but only those mentioning someone called Murchison. Did you come across him in your Middle Eastern travels?"

"No, I don't recognise the name. Who is he?"

"An Omani involved in construction materials. I'm about to check him out. Apparently, Leonard called him a 'carpetbagger'. That word has several connotations."

Her guest stood up. "While you do that, I'm going into

London for my meeting with the committee organising the Olympics. Some of us are flying out on Saturday to look at the facilities before the decision on where to hold the 2040 Summer Olympics is made. I'll be back on Tuesday. It's been great meeting you."

"Likewise, I'll keep you informed. That's if I can get a toehold on this case."

"Not something I'd be good at," he responded, beaming.

She walked over to the door, opened it for him and then watched him make his way to his car.

CHAPTER FOUR

Around 3,500 miles to the southeast of Mike's cabin, the two brothers were in a panic. Their father dying wasn't part of any plan, and they had never talked about it with him; he was only fifty-two years old.

It hadn't taken long for them to check for a pulse and breathing. He was cold and patently dead. Harper and Callum had only left him early that morning to go down to finish off their work. What had happened? There were no signs of violence, and he was sitting in a normal pose, staring into the middle distance.

After the fact that he was beyond saving had sunk in, they were trying to work out who to call first. They settled on Mohammed, their father's fixer, who told them to stay in the villa. He would be with them in forty minutes, he had said, and they weren't to phone the police. This made the boys panic further as the idea of phoning the police hadn't entered their heads.

They stared at each other in disbelief.

"Where does he want to be buried?" Callum asked rather randomly.

"What? No idea. Would he prefer here or in Victoria?" Harper answered his brother.

"Aren't Muslims buried quickly?"

"Yes, but ... does that mean we can't fly him back home?"

They were standing in a side study, having left their father where they had found him in the adjoining room.

"Where's his will?" Callum was the most practical of the brothers.

"No idea. In the safe?"

Their stares merely intensified as it dawned on them that they didn't know what was in the safe; they had never needed to know.

"Mum would be laughing." Callum was beginning to let the enormity of the situation that was to come further down the line sink in.

Harper, who had been the most affected by their mother's death, frowned at his younger brother and walked out of the room.

———

Mohammed, a native Omani, came into the entrance hall just after 7.30pm. He was a stocky man with deep-set eyes, and he was wearing a white *dishdasha* with embroidered cuffs and on his head was a multicoloured headdress known as a *massar*.

"I am so sorry." He hugged both sons. "Where is your father?" He muttered some plea to Allah under his breath.

Harper pointed to where his father was, but he remained rooted to the spot and didn't attempt to accompany or follow him.

Mohammed headed in the direction indicated, and nothing was said until he reappeared and took out his phone in anticipation of a busy few hours.

"What happens next?" Callum was needing some guidance, some structure, to keep him from freaking out even more.

"I'll call a local policeman near the works; he is my friend, and we'll organise for the body to be taken to the morgue. As a Muslim, your father will be buried tomorrow ... unless his wish is to be buried in Canada?"

"But how did he die?" Harper couldn't come to terms with any of it.

"Natural causes. The death certificate will say natural causes. It will be issued after the burial. Unless you want him to be flown back to Victoria, but that will probably take two weeks."

"Why so long?" Callum asked.

"There will be an initial death certificate, he'll be taken to a morgue, and there will be a lot of paperwork. The police will have to stamp a No Objection Certificate (NOC) – actually, several. It all gets more complicated." He stopped as something came into his mind: "What does his will say?"

Mohammed had become good friends with Habib Murchison and would help the sons in this difficult time, but he was also thinking of the major changes to his own life now his employer was dead.

"We haven't looked. Is it in the safe?" Harper asked.

"We should look."

Mohammed walked over to a bookcase with them. Callum pulled at one edge, and it pivoted into the room, like a door, to reveal a large safe. He put in the combination, which was a mixture of his and Harper's birth dates. At least their father had told them the combination, though he never really expected they would need it. Under piles of envelopes, he found one marked "The Last Will and Testament of Habib Murchison".

They gathered around a desk, and Harper and Mohammed looked on as Callum opened the envelope with the silver dagger his father always used. Callum began to read, "'I, Habib Murchison, formerly known as Cameron Henry Murchison ...'"

———

It had been eight years since Cameron Murchison had converted to Islam and become an Omani citizen. His two sons had emigrated at the same time, but they had no interest in Islam, Christianity or indeed any religion. They loved their father, but they never really got to the bottom of what had convinced a man barely into his forties to adopt a new faith. The Murchisons had been a happy family in Victoria, the state capital of British Columbia on the Pacific coast of Canada. They had the wealth, the status, the sixty-foot yacht and a business empire based on international construction. Suddenly and unexpectedly, Cameron's wife, Mary, had died; Callum was eighteen and Harper was twenty.

What happened next had filled the newspapers for weeks. After the funeral, Cameron had announced he was selling his houses in Canada and moving to the Middle East, where his businesses were based. Harper was at university in London and Callum was about to start at Edinburgh University. The family effectively buried their mother in Victoria and left the country. Even more bizarre was Cameron's conversion to Islam and adoption of a new name. Though he had always been a deeply philosophical man, he had never displayed any leanings in this direction before, despite loving Oman and having many friends there.

Over a decade of him living in the sultanate of Oman, the Murchison business empire – now known as Murchison Arabco – grew exponentially, supplying the materials for the property and construction boom throughout the Middle East. Habib Murchison chose to live in a villa that he had commissioned and built high up in the Hajar Mountains in the

Musandam Peninsula, overlooking the Persian Gulf and the Gulf of Oman. It was conveniently on the UAE–Oman border, but there was no one living anywhere near him, apart from the goat herders further down in the valleys.

The two sons hadn't followed their father to Oman. They were, however, infrequent visitors from London, where they both now lived. Harper had married and divorced within two years. Callum had dated many girlfriends, but he hadn't let any of them get close to him; he was fiercely private.

———

"He wants to be buried in Canada," Callum said out loud.

"Really? But he's a Muslim. I had thought that he would want to be buried here. OK, I will organise everything. This will all take much longer." Mohammed had been scanning the text and was very pleased with the financial provision he would receive under the terms of the will.

"Apart from four bequests, everything is left to you and me, Callum." Harper was getting to grips with the magnitude of them having to manage an international group of companies that employed 2,000 people.

"That is good because at least two-thirds of the assets must be left to the family under Sharia law." Mohammed was just about to begin a round of phone calls. "I will be back in an hour after making the arrangements. Please do not speak to anyone until I have set everything up."

———

Completely unaware that Habib Murchison had died minutes earlier, Mike Kingdom was about to undertake a search of her usual restricted databases and sources. This had yet to happen as she had got no further than the mountains of press and social media coverage of his personal and business life. The speculation over the sudden death of his wife, Mary, and the reasons for his apparently hasty departure from Canada dominated. His repeated explanation that it was too painful for him to stay where he had so many memories was never accepted, it seemed. The cause of her death was given as drowning. She had been a member of a group of women who regularly sailed Lasers (single person dinghies), and it was only a mild surprise that she had gone off in one alone, although that wasn't entirely without precedent.

Mike made a few notes and transferred her focus to the move across the Atlantic to Oman and his religious conversion. All of it was so unexpected, yet well documented; despite this, she was struggling to form an impression of the man. And why were Leonard and Barbara Aumonier interested in him?

The Canadian connection between Barbara and Habib Murchison stood out, but where did it lead? Mike had checked her past and noted that she had been attached to the commercial wing of the Canadian embassies in Saudi Arabia and Qatar. She and Habib would probably have met, and she may have been a great help to him, but what was relevant to her search? Was he blackmailing her? Was she receiving money from him for services rendered? Mike had no answers.

And what had this got to do with any of the Five Eyes, the Agency or Leonard?

A grey squirrel scampered across her roof and appeared at her picture window, only to disappear as she stood up to walk around the room. She noticed her kitchen clock had stopped. After lifting it down, she took out a fresh AA battery from a drawer, removed the old one from the clock and set it going again.

With her mind cleared, she stopped her delaying tactics and took stock. Firstly, there was plenty of mud flying about, but not much had stuck to Cameron Murchison or Habib or whatever he was now called. This was surprising given his life and incredible wealth. Secondly, both he and 'Barbie' were Canadian. How did this manifest itself in a way that had international implications? *Oh*, she thought to herself, *and why did he choose Habib as his new name in Oman?* This last point might just be an irrelevancy, but it needed to be checked.

She sat down for what would be a long session.

Habib's business interests took a long time to untangle. Murchison Arabco was an international holding company registered in the Turks and Caicos Islands. The largest of its companies was based in Ras Al Khaimah, the emirate that adjoined Oman, in which his quarry and cement works were based. The quarry not only supplied the raw material for the two works but also 50 million tons of crushed rock per year.

"*What?*" she suddenly exclaimed as she continued reading that the cement and aggregate lorries leaving the area every day were nose-to-tail for miles and miles and miles. They resembled train carriages as they made their way south towards Dubai and Abu Dhabi. In fact, the law said that they could only drive from 5.30am to 8.30am, and from 3pm to 8pm. At the end of each session, they all had to pull over to the side of the road in unison to allow the locals to pass, cross and undertake their daily business.

After two hours, she walked to the picture window to stare at the pine forest and to give her eyes a rest from the screen – one of the hazards of being an analyst. The trees looked beautiful in the warm evening sunshine.

When she resumed, she decided to change tack and to concentrate on the man himself. What was Habib Murchison like?

There were so many photographs of him with emirs and other world leaders, sheikhs, and local Arab dignitaries. He sometimes wore Western dress (mostly suits) and sometimes *dishdashas* with white *djellabas* flicked back to reveal his pale-ginger hair. He had prominent eyebrows and a kindly, if slightly unnatural, smile. He was fifty-two years old and widowed.

Mike found it easier to search for someone when she had an idea what they looked like. There was no logical reason for this.

Next, she checked out where he lived and was surprised that he didn't have houses all over the world – or even in Canada – and didn't own a superyacht. He did have his enormous villa, which wasn't too far from the quarry, works and port. It was neatly perched at the top of a valley, up in the mountains. She called up a satellite view and tried to imagine who lived there and what he got up to. He certainly didn't have any neighbours, and no one was likely to sneak up and surprise him – although Iran was less than thirty miles away across the Strait of Hormuz.

Did he live there alone? Mike wondered, *Where are his sons and what role do they play in this so-called 'family conglomerate'?*

After a little research on their time at university, Harper's failed marriage and where they lived in two London houses (one in Chelsea and the other in Docklands), she sat back, slightly surprised that they weren't involved in any of the businesses. "It looks like I can cross the two of you off of my list," she said out loud.

———

Callum and Harper were in a lounge with floor-to-ceiling windows that offered stunning views down towards the sea, which was almost half a mile beneath them; it was dark, but the lights of oil and gas tankers could be seen as they approached the choke point of the Strait of Hormuz. A third of the world's liquefied natural gas and a quarter of the world's oil pass through this narrow channel every year, despite it being only twenty-five miles wide and one of the busiest and most dangerous waterways in the world. It has two sea lanes, one for inbound and one for outbound vessels; each lane was two miles wide and they were separated by a two-mile safety zone. However, despite the fact that Iran asserts ownership and control of the northern half of the strait and Oman the southern half, most countries – including the USA – don't accept these claims.

Harper was watching the twinkling stars and the lights of planes flying up the Persian Gulf to Dubai and Europe beyond. He and his brother were drinking cardamom tea together and trying to absorb what had just happened. Mohammed had yet to return, not having finished his calls or making the arrangements.

"We're going to have to stay out here for a while to sort things out," Harper suggested. He had originally planned to fly back tomorrow.

"Great." Callum sounded ironically enthusiastic. "I hate the place even more now."

"You and I only come out here for one reason, and that's not changing."

They returned to silence for a few seconds, taking in the panorama, both preoccupied.

"Mohammed said natural causes. The death certificate will say natural causes." Callum paused. "Why did he say that?"

"No idea. Does it matter what they put on the death certificate? We can all see that Father had a heart attack. Why does it matter? He's dead."

"It sounded strange to me that the death certificate will say natural causes."

CHAPTER FIVE

It was 10.30am the day after the sudden death of his employer, and Mohammed had already been on the phone for hours. He was now standing alongside the two sons in the echoing entrance hall. The tall front doors were wide open, allowing the warm mountain air from outside to swirl around.

"Are you ready?" he asked.

The boys nodded silently, appearing to have regressed to their childhood while waiting for the body of their father to be carried past them and down the marble steps to the waiting black van. Harper, displaying little emotion, stared as the men walked by carrying the body wrapped in a cloth; he was trying to avoid thinking about the reality of the situation and looked numb. Callum's eyes began to water, and he turned away at the last minute as Mohammed closed the doors slowly. They stood there in silence until the van drove off down the long drive, went through the gates and started its protracted descent to the coastal plain. Within an hour, Habib Murchison would be in the police morgue, where he would stay until the arrangements for the release of his body for his final flight back to the country of his birth were in place.

At the villa, the three men retreated to a small lounge.

"Are you OK to visit the works at 2pm?" Mohammed was checking whether the sons were still up to meeting both the CEO and general manager in their offices at the cement works after lunch.

"Sure," Harper answered for them both.

"I've spoken to my local policeman friend, Nabil. When the body of your father has reached the police morgue, they'll file a report, and the body will be taken to the hospital. A doctor will determine the cause of death and produce a death-certificate declaration. There's no suspicion of foul play; therefore, it should be straightforward. I've asked for it to be sent here. After that, I submit some paperwork – your father's passport, for example – and with an NOC, which is the No Objection Certificate I mentioned, we'll get a death certificate. Then we'll begin the process of releasing the body for transportation." He took a breath and continued, "You'll need to contact the Canadian Embassy; I won't be able to deal with that end of things. I believe they cancel the passport and register the death in Canada. I'm not sure about that; this is all new to me too."

"Are you paid directly by my father or through the company?" Callum was always practical. "We would like you to go on helping us for the foreseeable future."

"Through the company, and thank you, I would like to help you. There will be a lot to arrange over the next few months, I expect. How long are you intending to stay out here?"

"As long as it takes. I have a feeling that we'll end up flying back to London and straight on to Vancouver." Callum had already thought about this.

Mohammed refilled their cups, and they drank some tea.

"Before we meet at the works, do you want to think about how and when you should announce your father's death?"

Mohammed said as he stood up. "I want to deal with some other matters before then, if you would excuse me?"

The sons also stood and thanked the man who had taken a great weight off their shoulders.

"See you at 2.00pm," Callum confirmed.

———

A cream-coloured limousine with a red roof was making its way up the road into the Hajar Mountains; it was one of the luxury taxis from Dubai airport. The passenger in the back was enjoying the air conditioning turned up to maximum; he wasn't a lover of the heat. Already bored by the journey before the shopping malls of Dubai bordering the road had petered out, he was now hypnotised by the repetition of the semicircular drill marks in the rock faces where explosives had been used to blast a route for the road up through the orange-grey limestone peaks.

He was being swung from one side to the other as the driver navigated the smooth bends, gripping and spinning the wheel as if the car didn't have power steering.

"*Sheesh!*" he had shouted as the driver swerved to miss a black van hurtling down the road towards them, "*has he got a death wish?*"

Sensibly, the taxi driver kept quiet and continued thinking about the gentlemen's club he would frequent that evening – a once-a-month treat.

Having turned off the main road onto a single-track road that climbed gently ever higher into the mountains, the car eventually stopped at an impressive pair of gates. A man stepped out of a door in the perimeter wall and approached the driver's window. There was an exchange in Arabic that didn't sound promising. Various attempts at translation led to the rear door being opened and the visitor directed to a telephone.

"Who is it?" a voice asked firmly in a confident Canadian accent.

"I have an appointment at 11.30am with Mr Habib Murchison."

"Sorry, you've just missed him." Harper would never know that this was literally true.

"I've just flown into Dubai for this meeting. Habib wouldn't have forgotten about it. It was *him* who asked *me* to come out here."

"What's the meeting about?"

"How the ...? How am I supposed to know? I don't usually have this problem when he calls me out here. Whom am I speaking to?

"His son, Harper. I'm sorry, it's not a good time, and he's not here."

"Harper, I'm Donald Reeve, may I come in for a few minutes? I've been travelling all day." The visitor was at his most appealing with his soft Alabaman accent.

"It will have to be very brief, and I don't know how I can help you."

The gates were opened, and the taxi drove Leonard de Vries up to the villa. He told the taxi to wait as agreed. Was it really only two days since he had done the same at The Greedy Pelican? He walked slowly up the steps to be met by a tall, ginger-haired and bearded young man.

"Hello, I'm Harper Murchison."

"Donald Reeve. Very pleased to meet you."

"Come in. Unfortunately, I can only give you a few minutes as we have to leave for an important appointment."

"Thanks again. This isn't like your father to forget a meeting. He and I go back a long way." Leonard was regaining his breath after walking up the steps outside.

"What did he want to see you about?"

Leonard couldn't tell Habib's son the truth, so he needed to swerve the question. "I don't know exactly, but we usually meet up two or three times a year for a chat here or in London."

Something about the harmless-looking, overweight, middle-aged American made Harper decide to tell the truth. The visitor would find out in a matter of hours when the press release hit the media in any event.

"Sadly, my father died yesterday. It has all come as a bit of a shock."

"Jeez!" Leonard was equally shocked. "I'm so sorry for your loss. I won't delay you; I'm sure you have a million things to process. How did he die?"

"Heart attack, we think. There were no indications. My brother Callum and I left him for a few hours yesterday and came back to find him dead in his chair."

"Where is he now?"

"They've taken him down to the morgue. There's a load of paperwork that has to be sorted out before we fly him back to Canada." He lost his train of thought. "Look, I'm sorry your long trip has been wasted. By the way, we haven't told anybody yet."

"Not your fault; not your fault. I won't say anything until it's public knowledge." Leonard reached into his pocket. "Here's my card. Ring me if you need anything. I'm in London. You and your brother both live in London – your father told me, I think?"

"Thank you, that's kind. Yes, we do."

Leonard was thinking on his feet. "I don't know how to say this, but I promised your father that, if anything happened to him, I would make sure you and Callum were OK. If things get messy out here, you will phone me straight away, won't you? I might be able to help."

"Messy? What do you mean by 'messy'?"

"Harper, trust me; you'll know messy if it happens."

He shook Harper's hand and turned back to the large doors. A couple of minutes later, he was back in the taxi.

———

After only a short distance into the return journey through the mountains, Leonard asked the driver to stop in a layby on the outside of a bend that gave stomach-churning views down to a concrete dam and the reservoir behind it. He stood back from the low wall and away from the taxi and its driver. There was no shade to be found, and the sun was beating down. He had one of his phones pressed to his ear, having dialled a UK number.

"Are you suspended?"

"Yes, naked over a tank of piranhas."

"Leonard, that isn't something I'm keen to visualise. Where are you?" Mike was very curious.

"I'm in the field, and it has *not* been a roaring success. I was trying to beat the clock."

"You're playing football?"

"I was having one last try to sort things out, but it's all gone down the tubes. I've been sort of suspended, and it will stay that way unless you've done something miraculous in the last forty-eight hours."

"I've been checking up on a Canadian who loves the desert." She was avoiding using key words and names on an open line.

"So was I until half an hour ago. He's dead. No one knows yet. I've just left his place."

"Really? You're in the desert? What do you mean '*He's dead*'? Is he – or was he – key to all this?"

"He probably had the answers, but I was a day late."

"Natural causes?"

"Yes, officially, but I'm not buying it."

"What next?"

"I'm gonna stay out here for a day or two and do some digging ... you know, fieldwork."

"I prefer it this way round with you in the field." Her voice barely concealed a smile.

"Have you contacted the friend I suggested?" he asked.

"Yes."

"You might need him."

"I'm *not* going into the field. I'll go on searching. Give me a steer on our late friend before you disappear."

"I'll tell you when I see you face to face. I'll just say that we usually chat about what he can see out of his window. I gotta get back to my hotel. *Tâ ba'd.*"

With that, he was gone.

———

Just before 2.00pm, the chauffeur dropped off Callum and Harper directly outside the pale-grey office complex located strategically at the entrance to both cement works and on the access road to the port. There was no disguising that this was a collection of Portakabins configured over two floors. There were four plant containers full of flowers, which required the undivided attention of someone in the workforce to be able to fight the elements all day. Apart from a few palms, there was no other vegetation worth mentioning for half a mile. The steps up to the door had a metal balustrade that displayed the name Murchison Arabco in English on one side and in Arabic on the other.

As he reached the top of the steps, but before opening the door, Harper turned to Callum and whispered, "We own this now."

Once inside, they were greeted by a Syrian called Kamal

Khalil, the British-born CEO of the companies in the group covering the Middle East. They had met many times before, and he hugged them both, searching desperately for the right words. They were standing in what passed as the office reception – a small, white room with a black leather armchair, a pot plant and a water cooler. The ubiquitous framed photograph of the emir had pride of place above the door through which they walked into a long, windowless corridor. After passing several offices, they entered Kamal's room, which was right at the end.

"Please," he said, indicating for his visitors to take a seat in front of his extensive, dark-brown desk with its thick glass top. "I don't know where to start. This was so unexpected."

"We want you to know that we don't want anything to change. We aren't going to pretend we know the businesses, so we want the status quo to be maintained. Please rest assured that we value you and the team." Harper was keen to reassure Kamal, who bowed his head slightly in acknowledgement.

"Is there anything we should know in the short term, and is there anything that you urgently need from us?" Callum asked.

"No, there's nothing that needs your input at the moment. The annual budgets have been agreed, the cashflow is very good, and we have no borrowings. Sales are off the chart – we can't produce enough aggregate, blocks or cement. The next big event is the annual maintenance shutdown of number one kiln, which is seven months away. Unless something really unexpected happens, you can leave us to run the operation out here in the Middle East," Kamal offered.

"That's a great relief," replied Callum. "We'll hang around at the villa until our father's body is released and can be flown to Vancouver. We'll fly there via London for the funeral. We're seeing our lawyers in London and then Canada to deal with the formal transfer of all the assets. We'll keep you informed."

"I can't think of anything that might require your signatures in the short term." Kamal was comfortable with running the quarry, cement works and port. There was, however, one area where he was in the dark. "I'm assuming there are to be no changes and no increase in power demand, for example, at the farm?"

"That was one of the reasons we were out here to see Father. We wanted to discuss extending the farm ... and that would require more power," Harper said.

"It can wait until after the funeral." Callum didn't want to upset Kamal.

"But not *too* long." Harper was more impatient.

CHAPTER SIX

Rain was driving against the picture window in the gable end of the cabin; it sounded gritty. The sky was sufficiently dark and threatening that Mike Kingdom had turned on the light, even though it was lunchtime. She had a slice of bread and butter in her hand and was trying to use the keyboard of her computer with the other. To say that she found Leonard exasperating would be a waste of breath, he was just ... There weren't words. He was also unpredictable. What was he doing in the field? Those days were well over – although the fact that he had got on a plane and flown to the Middle East showed her how important this all was.

At least she had the comfort of knowing that Habib Murchison, the person Tom had told her about, was centrally important to, well, what? Undeniably, to something. Her hours of research hadn't been wasted – other than that, as she now knew, he was dead.

Leonard had said that 'it' – whatever 'it' was – probably concerned something that could be seen outside of Murchison's window. What did that mean? She called up his villa on an aerial photograph and tried to imagine what might be visible from such an elevated spot. *To the west, could he see down to his quarry, cement works or port? To the north, could he see the Strait of Hormuz and Iran? And to the south-east, could he see ...? What's that?* She zoomed in to reveal what looked like a white golf ball on the top of a mountain.

Mike now had a list, although it might be incomplete: quarry, works, port, strait, Iran and listening station. Did the latter belong to the UAE? Oman? The Brits? The Americans?

Her mind wandered off: *He's a Muslim. He'll be buried today or tomorrow, won't he? Is Leonard going to attend the funeral or wake or whatever Muslims do?* She didn't know. Leonard had said that Murchison had died of natural causes, but he wasn't buying this explanation. There was nothing that she could do from 3,500 miles away about proving or disproving the cause of death. Or was there? She had an idea, but she needed Murchison's phone number.

A sudden gust of wind shook the cabin, and the pine boarding made a strange creaking sound. Mike phoned Tom's sister and asked her to pass on a message asking for Murchison's number, plus his email addresses, passwords and, in fact, anything that would help her. His sister, Carol, made it clear she had been told by Tom how to approach him by getting him to phone her back.

Tom was about to have his lunch break. This was convenient timing as he sent the information to Mike half an hour later by WhatsApp from his personal phone as he sat on a park bench. No wonder Leonard never wanted to lose Tom as his assistant at Five Eyes.

In the intervening time, Mike was searching online and came across the press release announcing Habib Murchison's death. It said he had died peacefully at home with his family around him and he was to be buried as per his wishes in Victoria, where he was born. *Does this mean the two sons are at the villa?* Mike was curious and wondered what their role was in all this.

He also isn't being buried quickly as per tradition but is to be flown to Canada. What does that mean?

The rain was easing, and the sky was brightening. Using the information Tom had provided, she accessed Habib Murchison's phone and checked whether this gave her a route to the security cameras around his villa. Rather frustratingly, it didn't at first, but – and this is where the dogged persistence of the analyst paid off – she did eventually find another way for her to watch the security videos and, as an added bonus, access a timeline and his photographs.

She started with the videos from Monday, which gave her an introduction to the normal routine of the household and staff. On Tuesday, she saw Callum arrive in a black Mercedes at 7.30pm and leave immediately with Harper. Mike had checked elsewhere for images of the two sons, and was therefore confident it was them, but she couldn't help wondering where they were going so urgently after Callum's arrival. He hadn't even gone into the villa to greet his father. An hour and a half later, they were back at the villa. Wherever they had gone, it couldn't have been far away in that mountainous region.

Apart from what looked like a changeover of staff, nobody had entered or left until the next day. Callum and Harper had got back into the chauffeur-driven car early that Wednesday morning and had been driven out through the gates. They returned at 6.45pm.

Earlier that day, at 8.44am, Habib Murchison, wearing a dark suit with open-necked white shirt, had been picked up in a silver Range Rover; there was what looked like someone providing protection sitting next to the chauffeur and wearing dark glasses. Habib had returned just after 4.00pm and walked back into the villa. Nobody except for what looked like staff in a people carrier, laughing and joking while their master was away, came or went in the intervening period, apart from a refrigerated food van that unloaded at the service entrance.

At 4.32pm, a white pickup had arrived and disgorged two men in Omani dress, who had stayed for twenty minutes and then left.

Mike could see no other movement of people in and/or out.

She broke off to go to the bathroom, and while staring at the knotholes in the pine cladding, she decided to check the photographs on Habib's phone when she returned to her desk.

There was only one from the Wednesday on which he died; it was a photograph taken at 1.03pm in what looked like a restaurant with views beyond of a city and the sea. It had been taken by someone else and showed Habib standing next to a man, who was also in Western dress. Was it taken in Dubai or in Abu Dhabi? Could he have travelled there in time? She checked and decided that it was most likely Dubai if he had gone for lunch. She didn't need to speculate; she could check his phone's location that morning – this was the easiest way for her to pin down the location. After leaving the villa, he had been driven to Ras Al Khaimah airport, and one and a half hours later, he was landing at Doha in Qatar. She had forgotten that he probably owned or had access to private jets.

What had Habib been doing in Doha?

Mike read his messages and emails; fortunately, he still wrote in English. Only one caught her eye as it referred to the need to change the restaurant. It was from someone identified in the phone as 'BlueStar'. This sort of searching was laborious, and she now had to find out who the phone number belonged to. Here, she hit a brick wall. The phone was registered in a false name to a non-existent company.

Finding the real owner wasn't insurmountable, but it would take more work and would most likely come via messages on Habib's phone. She needed the bathroom again, and this reminded her how long she had been sitting at the computer screen.

Staring at the grain of the pine boards, the knots, and the tongue-and-groove pattern in the bathroom proved to be productive yet again. She walked back into her lounge, wondering how long Habib must have spent in the restaurant. She would check this in detail later, but just taking a wild stab at it seemed to suggest he couldn't have been at the restaurant for more than half an hour. Why fly to Doha for thirty minutes to be with one or more people? Was the man in the photograph with Habib the aforementioned BlueStar? Was the photographer a waiter or a third member of the party? Were there other diners at the table? There was so much for her to find answers to that it was obvious she would be up most of the day and night.

Mike wondered what Leonard was doing at that moment. *What were his parting words?* "Tâ ba'd"?

She checked. It meant 'until later' in Farsi, the primary language in Iran.

———

Tom had been summoned by his new boss. On entering her office, he was confronted not only by Barbara Aumonier sitting at her desk but also by two men standing in front of the window. She didn't bother to introduce them formally, which is never a good sign.

"Tom, I would like you to give every help to my two colleagues. Please give them access to everything they wish to see. They're cleared to the highest level. I suggest you take them back to your office."

With that, the two men stepped forwards, and they followed Tom as he left Barbara's office and went down the corridor to his room. He had no chairs for visitors, but they seemed happy to stand either side of him as he operated his keyboard and called up files onto his screens.

"Can we see Leonard's search history for the last month?" the taller man asked in a Canadian or American accent.

Tom got it onscreen, but he failed to tell them that Leonard invariably asked him to undertake searches, so not much would appear in Leonard's search history.

"Look how often he checked the basketball scores," the shorter man commented, noting the predominance of sporting websites.

"Will you print that out for us and also put it on a memory stick?" the other man requested.

"Y-yes," Tom said, wondering who still used memory sticks. He was trying not to speak too much as his stuttering would be off the scale; he was feeling nervous and threatened. His loyalty to Leonard was growing in the light of all this inquisition.

"How do we find a list of the files he either searched for, opened" – the shorter man paused – "or asked to be signed out of Registry?"

"I don't know about R-Registry," Tom lied, "This is the l-list of what he opened on his c-computer."

"Will you add the list to the memory stick as well?" asked the taller man, who had hair cut high above his ears as if he had recently found Jesus.

"N-no problem."

"Did Leonard search for Project Ortolan?" questioned the shorter man with the bright-white teeth and fake tan.

"Y-yes, it's one of the m-most active p-projects."

"Can I see the search history?"

"Y-yes." Tom tapped the keyboard. "This is the history of everyone who's accessed the file, including the new director, yesterday and this m-morning." Tom couldn't bring himself to use Barbara Aumonier's name. He also didn't know the exact allegiance of the investigating duo.

Eventually, the invasion of his office came to an end, but

not before the man with the tan had pointed out how much Tom looked like the model of Woody on his desk. After the men had left and the door to his office had closed, Tom stared at it for a long while, wondering what had happened that had disrupted his life and that of his colleagues in Five Eyes in the last couple of weeks.

I wonder where Leonard is? Tom thought to himself. He was feeling a certain nostalgia.

"Crap!" Leonard had, at that very moment, cut his finger while trying to open a bottle from the minibar. He was staying in what had been described as a 'modestly priced room' in Dubai. He was paying for it out of his own pocket and was now starkly aware of what you get when you reduce your accommodation budget by eighty per cent. The room was spacious but virtually devoid of furniture or basic comforts, and it overlooked a roof that was littered with air-conditioning units. The room faced away from the sea, instead overlooking modern buildings that were engulfed in a grey-brown smog.

"Double crap!" He bent over as a sharp pain pierced his left side. He stood up and walked slowly around the room while bending just enough to make the pain tolerable. He swallowed two tablets with a swig of whisky directly from the bottle and sat down at the desk, pushing the tray with the kettle and a selection of teas, coffees and sugars to the side. He had already eaten the little pack of shortbread biscuits.

Many years previously, Habib Murchison – or Cameron, as Leonard knew him – had asked only one thing: that Leonard would look after the boys if anything should happen to him. This had always seemed strange as they were likely to inherit millions, if not billions, should anything befall him. Yet this unlikely event had happened, and Leonard was in the odd position of not being able to tell the sons what their father had been involved in.

Leonard was never one to dwell on the past or regret missed opportunities, but he couldn't help reflecting on the fact that he had been twenty-four hours too late. Someone had got to Cameron first; he would never be able to think of him as Habib, he realised. And this someone may have the sons in their sights, perhaps putting pressure on the Murchison Arabco business in the Middle East.

Cameron wanted to be buried back in Canada with his late wife, Mary – a wonderful woman whom Leonard knew from his days at Langley. This didn't surprise him, even if the interment of a Christian and Muslim together might raise a few eyebrows. He finished the miniature bottle of whisky and consoled himself that at least this wasn't the worst thing he now had to think about. *Nobody died,* as he liked to say to his staff around the world when they had suffered a setback. Sadly, this time someone had died, but would putting their bodies in the same grave really offend God? Wouldn't God be more interested in what Cameron and Mary had been trying to avert?

CHAPTER SEVEN

"I need an autopsy doing." Leonard was on one of his phones to Mike.

"Trust me, Leonard, if you can ask for one, you don't need one."

"I need it carried out on our Canadian friend. He won't be flown out of here for a few days."

"Can't you ring in the request to your lords and masters? They must be able to pull a few strings through the embassy." She didn't understand his difficulty.

"I have a slight problem with that."

"Leonard, are you out there officially or unofficially?"

"Sort of unofficially."

"We've had this conversation before. I would prefer a simple yes or no." She broke off as a loud noise came down the phone line. "What's that?"

"My room faces straight at the speakers high up on a minaret. It's Friday prayers."

"So? Is it a yes or a no?"

He didn't answer directly, but having walked to the innermost corner of his room, he said, "I'm on my way back to the US."

"Your geography is way off. What did you do? Buy a round-the-world ticket?"

"Would you drop some hints to the Canadian Embassy out here and the media that he was murdered? You know, making sure there's no trail."

"Leonard, I've been up all night and need some sleep. There's a lot I've found out that I would like to tell you about. When are you back in London? I'm assuming that you're flying this way back to the US?"

"I'm not going to be back in London. Maybe never."

She thought about this. "How do I send you stuff?"

"That's tough. Why not fly out here for the three days until I leave?"

"No!"

"I'm in the Royal Manta Hotel. By the way, if you look on the back of that card I gave you at The Greedy Pelican, you'll see a requisition code. It's good for $20,000. It's already signed off. It's kosher, and it doesn't matter what happens to me. Book a flight."

"No."

"Think about it."

No."

———

Mike was halfway down her external stairs, in desperate need of a walk in the forest to calm her down, when her phone rang.

"Hi, any developments?" Chris was sounding very jolly.

"Oh, hello, Chris. Yes, lots ... but it will be difficult to communicate them to you over the phone."

"How about I call in? In a few minutes, I'm setting off for a hotel at Heathrow ready for a flight tomorrow."

"Sure. What time?"

"How about I bring lunch? I'll pick up a pizza on my way; 1pm?"

"Great." Mike would enjoy seeing him again.

"You allergic to anything?"

"Leonard," she said, and he laughed. "No, I eat everything."

"Perfect. See you soon." He rang off.

She bounced down the stairs and headed for the pine trees with her mood already improved having spoken to an enthusiastic and positive human being. While walking along a grassy ride that acted as both a firebreak and as an access route for the forester, all she could hear was a jay's rasping call and the buzz of insects; a pile of cut logs provided a place to sit and soak up the sunshine. Mike had grown to love her solitary existence, but one of the downsides was that she didn't have much to distract her. Like a song that won't leave your mind, some thoughts just kept flooding back however much she attempted to push them away. Distraction techniques such as picking at the soft, red bark of the logs with her nails only worked for a few seconds.

"Damn!" She jumped up and set off back to the cabin, travelling down a different path and disturbing a snipe or woodcock, which flew rapidly away. Her thoughts had returned to Leonard. Didn't they always? There was no point fighting it, she would do as he asked and disseminate misinformation and suspicion about Habib Murchison's death; this wasn't difficult for her to do using routes via the dark web. Mike could see this death was of critical importance to Leonard, but she couldn't yet see why. He had even diverted to Dubai on his way back to Langley; presumably, he had been recalled there to face the music. Would she ever see him again?

She was thinking about the fact that Leonard had already set up a payment to her for $20,000 even before they had met in that awful pub near Heathrow when the cabin appeared through the trees and a pair of pigeons flew off from the roof. Subconsciously, she was already running through ideas to provoke the authorities into questioning the death – she couldn't stop herself.

Once back inside the cool of her room, she started to interact with the Canadian Embassy websites in Abu Dhabi, Doha and Riyadh; next, she did the same for the Canadian consulates in Dubai and Muscat and, finally, the High Commission of Canada in London. Once a foundation had been laid and a history created, this was promoted and cross-referenced. The story developed a life of its own. She sent press releases to a dozen TV channels and newspapers in the UK and the Middle East, again linking these to each other. She quickly set up a social media campaign demanding an autopsy before Habib was buried in Victoria. *That should put the cat among the pigeons,* she was thinking as she heard a car pull up outside. Hours had passed unnoticed.

Mike quickly changed into her red wig, opened the door, and went down to collect the pizzas and carry them back up. Chris, in a yellow polo shirt and dark-blue trousers, pulled himself up the stairs behind her.

"We'd better eat the pizzas before they get cold," he said.

"I'm starving. I was up all night, and Leonard's had me running around all morning." She stopped herself. "I'll fill you in after the food."

They opened the two boxes and munched on slices of margherita pizza with added extra olives.

"Where are you flying to tomorrow?" she asked while trying to pinch a stringy bit of mozzarella between her fingers.

"Dubai and on to Doha a day or two later."

She stopped chewing and put the remains of the slice back into the box. "*What?*" she almost shouted, and several seconds passed. "Dubai? I'll kill Leonard. How long has he known that you're going to Dubai?"

"I'm not sure he knows."

"I don't buy it. I don't do coincidences. He's just asked me to fly to Dubai for three days. By the way, he's there at the Royal Manta Hotel."

"Leonard's in Dubai?" All this was a lot to take in. "You'd better start at the beginning."

Mike updated Chris on Leonard's requests and what she had done to sow seeds of doubt around the Middle East and beyond. She also explained that he was on his way back to head office in Langley, probably to be chastised and suspended.

"It's possible he knew I was going to Dubai," Chris conceded. "It's a huge international delegation with the usual dignitaries that's been in the diary for six months. This is where the IOC [International Olympic Committee] checks all the facilities and sites for the countries bidding for the 2040 Summer Olympics. It's a big, big deal."

Mike looked suspicious. "How is Leonard paying you?"

It was Chris's turn to look suspicious. "I was going to raise that later. He said you would pay me."

"What? We've totally been set up by ... by ..." She didn't bother to fill in the name or accompanying expletives. "Leonard told me this morning that I have an approved requisition order for $20,000. The number is on the piece of card he gave me on Tuesday."

Chris swallowed his last bite, took a mouthful of water and closed the cardboard lid. "Will you go out to Dubai?"

Mike carried the rubbish over towards the sink and rested the boxes on top of her waste bin. "I feel like my life is being manipulated. Knowing that you're out there is great, but I expect you'll be tied up for most of the time and in a hotel on the other side of the city. The upside is that I get to speak to Leonard face to face. With his current status at the Agency, it's impossible to speak to him in any depth on his phone – we end up speaking in code; you know how it is."

"I do."

"The death of Habib Murchison has changed things substantially; I just have this feeling. I can tell from Leonard that something has gone terribly wrong. He didn't fly out there for the fun of it." She lifted her glass of water. "He said, in his coded way, that this whole thing was about something that Habib Murchison could see from his villa window. I've been searching half a dozen things."

"Such as?"

"Well, so far, I've been checking quarries, cement works, ports, the Strait of Hormuz, Iran and a British listening station. There's a small chance he might be able to see an exclusive beach resort accessible only by four-wheel drive or by paraglider, but I doubt that."

"I can't believe all this is about anything industrial. It must be about the strait, Iran or the listening post, surely?" Chris was weighing up the possibilities.

"I agree, but I haven't found anything yet."

"Was Leonard ever a field agent? Only this all seems a bit 'boots on the ground'."

"Well, I think he must have been one 100 years ago. If he was an analyst, we might as well all go home. He can barely type."

"So?" Chris looked at her across her kitchen table.

"I know I've been set up by him again, but ... I will go. There's no point doing half a job here." She looked around at the cabin.

"Great. I fly at 9am tomorrow. It arrives in the evening. We're all on a special British Airways flight."

"In a minute, I'll book an Emirates flight from Heathrow for about the same time," she said, with the decision made.

———

Callum's splayed fingers were gripping the wire mesh. Together with Harper, he was in a protective metal cage at the top of the quarry in the blistering heat. This was a viewing platform normally only used by visiting dignitaries; it was perched on the top rock bench with a panorama normally only seen from a plane window. Far below were the cement works, the port and their own nondescript computer building, separated by a stretch of Persian Gulf shoreline.

"Harper, we own all of this." Callum was trying to come to terms with everything.

"I preferred it when Father did."

"Me too. How much longer can we keep this place secret?"

"We've managed it pretty well so far. Once the funeral is over, nobody will be interested in who owns some bits of old industrial plant."

They both laughed at the idea of describing their father's pride and joy as 'some bits of old industrial plant'. Far below them, they could see thirty of the dump trucks negotiating their way up haul routes and along twenty miles of rock benches – each truck could carry ninety tons of rock. Every day, 120,000 tons was crushed and transported down to the cement works, the loading bays and the port. It was one vast ant colony in perpetual motion. Despite the noise and the dust (and even the regular explosions as the working faces were blasted), a pair of falcons circled in front of the brothers, almost 2,000 feet above sea level in the hot desert air.

"You do still want to keep going, don't you?" Callum asked.

"Of course ... I can't give up now."

"You know that means we can't sell Father's company? We need the cover. We need the energy."

"If we sell, we sell it all ... but who would buy the farm without control of the energy supply?"

"Let's take a big dividend from the company and continue the way we are. I'm enjoying it."

"Agreed. We did our best to hide the farm, we put up enough barriers and disguised it as well as we could."

"Let's go back to the villa. I need a drink."

The two brothers fist bumped and turned to leave the viewpoint. Fifty yards away, a silver Range Rover was waiting for them, its engine running and the air conditioning on full.

If they'd been more attentive, they would have seen two men with binoculars on the opposite rim of the quarry. They weren't watching falcons.

———

After the heat and dust of the quarry, they both felt like having a quick shower. As they walked around the cool villa, there was a silence that only served to emphasise the missing presence of their father. Some of this was undoubtedly down to guilt. While they had their own bedroom suites with wardrobes full of clothes, they had chosen never to treat it as home. They would turn up with suitcases, almost to make the point. As if the death of their mother hadn't been traumatic enough, they never understood their father's move to the Middle East and his conversion to Islam. They still saw themselves as Canadians who had been educated in the UK and now lived happily in London.

There had been big arguments, but somehow, the distances between Edinburgh, London and Oman provided enough space for a working relationship to be maintained. Of course, their father's natural desire to engage with his sons and encourage them in whatever field or fields they chose smoothed over much of the tension.

Callum had come back downstairs first and had been sitting in the smaller of the lounges while on the phone to the lawyers in London, running through what needed to be done, especially in regard to ownership transfer in the Turks and

Caicos. Next, he would repeat the exercise with their lawyers in Canada re dealing with the remaining holdings, but mostly with the validation of the will. He was pouring a bottle of beer into an ice-cold glass when his brother walked in wearing a patterned cotton shirt and rubbing his still-wet ginger hair.

"I need one of those," Harper said.

"I think we may be drinking quite a few."

Harper located a control on the wall that lowered the oriental-looking blinds on all the windows to about half mast. Even through the partially tinted glass, the glare from outside was unavoidable. The psychological effect of lowering the blinds was immediate. Without the need to say anything, they were aware that they never spent this much time together in London.

Callum was pouring his brother a beer, which he'd found in a fridge cunningly disguised and hidden in a pale-walnut cabinet, when his phone rang.

It was Mohammed.

"Hi," Callum answered.

"I need to come up to the villa. The news channels are saying that your father was murdered. This is crazy."

CHAPTER EIGHT

Heathrow on a Saturday morning was busy. Mike had checked in her battered suitcase at the Emirates' desk and had made her way through security. Ignoring all the shops, she wandered around aimlessly with her rucksack on her back. She had woken early and was in desperate need of caffeine. When she was finally sitting with an Americano and slice of millionaire's shortbread, she texted Chris to see if he'd also had a relatively stress-free passage to the lounge. A few minutes later, he walked into the coffee shop and sat down next to her. He was dressed in beige trousers, a dark-blue blazer, a white shirt and a tie that looked as if the Stars and Stripes flag had been sliced up and sown back together randomly.

"You scrub up well," she said. "Would you like a coffee? I need another one."

"No, thanks; I only have ten minutes. I'll need to rejoin the others. It took me a while to get through security. It's never easy for me, what with the legs and everything."

She drained the last mouthful of cold coffee from the paper cup, but she could think of nothing to say.

"Well, you've certainly stirred everything up if the news

programmes and social media are anything to go by," he said, rotating the maroon tray to align with the table edge.

"Better than I expected. I hope his lordship is happy. I've arranged dinner with him tonight." They both knew they would need to talk obliquely, not mentioning names.

"I'm sorry I can't join you tonight, but I saw that your hotel is only a ten-minute cab ride from ours."

"When's your first visit?"

"Tomorrow evening."

"Do you know when they'll announce who's been awarded the Summer Olympics?"

"No, it's not been decided yet, but it's between Montreal, Istanbul, Mexico, Doha and Nusantara."

"Nusantara? Where is that?" Mike had never heard of it.

"Indonesia. It's the new capital that's under construction now. Remember that this is for 2040."

"True, that's a long way off. I think I'd better worry about the next three days ... which are to be spent in the same hotel as you-know-who."

"Things have clearly developed since he met you originally. The fact that he'll be able to speak freely and tell you what's really happening is a great advantage."

"I hope so. I'll fill you in when we next meet up."

"Perfect. I'd better get back to the business lounge. Stay safe."

"No running off with a gorgeous Serbian weightlifter," she ribbed him.

"Unlikely on several fronts." He winked, stood up and negotiated his way through the tables, vanishing into the crowd.

———

"I'll do my best." Mohammed was standing in what had been Habib's office and was talking with the two sons.

"He had a heart attack. Where did all these rumours start?" Callum was visibly red around his neck and sweating despite the air conditioning. "Can't we kill all of this nonsense?"

"As I said, I'll do my best, but another one of my police friends – a chief inspector here in Oman – wants to come up here and interview you both. He's under pressure from above. He must be seen to be investigating."

"What do you mean by 'from above'?" Harper asked.

"I mean 'the top'. Various ambassadors and the press have been asking questions of our Deputy PM. He is also our Minister for Relations and International Cooperation Affairs."

"But it's just stupid speculation by some shit-stirrer." Callum was exasperated.

"Maybe, but it can no longer be swept under the carpet." Mohammed was doing his best to keep things calm.

Harper walked around a desk and sat down. "Who gains from all of this? I can't think of anyone. Did my father have enemies?"

"No enemies who would want to kill him, I think, but many commercial competitors."

"But Father's dead. What do they gain from all this? He's gone. He's no longer a threat of any kind." Callum could see no logic in this.

"Perhaps they want to make it difficult for you two?" Mohammed suggested.

"Why?" Harper asked, but there was no reply. "And what would an autopsy prove? Only that he had a heart attack or had a congenital heart problem." He was also at a loss to understand.

Mohammed kept quiet for a few seconds to let the sons vent their frustration, then responded, "With the greatest respect, we don't need to speculate. Please compose yourself for when the chief inspector is here later. If he's happy when he leaves, he'll file his report, and there will be no autopsy or delay." He paused. "Again, he's my friend and he knew your father."

"Thanks, Mohammed, we understand." Callum had now begun to see a way forward.

———

While Leonard may have been disappointed by the Royal Manta Hotel, Mike was impressed due to her life not having consisted of first-class air travel and five-star hotels. She marvelled at the central sculpture in the atrium. In fact, she wasn't sure that it was a sculpture; it was a six-foot-wide tower of large pebbles held together by chicken wire extending up seven storeys. Having travelled up in the inward-facing glass lifts, she entered her room on the fourth floor to be confronted with a corner view of the city and the desert hinterland. It took her two minutes to open the minibar and drink a can of ice-cold orange juice. The contrast with her cabin was enough for her to enjoy every sight, smell and sound.

She began unpacking her suitcase, realising that every piece of clothing she had ever owned would fit in the room's three wardrobes with their sliding doors. However, there was nowhere to mount her three wigs and nothing that she could adopt or adapt. They would have to stay inside her emptied suitcase.

Her various pieces of computer hardware were distributed between the safe and the top of the bathroom cabinets. Her late husband Dylan's breaking and entering equipment didn't need hiding; these items were disguised as the simplest of everyday objects. She sat back on the bed, satisfied with her work, and decided to have a shower. The telephone on her bedside table rang.

"Four zero four," she said.

"Isn't that an error message?"

"Hello, Leonard, you might make an analyst yet. I've just arrived." She didn't bother to ask how he knew she was in room 404.

"Can I come over?"

"Sure."

"See you in five."

The last bit of unpacking needed to be done before he arrived, and therefore she hung some more clothes in the wardrobe and took her washbag into the bathroom. After reopening her suitcase, she grabbed her red wig. There was a tap at her door as she was turning up the fan on the air conditioning.

"Hey, your room's better than mine," he said on being invited to enter, not bothering to say hello, "and mine needs redecorating."

Well, it will after you've been in it a week, Mike thought to herself. "Make yourself at home," was what actually came out of her mouth.

"Have you eaten yet?" It was almost 9.00pm in Dubai.

"No, but I ate on the plane."

"Shame. I was thinking we might order room service."

His face looked a little drawn, and there were bags under his eyes. His sleeves were rolled up, and there was a sweaty sheen on his skin. Mike felt a pity for him that came from some deep respect that had been building over the years. While revolting in so many ways, he was a good man at heart, and he was clearly suffering.

"Let's do that, then you can cut the BS and tell me the whole story. I flew out here, by the way."

"Thanks, I noticed. They do a great sirloin steak sandwich with fries." There was no pause between the acknowledgement and the menu recommendations.

The next five minutes could have been avoided if they had listed what he *didn't* want from the room-service menu rather than what he did. His order placed, he slumped back in an armchair that was too small for him, a gin and tonic from the minibar in his hand. Mike made herself comfortable on the bed, nursing a bottle of Sprite.

"Right. Shoot!" she demanded, "From the beginning. Do I need to repeat the terms and conditions?"

"No." He screwed up his face as if the tonic were a little too bitter. "Cam Murchison was a friend of mine. We met a long time ago when he was still in Canada, and I was still in Washington, DC. His wife, Mary, had been a key source for me. Her parents were Assyrian refugees who ended up in Toronto; there's a load of them there. She would do anything to change Iran back into a state that genuinely accepted Assyrians. She hated the Shah, the Ayatollahs and most of the Shias, who didn't see her ... tribe, whatever ... as Persian; you know, Iranian."

He took a sip, but Mike didn't notice as she was starting to draw up a long list of questions in her head before he continued.

"She gave everything for the cause. We, at the Agency, couldn't believe what she did, even with a young family." Leonard stopped and stared at his near empty glass. "Then she drowned, and I always thought we'd let her down." He stood up awkwardly and paced slowly around the room, stretching his back; this wasn't the Leonard that Mike knew of old. This wasn't the buffoon.

She walked over to the minibar without saying anything, took out a can of beer and returned to the bed.

"Cam had been the very best cover for her, but it had gone wrong. The MOIS – they're the Iranian Ministry of Intelligence and Security – killed her, but nothing could be proved, and the West couldn't reveal what she had been doing for us.

Cam changed. Hey, who wouldn't? He sold up shop and moved to Oman. He very discreetly took up the challenge."

He returned to his chair and they both took a sip.

"Normally, you have to encourage a Joe, but not Cam. I couldn't hold him back."

"Were you in London by then?"

"Yes, just moving across. He said he was converting to Islam and that it was for genuine reasons. I told him that was the stupidest idea I'd ever heard, but he did it so perfectly and, of course, believably. He became the Agency's best source in the Middle East. A widowed multimillionaire businessman who appeared to have run away and hidden himself with his money, but actually, he was as active as anyone."

"So, that's what you meant by telling me he could see the problem from his villa?"

"Yeah, but it's a bit more complicated than that."

"Ain't it always so?"

Leonard went on explaining the background until there was a rap at the door. With food to distract him, he stopped. For the next few minutes, they sat opposite each other, eating from the two trays that had been delivered. Despite the air conditioning, the room began to smell of steak, fries and onions.

"How do the sons feature in all this?" Mike changed her approach slightly.

"Until Harper answered the door on Thursday, I'd never met them. Cam kept them separate and at a distance in London. I don't think they come out here much. Obviously, they know nothing of his activities ... or their mother's."

"Why did you come out to see him?"

As it was so often with Leonard, he didn't answer the question directly. "We installed the usual kit in the villa for him. It made communications easy, especially having that British listening station nearby. Handy that. To keep the relationship personal – you know the drill – we would meet up a couple times a year, mostly in London but occasionally out here." He paused as something crossed his mind. "We need to get that kit out of the villa." Who 'we' referred to wasn't specified.

"Your trip was pre-arranged, then?"

"Sort of."

"Leonard!"

"OK, OK; it was off the record. He specifically asked me to visit, and I came out here off my own bat because I can't trust London ... and by 'London', I mean both our HQ and Chiswick. He said he would have something big for me by the time I arrived. I was going to use the trip to warn Cam that he might be compromised. I was a day too late."

"Who killed him?"

"The Iranians, I presume, but I can't be certain."

It was Mike's turn to go quiet and think before speaking. "When you asked me to look for who might be compromised among Five Eyes, did you suspect your contacts were in danger?"

"Yes, that's why I want you to find out who it is. I can't use my crew in London, and I may not be around much after this trip out here."

"If you've been suspended, how come they've let you come out here?"

"I haven't been suspended; it's more that I've been called back to explain why I shouldn't be suspended."

"What do you expect me to do?"

"Find out who's compromised and find out who killed Cam. They're probably linked." It was Leonard's turn to change tack: "By the way, good work on the disinformation. They really should be under pressure to check out the cause of death, but who knows? They might just kick it into the long grass."

"Is there anything else I can do to stir it up?" Mike wanted as much of a steer as possible.

"Just keep pouring gasoline on the fire. The royal families out here don't want murdered businessmen as the main story. Make sure it doesn't drop down the page."

"No problem."

"And in your spare time, could you check out the two sons? You know how we don't like coincidences. Why was he murdered when they were both out here?"

Mike moved on to BlueStar, who had attended – or at least arranged – the lunch in Doha with Cam/Habib. She pulled up the photograph on her phone and showed it to Leonard.

"Do you know a BlueStar? Do you know who this is?"

"No. All new to me, but Cam was very precious about his contacts."

"How about these two men turning up half an hour after Cam returns from Doha and half an hour before the sons find him dead?"

"Nope. They didn't stay long, did they? They were let in through the gate, so someone knows about them."

"That's what I thought."

They went on chatting for a few minutes and agreed to meet for breakfast downstairs the next morning. Leonard looked weary, and Mike was very tired after her long day. When he had left, she quickly cleaned her teeth, put her phone on flight mode and fell into a deep sleep.

CHAPTER NINE

It was 9.00am, and Callum and Harper were awaiting the arrival of the chief inspector.

Mohammed had suggested that they stayed in a lounge and allowed him time to greet the officer at the front door. The room was on the south side of the villa, which necessitated opaque glass in the windows; this was irrelevant as the floor-to-ceiling gold curtains were permanently closed. Callum was sitting in an ornate armchair while Harper walked around, seemingly obsessed with the patterns of the silk rugs scattered across the marble floor. He stopped in front of a carved mantlepiece, below which there was a hearth that had never been sullied by soot or smoke. The large painting on the chimney breast took his eye; he had never noticed it before. It was by Juan Gris and looked incongruous in such a classically decorated room. It didn't appeal to Harper's logical mind. "Why try to paint bottles and plates only using triangles and three colours?" he asked Callum.

He never received a reply, as the double doors opened and a man who looked more military than police entered, followed by Mohammed. He had a black peaked cap with silver decoration on it under one arm, epaulettes and tags on his lapels. He offered his hand first to Callum, who had jumped up, and then to Harper.

"I'm Chief Inspector Saeed; I'm pleased to meet you." His face had baggy, sallow skin with dark-brown eyes that displayed warmth but a certain aloofness. His English was good, partly as a consequence of years at the Royal Military Academy at Sandhurst in Berkshire before he joined the Royal Oman Police.

After the introductions and the condolences, the four men sat in the armchairs and waited while a servant placed water and dates on a low table between them.

"How may we help you, Chief Inspector?" Callum asked. "This is a distressing time for my brother and me."

"I've spoken to Mohammed. I wish to speak frankly with you both. I need you to describe in detail what happened to your father and how you found him. There's increasing pressure on me to ask for an autopsy, which I'm sure you don't want?"

He didn't specify where this pressure was coming from, but it could only be from above and probably right from the top. While Mohammed drank some water, Callum described the events of the previous Wednesday; it didn't take long. Harper spoke only to confirm what had been said and to ask why there was any suspicion of foul play.

"As I understand it, your father had no history of heart or other medical problems. His doctor tells me that he was fit and healthy. So why did he die suddenly?"

"Chief Inspector, we don't know, but how else did he die?"

There was no reply to this question; instead, the chief inspector asked, "Why did he fly to Doha for lunch on Wednesday?"

The brothers looked at each other. "No idea; we weren't here."

"Do you have CCTV cameras in the villa and grounds?"

"Probably. You must understand that Harper and I don't live here; we are – were – visiting our father from England."

The policeman turned to Mohammed. "Can you provide my office with any CCTV footage?"

"Of course."

"Where were the two of you all day Wednesday?" The chief inspector's attention had turned back to the sons.

"At the works ... the cement works, I mean." Callum sounded nervous.

"Did your father have any enemies?"

"None that we know of ... but we live in England. We aren't involved in the businesses," Harper answered, sticking to the easier questions.

"Then what were you doing at the works all day?"

Neither son replied instantly.

"We have an office down there that we use when we're out here." Callum was hoping this was enough for the chief inspector, who was looking at them suspiciously.

"Presumably you both inherit the businesses?"

"Yes," Harper said. "It will be a steep learning curve, but we have Mohammed here and Kamal Khalil as CEO. I'm sure there will be a smooth transition."

"What was your relationship like with your father?"

"We loved him very much. Everyone liked him. However, we never fitted in out here." Callum realised too late that this might sound offensive, but he continued, "Since we left Canada, our lives have been in the UK."

The chief inspector picked up his hat and indicated that he wanted to bring the interview to an end. He paused on standing up. "I'm sorry for your loss, but from what I've heard, there should be an autopsy. This will take some time, as I'm sure you can understand. Your father's body is now in the UAE. Why did you send him there?"

The two boys said nothing, hoping that Mohammed would explain.

"It was the nearest hospital," was all Mohammed said. He had tried to cut corners, and it hadn't worked.

"I'll talk to my superiors. I don't know whether your father will need to be transferred back to Oman or whether the autopsy can be undertaken in the UAE. It's become complicated." He turned to Mohammed: "Please get the CCTV footage, and I'll speak to Kamal Khalil. Clearly, the works are in the UAE and also not in my jurisdiction."

The boys looked at each other as the two men left the room. Things were not going well.

———

Something didn't quite gel, if you excluded the grease on the eggs and turkey bacon at the serving stations. Perhaps it was the smell of hot fried food in a very cold restaurant. Either way, Mike was sitting at a corner table, glad she was wearing sleeves but regretting not wearing sunglasses. Why was everywhere so bright? Was it the excess of lighting using the cheap electricity or the love of shiny surfaces? She was in the restaurant, tucking into cold meats, cheese and croissants, but holding on to the mug of tea for warmth. As soon as Leonard arrived, he could answer the question she had forgotten to ask last night: had he known all along that Chris was coming to Dubai and Doha for the visits to the potential Olympic sites?

They had agreed to meet at 9.00am for breakfast and, as it involved food, Leonard was unlikely to be late. There had been a missed call from Leonard not long after he had left her room last evening; there was no message, and he hadn't rung back, so it couldn't have been important. She ordered another pot of tea from the attentive waiters in their red waistcoats and, at the last minute, added some more croissants to her order. There were five small glass jars of different jams in the middle of the table, and she rotated them to decide which one she would spread on her croissants – that's if she could open the lid.

At 9.20am, she was convinced that Leonard was on some important call and couldn't get away. Ten minutes later, she sent him a row of emojis featuring food that would surely speed up his arrival. She was now full to the limit with blueberry jam and tea. The labels of everything on the table had been read twice, and she was even trying to equate the Arabic with the English translation on the jars and the menu. The live updates from CNN and the BBC on her phone were no longer keeping her occupied.

She dialled the cell phone number that Leonard had given her; it rang, but there was no response.

She managed to distract herself for another few minutes before she stood up and made her way out of the restaurant into an echoing marble hall. A lift was available, and it took her up to Leonard's floor. Along the carpeted corridor, she could see a cleaner's trolley was outside his room and the door was open. Voices could be heard inside, but perhaps these were from a TV.

Mike hesitated before tapping on the opened door, which was being held ajar by a piece of black hand luggage. She walked in confidently, expecting to see Leonard, but was faced by a young man with a trimmed black beard. He was part of the hotel management team, which was confirmed by his gold name badge. He was giving instructions to a cleaner.

"May I help?" he asked.

Mike scanned the room quickly. Some of Leonard's belongings were on the bed and on the desk, including two phones. His suit jacket was on the back of a chair.

"I came to see my father. We're going for breakfast," she replied.

The man stared, assessing her before speaking. "Your father is not well; I'm sorry."

"Where is he?" She tried to sound concerned. "He hasn't called me."

"Ah ... he has been taken to hospital; I am sorry."

"What?"

"He requested an ambulance late last night. It has taken him to hospital." He repeated, "I am so sorry."

"Which hospital?"

"The Mena General Hospital, I expect. Everyone is taken there."

"What happened? Did he have a heart attack?"

"I am sorry; I don't know. I am here to collect his things and put them into storage. He was only booked in until tomorrow."

Mike stood there, dumbfounded.

"May I ask if you are staying with us?"

"Yes, I'm Michaela Kingdom. I'm in 404." She paused. "You can move his things into my room if you like. I'm worried about his wallet and phones."

The man rubbed his beard while thinking. "I'm sorry ... I don't think ..."

He never finished his thoughts as one of Leonard's phones began ringing on the desk next to Mike.

She picked it up and swiped the screen. "Hello, this is Mike; how may I help?"

The male voice on the other end hesitated. "I wanted to speak to Donald."

"He's not here right now; this is his daughter, Michaela. Who's speaking?"

"Harper, Harper Murchison."

"Oh, hi. Dad mentioned you. Is it urgent? May I give him a message?"

"No. Well, yes, could you get him to call me?"

"I will. Thanks for calling."

Mike took out her own phone and entered Harper's number, and then she put all the phones in her pocket without looking at the junior manager. She turned, focused on him and took control. "OK, put Dad's stuff in your secure storage. I'm going to the hospital. Oh, what's your name?" She leant forwards and read the badge. "Thanks, Rohan, I'll come and see you when I get back."

She turned and walked out into the corridor.

———

Mike hadn't calmed down by the time she reached her room. She had been mentally floating just above the very spongy carpet in the corridor and following the rather pointless dado rails that served only to separate the beige paint on the lower half of the walls from the flocked wallpaper. The door to her room shut behind her with a reassuring click. What had just happened?

She didn't even bother to answer that question; she had a long list of things to do that might throw some light on to events. Leonard's two burner phones were weighing heavily in her pocket. She smiled to herself at the thought that she had managed to slip them in her pocket. It was her casual disinterest in Leonard's other personal belongings, washbag and hand luggage that had reassured Rohan that she was, indeed, Leonard's daughter.

Dylan's voice echoed in her head for no apparent reason: "*Hide the phones!*"

She put them on top of the wardrobe and took stock by ticking things off in her mind.

Firstly, she felt an enormous guilt that she had missed Leonard's call; this made her shudder. What if he had died because of this? It didn't bear thinking about.

Secondly, she believed that Rohan was for real. He was junior hotel management and had been called to deal with a sick guest who had been taken to hospital. His instructions were to gather up Leonard's belongings, put them in safe storage and get the room cleaned ready for the next guest.

One thing she now knew almost certainly was that Leonard had been taken to the Mena General Hospital by ambulance. What was wrong with him? Given his lifestyle and the stress he was under, probably several things. He had left his phones in his room, so it had been an emergency. He was also in Dubai incognito, and Leonard was so experienced that, if he wanted to disappear, he knew more than anybody how to stay under the radar. There would be no one looking for him.

She began to think about the stress Leonard must have been under that meant he had flown to Dubai to sort out whatever it was without telling his bosses. Mike stopped speculating. There were phone calls to be made.

Reception at Mena General Hospital was very efficient, but despite providing several ways to track him, they failed to find Sir Donald Reeve, Leonard de Vries or anyone brought into the hospital from the Royal Manta Hotel that morning or the previous evening. This was a surprise to Mike, who immediately rang Rohan to ask for the name of the ambulance service that had collected Leonard. It was at this point that Mike began to get worried. Rohan said it wasn't the hotel that had made the calls, but that he did know the name of the ambulance company, and he gave the number to her.

After another surprisingly helpful conversation, the company explained to Mike that her father had been taken to the hospital on the Al Dhafra Air Base in Dubai.

That he was on a US Air Force (USAF) air base appeared at first to be good news, but then again, she wondered what had happened and how the American military got involved or even knew he needed help. He had purposely flown out to the Middle East without telling anyone.

There was no time to think. Should she call the USAF base? Probably not. He was safe and getting the best medical treatment. There was nothing she could do to help him. What would Leonard want her to do next? "Complete the task you asked me to do," she said out loud to herself.

It all centred on the death of Habib Murchison and on his sons; this was self-evident. She picked up her phone and dialled the number Harper had used to try to call Leonard.

"Hi, Harper, it's Mike ... Michaela .... Donald Reeve's daughter." She needed to remember Leonard's alias.

"Hi, is Donald around?"

"Unfortunately, he's been taken ill, but can I ask you to do something a bit weird? Can I ask you to trust me? I know all about your father, and if there's anything I can do to help, please ask."

"What? I don't know Donald, but he came to the villa just after my father died and asked me to call him if things got messy. He seemed to suspect there would be problems and so it has turned out."

"Let's not speak on the phone. Let's meet as quickly as possible. Shall I come to your villa? I'm in Dubai. Trust me, I really can help."

"What? How can you help?" Harper was letting this all sink in, but he decided that he should pursue every avenue. "I'll send a limo taxi to pick you up. Our driver can return you afterwards."

"I'm in room 404 at the Royal Manta Hotel."

"I'll book the taxi for you. It won't take long ... I mean, it won't take long to arrive; the journey here takes two hours, unfortunately."

"I look forward to meeting you and Callum."

CHAPTER TEN

Mike was in her hotel room, where she was adjusting her black wig in a mirror, the surround of which was gold coloured with what appeared to be hieroglyphics as ornamentation. It made her reflection look like a promotional poster for a production of *Antony and Cleopatra*. Ever prepared, her gizmos and tools were already packed in her rucksack, and she was ready to go down to reception to wait for the taxi to arrive. At the last minute, she decided to phone Chris; if he was tied up, she'd leave a message.

"How are you doing?" He had picked up immediately, and she, as usual, had to resort to the irritating default of speaking in bland statements.

"I wanted you to know I'm about to get in a taxi to the villa. I've been speaking to the sons. I'll be back this evening. But the main reason for phoning is to tell you that our beloved uncle has been taken ill. He's now at the USAF hospital. I have no details."

"Really? Did you speak to him? What's wrong?"

"No idea. I'll tell you about it when we meet. I stumbled across it. When do you fly back to London?"

"I'm off to Doha this afternoon. We're looking at progress on the various arenas and facilities. I fly back Tuesday."

"If you had to stay out here a couple of nights, would that be difficult?" she queried.

"Well ... it's possible. Will you let me know how your visit goes?"

"Will do."

"Be careful."

"Always."

For no apparent reason, the air conditioning in the room cut out and the sound of hotel staff appeared in the background. As if this was a cue, Mike collected Leonard's phones, grabbed her rucksack and opened the door. She walked along the corridor to the lift, musing on why we all end up in places that were never part of the plan (as if we had one). From the internal lift, the view of the gravity-defying, sculptural pile of stones at the centre of the atrium only served to convince her that nothing was what it seemed.

There was a surfeit of staff on duty at reception, eagerly waiting for a guest with a problem. She was walking by when she spotted Rohan smiling at her from behind a long counter. He lifted a hinged part and stepped towards her.

"Have you heard from your father?" His concern sounded genuine.

"I'm going there now," she lied.

"Please let us know if we can help. Do you have a taxi booked?"

"Yes, it should be here in the next few minutes."

He encouraged her to walk to some seats near the main entrance, purposely located there for such situations. He said something in a language she didn't recognise to a colleague, who walked outside, she assumed to look for the taxi.

A large American car turned up within minutes, almost blocking the entrance. After some nodding among staff, Rohan told her this was her taxi. The door was opened for her, and she sat in the back, almost swallowed up by the folds of beige leather. In twenty minutes, the view from the car had transformed from skyscrapers to sandy desert with random fences and the occasional scrawny camel. The panorama behind showed the high-rise centre of Dubai against a perfect spray-painted sky of browns and blues. The driver, who was an ex-NCO from the Indian army, sported a fine handlebar moustache, but he said little. The car gave the impression that it was driving itself along the smooth, sweeping motorway.

After an hour and a half, Mike's ears popped as the road climbed steadily through the mountains, travelling north-east. Apart from a boy with a herd of brown, white and black goats, all she saw was the constant stream of aggregate and cement lorries heading downhill to Dubai and beyond. The quarry, works and port were below and to her left, but she never saw them behind the landform and screening banks.

———

At that exact moment, Chief Inspector Saeed was on the phone to Kamal Khalil, the CEO, at the works 1,000 feet below Mike and to the west. The men were speaking in Arabic.

"Thank you for confirming that," the policeman was saying, "I'm trying to establish the movements of everyone involved on that day. And you are saying that there's no way the sons could have left the works and returned to the villa?"

"No, they have to pass this office in which all vehicle movements are logged and filmed on CCTV. That's every vehicle — cars, lorries and vans," the CEO explained. "They came here in the morning and left with their driver at 6.25pm, having been here the entire time."

"What were they doing all day? They aren't actively involved in your construction material businesses, are they?"

"They are now – they've inherited it all." He took a breath while he thought things through. "They've always kept an office down here, which they use whenever they're out here visiting their father."

"Why do they need an office?"

"To run their UK affairs, I presume."

"Couldn't they do that from their father's villa? It must have ten spare rooms?"

"I don't know the answer to that."

The chief inspector changed the subject: "Did they get on well with their father?"

"Yes, they spoke fondly of each other. I never saw any animosity. May I ask why you suspect he's been killed?"

"Important people think Habib Murchison was murdered." He didn't bother to elaborate further. "They are now taking an interest. I've spoken this morning with my UAE counterparts, and Mr Murchison's body is being transferred to Oman for an autopsy. This will be undertaken in The Mortuary in Muscat" – here, he was using the facility's actual name – "to establish if there has been any foul play."

"Habib was a close friend of mine; as you know, I was – am – the CEO of his business empire here in the Middle East. I find talk of foul play distressing."

"I understand, and his death may prove to be from natural causes, but you're fully aware of the rumours and pressure coming from various important places. An autopsy will clear this up."

"Thank you. Is there anything else I can help you with at this stage?"

"No, you've been most helpful. Let's hope that it is natural causes, otherwise the implications are almost unthinkable. In fact, under such circumstances, who do you think might want to kill Mr Murchison?"

"Chief Inspector, of our commercial competitors, I cannot speak, but on a personal level, he was a much-respected man."

"You are implying that commercial competition may be a motive?"

"I won't lie to you. Our contracts are for tens of millions of dollars, but there's no real reason why these might lead to ... murder."

"Thank you." The chief inspector ended the call.

———

Mike hadn't expected the villa to be so high up in the mountains; the views, when available between peaks, were stunning. Her preparations had told her that Oman had a very small outlier, an isolated area of land within the UAE, which formed the northern end of the Hajar Mountains that face Iran across the strait. In reality, there were no borders, no barriers and no signs. She had no idea if she was in the UAE or Oman.

Entering the gates to the villa was like entering another world. The limousine drove along the paved road and pulled up outside the pillars of what she thought resembled the White House. After getting out, she walked up the steps and turned round at the top to take in the views. The doors opened and a tall, ginger-haired man appeared, holding out his hand in welcome.

"Harper," he said, and he moved back to let her enter the marble hall.

The private jobs that Mike had undertaken since her accident had meant she had been introduced to wealth and large private houses, but none of these prepared her for the over-the-top opulence of this villa. Despite the chandeliers; the long, gold drapes; and the high ceilings, it still managed to feel like a home and not a museum. In a lounge with small, white sofas and a long display cabinet full of tiny objects, many encrusted with diamonds, she sat while a servant poured her a glass of a red liquid.

"Thank you," she said, waiting until she was alone with Harper before continuing, "I'm so pleased you trusted me enough to let me come to see you. I'm not sure I would have if it had been the other way around."

Harper Murchison crossed his legs and evaluated his visitor, a thirty-something woman with a pock-marked face and a black Cleopatra wig, who had walked in with a slight limp.

"Are you Canadian?" he asked, slightly bemused by her accent.

"American, from Oregon ... via London."

"And how does your father know my father, and how can you help us?"

Mike looked at him directly and, having thought about it on the long journey, gave it to him straight: "He's not my father; he's my ex-boss. We're in intelligence. For the moment, please don't ask for any more detail on that. Your father was helping Donald" – here, she had to concentrate again so she kept the story straight and didn't use the wrong names – "and your mother was also in intelligence."

Mike had decided that, as both parents were dead, she could reveal enough that Harper, and Callum, would be so gobsmacked that they would be keen to help her.

She was right about the impact. Harper was already stressed out by his father's death and the chief inspector's visit; therefore, Mike's revelations served to turn his world upside down further.

He stood up. "I ... I'll go and get Callum. We should hear this together." He began to leave.

"Harper, I'm here to help."

While he was out of the room, Mike walked to a large window and stared down at what she presumed was the Strait of Hormuz. Living up to what she had read, four oil tankers could be seen on their way to the Indian Ocean, with a couple of small fishing boats giving scale to the scene.

Harper returned, accompanied by his younger brother.

After some cursory introductions, Callum said, "I think you'd better start at the beginning."

Mike managed to avoid mentioning the CIA, Five Eyes or Iran. Instead, she kept it as vague as possible and asked them to concentrate on the fact that it was likely their father had been murdered.

"This is all so surreal," Callum declared. "We came out here a few days ago, and since then, our father has been murdered, and now we've learnt that he and our mother were spies. *Unbelievable*."

"Donald" – she had almost called him Leonard – "spoke very highly of both your parents."

"Did you know my father?"

"No, I didn't; my job is to find out who killed him and to make sure both of you are safe."

This alarmed the brothers.

"Where is Donald?" Harper asked.

"He's in hospital, which is why I'm here now."

She failed to mention that her real task was to find a possible traitor in Five Eyes or its component organisations and to save Leonard's ass. She took a sip of the hibiscus juice just as Harper's phone rang.

"Hello. Hello, Chief Inspector," he answered. There was a long silence. "Of course, I'll tell my brother ... Really? Really, we had no plans to leave anyway. Please let us know the results as soon as you have them. Goodbye."

He turned to Callum and then to Mike. "That was Chief Inspector Saeed. Father's body is being transferred from the UAE to Muscat for an urgent autopsy. He'll phone us when he has the results. He asked us both not to leave Oman until he's spoken to us again."

"Shit." Callum put his head in his hands.

"Why's the body being transferred?" Mike was confused.

"We're right on the border here between the UAE and Oman. Technically, the villa is just in Oman. When Father died, Mohammed – his Mr Fixit – called up a friend and had the body taken down to the nearest hospital, which is in the UAE. It's so much easier to get to than taking the winding road over the mountains towards Muscat, which is five hours away. You have to remember that we all thought he'd suffered a heart attack," Harper explained.

There was a natural pause in proceedings.

"Have you heard of BlueStar?" Mike needed to know whether they were aware why their father had taken the long trip to Doha for a half-hour lunch.

"No," they said in unison.

"Is it a company?" Callum was curious.

"It could be. It's who your father had lunch with in Doha while you were at the works."

"We didn't know he was going to Doha; he didn't say."

Mike got out her phone and searched through until she found the photograph taken in the Doha restaurant. "Do you know this man with your father?"

"No," they said in unison once more.

She scrolled further in her photographs. "Do you know these two men?"

They both lifted from their chairs to look. Again, they said no.

"Why, are they important?" Callum asked.

"This is from the villa's CCTV. It was taken at 4.33pm, an hour or two before you both came back from the works. Did that vehicle pass you on the way down that afternoon?"

The sons looked at each other and said that they didn't remember seeing it.

"You know, unless a member of staff was involved, these two men could well be your father's killers. Nobody else entered the villa from the time you both left in the morning." She corrected herself: "That's excluding your father leaving and returning, obviously."

"We could ask Mohammed about all of these things," Callum offered.

"No, let's keep absolutely everything we talk about today strictly between the three of us. Maybe we can ask him later, once I've done some more investigation." Mike didn't know where Mohammed's or anyone else's allegiances lay. She was already trusting that Leonard had thoroughly checked out the sons.

Harper was looking bemused. "Who were our parents spying for? Canada? Who were they spying on? Oman? The UAE? I don't get it."

"I can't tell you that, and it's probably best you don't know."

"But you're American. Was father spying for the USA?" Harper enquired.

"Let's call it the West and leave it at that."

"What do you want us to do?" Callum was worried.

"Firstly, be careful. Secondly, let me know the moment anything happens or you think of something, however small. I'll stay in Dubai until this is all resolved."

"Do you think we should stay in the villa?"

"Well, do you need to go down to the works again?"

The two sons looked at each other but said nothing.

CHAPTER ELEVEN

It was Monday morning, and Mike was having breakfast. However, this wasn't croissants and jam in a freezing cold hotel restaurant; it was perfectly poached eggs in the dining room of the Murchison villa. The coffee was hot, and the toast was wrapped in a napkin to keep it moist and warm. She was on her own, admiring the dining room, as the sons had yet to make an appearance. The villa's decoration fascinated her – it was so eclectic, which was perhaps no surprise given the Scottish, Canadian and Omani history of its owner.

Having talked throughout the afternoon following lunch the previous day, the sons had suggested that she stayed the night rather than going back to her hotel. There was nothing Mike couldn't do from the villa that she could have done in Dubai. In fact, she was more likely to discover things here than 100 miles away in a hotel room. Yesterday, the sons had gradually warmed to their odd-looking visitor as the frightening reality of what may have happened to their father dawned on them, along with the idea that they might be next, and their visitor – whoever she was – might be their saviour. The conversation had gone in circles, always returning to the fact that they were vulnerable from some undefined individuals who might also want them dead.

Harper had, at one point, suggested that they ignore the chief inspector's instruction to stay in the villa and instead go to Dubai, jump on a waiting private jet and escape back to England. After all, money was no object, and there was no manned border on the road outside of the villa. Mike – backed up by Callum – had explained that this could only be seen as an admission of guilt and, furthermore, that they owed it to their father to establish how he died and, if it was murder, to help the authorities find the killers.

"There's no extradition treaty between the UK and Oman," Harper had said at one point, but this had been dismissed by Callum with a glance and a reminder that, in addition to finding the cause of death, they now owned the industrial complex down below them. Mike, of course, didn't pick up on the full implication of his use of the words 'industrial complex'.

While they might have been economical with the truth, so had Mike when they had pressed her several times to say who she was working for and what back-up she had at her disposal. She had used some weasel words and had failed to say that it was just her and a Paralympian currently visiting Doha.

———

With her eggs eaten, she poured another cup of coffee and leant against the back of the chair she was sitting in. Was the trip to Doha to meet someone, perhaps BlueStar, connected to the two men who had turned up and, most likely, killed Habib? They could be quite separate events. In fact, the more she thought about it, the more it seemed like the two events must be connected. The killers knew Habib would come back at a specific time, offering only a short window until the return of his sons. They must have known about the Doha trip. And how did the killers gain access through the front gate in their vehicle? She mused that they must be known to the man on security duty and had probably visited the villa before. The prospect of searching back through CCTV footage for weeks didn't appeal to her.

BlueStar was key, but who was he or it, if it was a company? If it was an individual, Mike needed to identify him, but she only had his code name, his phone number and his face – if indeed he was the man in the Doha restaurant photograph. The code name was of no use. It could be anything, and most code names were chosen specifically *not* to help anyone searching. She couldn't trace the phone number and wasn't sure yet whether she should call it, as this would be a do-or-die act. There would be no going back, and she didn't know whether BlueStar was friend or foe. She was at an impasse.

The young man who had been serving her came into the room and asked if she required any cakes or fruit. The idea of cakes at breakfast with strong coffee was very attractive, and Mike accepted. The dozen or so staff around the villa were very attentive; they were all acting as if their employer hadn't just died. They must have appreciated that their futures were likely in doubt. Did they all live on-site? There was no village anywhere nearby. Questions – she was swamped with too many questions. Which were the important ones?

Mike looked at her phone; it was showing 9.00am, which meant that it was 6.00am in London. She sent Tom's sister a message asking her to call her brother and ask him to make contact before he went to work.

Callum had already joined her for breakfast when her phone rang. She made no excuse, but she stood up and walked into a corridor.

"Tom, thank you for calling. Our old boss was taken into the USAF hospital very early yesterday morning. I'm hoping he's all right. If you hear how he is, please let me know. I'm currently at the villa with Habib's sons, who are now very scared that they might be next. I checked Habib's phone, and on the day he died, he had a quick lunch in Doha organised by, and possibly with, someone or some company known as BlueStar. If I give you a telephone number and send you a possible photograph of him from their meal, can you find out who he is? I think he is key."

"N-no problem. I'll b-backdate a request from our old b-boss that authorises me to search. I'll get b-back to you."

"While you're doing that, I'll contact the hospital."

"J-just to let you know that my new b-boss and two men have been investigating our old b-boss and his search history. I'll p-probably call you back at 12.30pm if I've found anything."

"Thanks, be careful."

"Y-you be c-careful."

The call ended, and she rejoined the breakfast that was gradually turning into brunch.

———

At the start of a new week, the staff were entering the Five Eyes' building. The weekend had been sunny, and there were plenty of stories to exchange before they got down to work. It was 10.00am before Tom could start his investigation into BlueStar, the phone number and the possible photograph of this individual. The first two tasks were easy as he had memorised the name and number; it was simply a matter of initiating a search using the enormous computer networks available to him. Checking the photograph was more difficult because he had to leave his personal phone at security. Instead, he used his office computer to search his own Instagram account where he had added the picture, which he then imported and started a check using face-recognition technology. This would all tick away in the background while he undertook his day job.

It turned out that his day job was about to change. Barbara called him into her office. "Tom, have you heard of Andrew Woodhouse or his son?"

"Um, n-no; well, yes. I've seen his name on m-many reports from Australia, but I don't know about his son."

"Did Leonard ask you specifically about Andrew Wood-house or his son? By which I mean recently."

Tom answered truthfully, "N-no, I don't think so. Mr Woodhouse's n-name was at the top of several reports from Australia, but Mr de V-Vries n-never asked me specifically to find any."

"Would you provide me with a list of any reports that mention Andrew Woodhouse and/or his son in the last three months?"

"N-no problem." Tom began to turn away.

"And Tom, will you provide me with a similar list of any reports that mention Harper and Callum Murchison? They're the sons of a Habib Murchison who's just died in Oman."

Tom took out a small pad and wrote down the names. His boss smiled at him with warm eyes and said that was all she needed for the moment.

———

Mike had several hours until Tom phoned her, assuming he found anything. She had a long list of items of her own to check, beginning with Leonard's location.

Something was bothering her about his unexpected illness and transfer to the hospital. If he had suddenly been taken ill in his hotel room, after he had tried her number, who did he call? Reception? The general emergency number in the UAE?

The US Embassy? The USAF hospital? If it was either of the first two of these, he would have ended up in Mena General Hospital like any expat or tourist who's taken seriously ill. If he had rung the US Embassy, he would have revealed he had gone rogue and was up to something in the Middle East. If he was having a heart attack, he probably didn't care about any of this. Did he ring an old CIA contact at the embassy? Would they have organised that he was sent to the military hospital? This was credible. He was unlikely to phone the military hospital himself; he would be dead before he had explained everything and had gotten through to the right person.

If she were right, someone at the US Embassy now knew he was in Dubai and would have told their superiors and colleagues. Given that he was being suspended or, at least, under suspicion, would they fly him directly back to the USA once he was stable?

If Leonard might be described as having 'gone rogue', she wasn't sure what her position would be called. Whatever it was, it meant she had to stay incognito, and that meant the US Embassy was out of bounds.

The USAF hospital was her only hope of checking what had happened to him, but she would need to be very careful. Firstly, he would be using his real name, as he would be there as a CIA director, and everything would be done according to the book. She decided to call as Michaela de Vries, his daughter.

To her surprise, she managed to be transferred to the correct ward with relative ease, and a captain in the nursing corps picked up the phone. Mike played her role as the concerned daughter well. The captain, who sounded like a woman in her forties, confirmed that her father had indeed been on the ward and that he had been stabilised. She had gone on to explain that he was soon to be put on board a USAF plane to Joint Base Langley–Eustis in the USA, where he would be transferred to a specialist hospital. She then said that he would have the operation that had previously been planned. It was a short but useful phone call, and Mike thanked the captain and, after ringing off, took a few seconds to digest what she had just heard.

He was safe – that was the most important thing.

After staring out of the window at some vulture soaring on the thermals among the rugged peaks, several thoughts came into her mind. She listed them: he had probably phoned the embassy, as there was no other likely way he could have ended up at that hospital – he was, after all, a CIA director; the embassy would have organised the ambulance; they now knew he had come to Dubai; the embassy would know he was being flown back to the USA; and they would go to the hotel to collect his belongings and check his room. This thought caused Mike to be thankful that she had his phones in her rucksack and hadn't left them on the top of her wardrobe at the hotel. In one way, this didn't matter as she couldn't easily open them, but at least the Agency wouldn't know they existed and would be unlikely to search his call history. He could make up any story about what he was doing in Dubai for a few days.

Although the conversation had been brief, it was the final sentence that lingered in Mike's mind: *"He will then have the operation that has previously been planned."* What did the captain mean?

At that moment, Callum tapped on her door and asked if she would like to join them for a drink before lunch.

Despite the number of rooms and the opulence of the villa, the sons had defaulted to sitting on barstools in the kitchen with some snacks before them on a granite worktop. They were pouring themselves drinks, making the staff uncertain how and when to serve.

"Have you made any progress?" Callum was probing in as gentle a way as possible.

"Donald's getting better, but he has flown home." Mike was less than specific.

"How about the people in the photographs you showed us?" Harper had moved on.

Mike was very honest: "Nothing yet, but watch this space. I'm expecting a call mid-afternoon."

"I remembered that the chief inspector also asked Mohammed for the CCTV footage from the villa. Perhaps he's identified them?" Callum chipped in.

That the Omani police were checking the two men was probably a good thing, and it showed they were still investigating the death.

As if on cue, Harper's phone rang.

"Hello, Chief Inspector," he answered. There was a short time during which Harper said nothing, and Mike and Callum stared at him, waiting for some sort of indication. "I agree; definitely. Yes, we'll arrange that immediately. Thank you again. Oh, is there anything else that you need from Mohammed or from me and my brother?" There was another pause. "Thank you, Chief Inspector. Goodbye."

He turned to his waiting audience. "Death from natural causes. Father had a heart attack, just like we all suspected."

"We're free to leave?" Callum asked.

"Yes, but not until you and I go to Muscat with some paperwork, passports and stuff to release the body for transport to Canada."

"OK, but that's great news" Callum leant forwards and clinked glasses – first, with his brother and, afterwards, with Mike.

"Yes, that's great news," she said. "Does that mean the police investigation is over?"

"Yes, he said it is. We now only need this No Objection

Certificate, or whatever it's called, and some other bits of paper. We'll get Mohammed on to it after lunch. Happy days."

The relief among the brothers was palpable.

Mike, however, was hiding her deep unease. She was feeling that everything was being conveniently swept under a very expensive carpet from Isfahan. It had even made her suspect Leonard's unexpected illness and medical evacuation flight to the US. The fact that she had told the sons that their father, and mother, were spies seemed to have been forgotten.

"Let's crack open some champagne." Harper had the look of somebody acquitted by a jury of a heinous crime.

"No," his more sensible brother said. "When father's body is on a plane and we're in international airspace, we can drink what we want."

Mike suddenly felt lost. She missed being able to speak to Leonard, and that was a thought she had never thought would pass through her mind. Her body shivered.

CHAPTER TWELVE

Tom had been counting down the minutes until lunch. He needed to communicate his findings to Mike and fill her in on Barbara's latest requests. He wasn't sure which was the most surprising: was it her interest in Andrew Woodhouse and his son, or was it her desire to investigate the Murchison brothers?

Down at the security station in the foyer, Tom collected his phone, logged out and left the building, as he did most days, to get some fresh air and a sandwich. He walked past a pop-up vegetable market and ended up leaning against the stone plinth supporting the statue of a soldier on a horse. There was no one in earshot, and so he dialled Mike's number.

"Hello, Tom."

"M-Mike, I could find, um, nothing on the phone number. It's well-hidden and p-probably untraceable without a lot of input from Cheltenham. Also, our system has nothing on anyone, or anything, called BlueStar; sorry."

"Tom, that's fine. Thanks so much for trying," Mike was at her most gentle and reassuring. In fact, she was probably only like this with Tom.

"I thought the name and phone number would come up

trumps, but ..." He sighed. "I did have some luck with the photograph."

"Really?" Mike was surprised.

"The m-man is Ahrun Yonan." He spelt it out slowly.

"Is he on anyone's system?" By which she meant any of the five services.

"Only at the lowest level as a s-sympathetic Iraqi contact."

"And there was nothing else about him?"

"The bio said that he was Assyrian and born in M-Mosul. Nothing else. Sorry, he's obviously not really on the radar."

"Don't say sorry, Tom; this is very helpful."

"Have you heard anything about Leonard?"

"He's being flown back to the USA to have an operation. I don't know anything else."

"Oh, g-good."

There was a silence interrupted by the voices of market traders selling fruit and veg from Tom's end of the line.

"Tom, I know how difficult this all is, so let me say a big thank you from Leonard and from me. I'll check out the man in the photograph."

The conversation had come to its natural conclusion.

"One m-more thing," Tom added, "my new b-boss asked me this m-morning to give her all the file references to the sons; do you understand?"

"Really? OK. No further explanation?"

"No, just provide a list of files."

Mike thanked Tom again and ended the call. Before rejoining the brothers, she sat and reflected on the new information.

It was no surprise that BlueStar, which she guessed was a code name for an agent, and his phone number were hidden and effectively untraceable. The fact that he was Assyrian intrigued her, given that Mary Murchison, the brothers' mother, was also of Assyrian extraction and was spying against the Iranians. Why had her husband Cameron Murchison, now Habib, flown to meet BlueStar for a half-hour lunch in Doha? It must have been to collect something from him or be told something that had to be said face to face. Mike decided to ask for a coffee and to begin looking into Ahrun Yonan and the whole Assyrian relationship with Iran.

While she was waiting for the young houseboy to bring her the drink, she also pondered why Barbara Aumonier was showing an interest in the sons. Of course, it might be harmless and the natural step in any investigation after Habib had been 'killed'; she might not know yet that the autopsy had concluded that the death was from natural causes.

With a coffee in her hand, Mike wondered whether Leonard had been breaking the rules, as usual, and had kept his friend Cameron Murchison separate or even hidden from the rest of the CIA system. If this was the case, Barbara wouldn't know about him. While holding the cup in both hands and sipping, she remembered that Barbara had been in Saudi Arabia and Qatar on previous postings. Had she met the Murchisons then or even BlueStar and any Assyrian network? Had she even met Mary Murchison in Canada? Mike needed to check the dates.

It was time for her to sit quietly at a computer and do some searching. She now knew that things were becoming urgent. The sons would leave the Middle East as quickly as they could once their father's body was on a plane to Victoria in Canada. She was feeling a slight nervousness about being in the villa; this wasn't from the sons or the staff but from a feeling that powerful forces were involved. She suspected Iran, which was less than thirty miles across the sea to the north, but her uneasiness was probably because the threat could come from one of many other directions.

An hour later, Mike was frustrated. She had spent some time sitting at her laptop searching for Ahrun Yonan with only minimal success. He was an accountant in a gas production company in Doha and married with two children. The only photograph of him came from the company yearbook. He may have been an anti-Iranian sympathiser, but where he fitted into the Murchison affair didn't seem straightforward. "Unless he's just a cut-out, a middleman, a courier ..." she said out loud as it occurred to her. "What did you pass to Habib Murchison? And where is it now?" she whispered at his black-bearded face on her screen.

If it was information passed on verbally, she was unlikely to find it now Habib was dead, unless he had written it down or had it on his system. This was highly improbable. He didn't fly all the way to Doha, avoiding communication channels, to return home and commit it to paper.

She rocked back in her chair and threw both arms back above her head. *If it had been something on a memory stick or similar, it would have been in his pocket, wouldn't it?* She let her mind race. *If not, it could have been in a shoulder bag, wallet or briefcase, say. What if he was sitting in his chair and heard his attackers or suspected something? Would he have hidden it quickly so they wouldn't find it? Or, unfortunately, had they killed him, checked his pockets and removed it? So many possibilities.*

Mike reduced the task in front of her to two basic questions, each of which had a yes/no answer: Did Habib bring some physical object from Doha to the villa? And did the two men who probably killed him know that this object existed?

If the answer to the first question was no, she knew she would have to find or meet Ahrun Yonan. This would involve a trip to Doha. If the answer was yes, the object entered the villa on that fateful afternoon.

If the answer to the second question was yes, the men had probably found it and took it with them, and she would again have to go to Doha. But if the answer was no, the object may still be in the villa. She needed to search his study and bedroom before she committed herself to a trip to Qatar. Should she tell or ask the sons? They had told her to make herself at home and use all the facilities. It wouldn't be difficult to wander into Habib's study, where he died, and into his bedroom. She made up her mind while, in the distance, she could hear Callum and Harper talking in the kitchen.

Carrying only her phone, she walked along the upstairs corridor from her room to find where Habib slept; this wasn't difficult as the corridor ended in a pair of large, ornate double doors. She listened outside and opened one of them gently. It had been cleaned and tidied as if he were coming back tomorrow. Even here, his love of an eclectic range of art was on display. Much of it was more personal and related to his past, such as landscape paintings of Scotland and Canada. On his dressing table was a gold-framed picture of him with Mary on their wedding day; sadly, there was no memory stick or notebook. A gold box looked promising, but it was full of cufflinks, pens and coins. She opened his wardrobes to check through the pockets of his suit jackets and trousers. She had hoped the staff had hung up his clothes without removing the contents of his pockets; however, they were empty, and his *dishdashas* equally yielded nothing.

Her eyes fell on the linen basket. Had they put his clothes in there when they had dressed him for the last time? Disappointingly, it was also empty, although she reached in to check that nothing had fallen out. She opened some drawers, but she could feel a growing nervousness, demonstrated by her sweaty scalp under her wig. It was time to leave. Dylan would have been proud of the efficient way she had searched the room. "*We'll make a field operative out of you one day,*" he had said many times.

Trying to walk normally, she left the room and made her way down the sweeping stairs towards where Habib's body had been found. The sons, who were still chatting in the kitchen, had pointed out their father's favourite room previously. No one, it seemed, was enthusiastic about going back in there.

The first thing Mike noticed was *The Running Man* bronze sculpture, which sat on the floor and faced the gold-upholstered chair in which he had died. She rubbed her hand on its head and tilted it to see if there was anything underneath. Nothing. There were several bookcases, but she could only scan the spines of the books quickly and nothing caught her inexperienced eye. Mike was famous – though perhaps 'reasonably well known' would be more accurate – within the CIA for developing the technique of searching for what's missing from a dataset rather than the more obvious searching for a specific name or word. She applied this technique to the task in hand. *What's missing? What should a study have? Where's the safe?* She wandered around the large room, thinking it all through. *It doesn't have to be in his study, and would he have had time to open and close it anyway?* She would ask the sons about it.

Mike never found the safe hidden behind the opening bookcase in the adjoining room, but she had decided he was probably sitting in his tall wingback chair when his attackers entered the villa. If this were the case, he would most definitely not have had any time even to stand up. There was nothing behind the small, loose cushion or, after undoing the zip, anything in it. Mike pushed her hands down the sides of the seat cushion, and on the left-hand side, she found and extracted a piece of folded paper. A noise outside the door spooked her, and she pushed it deep into her trouser pocket.

When Mohammed entered the room, she was standing over the Giacometti statue, *The Running Man*, taking a picture with her phone. He waited for her to speak.

"Do you think Callum and Harper will sell all these beautiful pieces of art?" She was desperately trying to sound calm and to give the impression that she was in the study photographing the sculptures and paintings.

"I have no idea," he sounded unfriendly, and his eyes were staring right through her.

"I'll ask them." And she walked past him and out of the room.

———

"*How much?*" Callum was eating a snack while sitting at the peninsula in the kitchen.

"It made $140 million," Mike replied. "That's the most expensive Giacometti ever sold, but there are plenty for one per cent of that price."

"What? That's still $1.5 million! I must admit that Father did have a good eye for art." Harper was impressed by Mike's knowledge of such things.

"It was his favourite. He always had it in front of him on the floor of his study." Callum took a bite of a sandwich.

Mohammed hadn't joined them in the kitchen as he was evidently dealing with staffing matters, much to Mike's relief. Her conversation with the sons was more to explain why she was in the study rather than a discussion on the subject of twentieth-century art. She had concluded that Habib was a complex and emotional man who used art to link himself to all the important things in his past and present. He was clearly *The Running Man*, running away from the death of his wife, from Canada and so much more. More interestingly, what was he running towards?

"We're leaving the day after tomorrow, Wednesday, to go back to London." Callum abruptly provided an update. "Father will be flown out tomorrow on a flight to Canada."

For some reason, Mike's mind followed a completely random course that had her hearing Leonard's voice saying that their father had been given some encryption equipment that would need to be retrieved. Was it in his safe? Should she try to find it? The sons would probably be receptive, if she played the 'your parents were wonderful patriots' card. She gave herself a mental slap and concentrated on the issues she was meant to be dealing with. Once the sons had left Oman and she was back in Dubai, she couldn't revisit the villa or area.

Callum pushed his plate containing a half-eaten sandwich across the marble top for someone else to remove – a privilege of his upbringing, which wasn't wasted on Mike, who had never had servants to clear up after her. "I'm going down to the works for an hour; it may be my last time for a while," he said. "Harper's going to sort out some last-minute stuff to do with the transportation."

"May I stay tonight and leave tomorrow?" She was thinking fast.

"Sure, leave when you want."

Mike had regained her composure after Mohammed's intrusion and was now standing in her default pose of leaning on the kitchen units, facing the brothers with her legs crossed at the ankles. "Thank you, I have some calls to make this afternoon."

"Shall we meet for dinner at 7pm?" Callum asked.

"Perfect."

"Mohammed will be here all afternoon, so if you need anything, just ask."

Over my dead body, was what she thought rather morbidly, but she kept it to herself and moved on quickly. "I will, thank you."

She presumed that Callum was going down to the works because they now owned them and there would be plenty of administrative matters; in this, she was wrong. Yes, there were administrative matters, but, no, that wasn't the real reason he needed to go down there.

The piece of paper was burning a hole in her pocket, and she made an excuse to return to her room. All the way back up the stairs and along the corridor, she was looking out for Mohammed, but he was nowhere to be seen. Once in her bedroom with the door closed, she took out the folded paper and sat at the dressing room table. Staring at the mirror before opening it, she came to a sudden realisation that, whatever it contained, this was most likely the reason why Habib went to his meeting in Doha with Ahrun Yonan. Also, whatever it contained could be the reason Habib called Leonard out to the villa, specifically to arrive the day after he had picked it up from BlueStar.

Leonard had never got to see its contents.

CHAPTER THIRTEEN

The piece of paper was, in fact, the top half of a receipt. It had been torn and folded over. It was also slightly crumpled from being pushed down the side of the seat cushion and crammed into Mike's pocket. She didn't waste any more time wondering about it.

It was from a restaurant in Doha, probably the one where the meeting had taken place. There was a series of numbers handwritten on it that could mean absolutely anything.

If Mike could have seen herself, she would have laughed at the cinematic parody of disappointment she was displaying – slumped back in an armchair with gritted teeth. She repeated in her mind what had become her mantra: *I'm not cut out for fieldwork.*

Resisting the urge to ask for some alcohol, she settled on taking a walk around her room instead, which provided no answers.

Feeling as if every door had slammed shut, she conceded to herself that it was all over. It was time to fly back to London from Dubai. The sons would also be back in the UK on Wednesday, and their father's body would already be on its way to Canada. She at least acknowledged to herself that she had tried. Oh, and Leonard would soon be safely back in the USA, having the best medical treatment.

Perhaps she would have that drink?

It wasn't needed. A quick internal pep talk made her begin to appreciate that this piece of paper was pushed down the side of a multimillionaire's chair in Oman or the UAE or whichever country she was in. People like Habib didn't care about restaurant receipts, let alone push them down the side of his favourite armchair. What was it doing there? It meant something important, surely? The desire for alcohol persisted.

Ten minutes later, the glass of whisky on ice that had been brought to her room rather reminded her where she was and the way other people lived. She picked up the receipt again, photographed it on her phone and typed the thirty or forty printed words (mostly food and drink items) and the hand-written numbers into her laptop so she could analyse them. Her mood improved as she had something to get her teeth into.

Her phone ringing on the table alongside her made her jump.

"Oh, hi," she said, answering it.

"Am I disturbing something?"

"Sorry, Chris, I'm five steps forwards and ten back at the moment."

"Can you speak?"

"Yes, but this isn't secure."

"Sure, no problem."

Mike updated him on the chief inspector's call, on the Murchison family travel arrangements for the next two days and that her work – if that's what it could be called – had been done. She would return to Dubai tomorrow. She didn't want to talk about BlueStar on the phone, so she merely said that she might need to go to Doha.

"Mike, is there anything I can do? I'm sitting in Doha doing nothing for a few hours."

"No; well, yes, but ..." She stopped. "I'll fly to Doha tomorrow morning. Can we meet?"

"Sure."

"I'll send you my flight details later. See you tomorrow."

After the call, she put the words and numbers written on the receipt into an AI search engine, and she wasn't surprised when it came up with only the most obvious conclusions. Pattern recognition software and code-breaking programmes also didn't come up with anything meaningful. As Sherlock Holmes most definitely did not say, once you've eliminated the obvious, *whatever remains* – no matter that it looks like a load of bollocks – is probably a load of bollocks.

She walked to a wall and rested her head against it. However much you're used to pursuing leads, when you reach a dead end, it's a big blow. She consoled herself that there was some story behind why a restaurant receipt was stuffed down the side of a millionaire's armchair in his private lounge, but did it have anything at all to do with his trip to Doha, his meeting with Leonard or, ultimately, with his death?

———

Mike had spent the remainder of the afternoon going round in circles and failing to make progress in any meaningful way. Her parents had both risen to high points in their respective careers as musicians, but they did so without making any large sums of money. Having neither excelled at anything nor made any amount of dollars that was worth talking about, she decided that she was a failure, and it hurt her. It was time to rethink.

There was still an hour until it was time to go downstairs to meet back up with the sons, and she decided to break off from her searches. Leonard had been uppermost in her mind. What would he do now? The thought led her to his two mobile phones, which were in her bag.

Was one phone official and the other to hide his trip to Dubai? Or were they both for non-CIA calls? She favoured the latter, as any official phone could be tracked and traced. Stretching her legs, she walked over and retrieved the phones before placing them neatly on her desk. Hacking into a CIA director's phone was probably a serious crime, but what the heck? She turned on the first phone and used a combination of factory reset and some useful software to unlock it. This always risked automatically deleting all his files and apps, but there were ways to restore these.

Unfortunately, this automatic deletion did happen, but at least she had unlocked it. It would now take her twenty minutes to restore his data; she was enjoying the process and mentally went into cruise control. Out of the blue, the other phone rang loudly, frightening her. It was a WhatsApp call, according to the banner at the top. She wrote down the number before it disappeared. It must be something to do with his secret trip to the Middle East, mustn't it?

Mostly on impulse and feeling that she had little to lose, she dialled it from her own phone and waited expectantly to hear who it was.

"Hello?" a male voice answered, but he was clearly being reticent due to not recognising her number.

"Hi, were you trying to get hold of Leonard just then?" She was hoping that he didn't know Leonard by any of his code names.

"Who is this?" he asked.

"His daughter, Michaela." She was speaking without thinking through the consequences.

"Oh" – the man stopped for a second, also pondering the situation – "is Leonard around?"

Mike had to decide quickly whether this was a trap or if the man genuinely didn't know where Leonard was. "He's in hospital." She hesitated before adding, "In the US."

"I know, Michaela. I was ringing to see how he was. He rang me. I ordered the ambulance for him."

"Who am I speaking to?"

"Kevin ... I'm at the British Embassy in Doha. I've worked with your father around the world."

Glaciers could have formed and melted before either of them spoke again.

"Kevin, we don't know each other. If you really are Kevin at the British Embassy in Doha, may I come to see you?"

"Of course, but it's a long flight from the USA. Why would you like to see me? We can talk on the phone."

"Well, firstly, I may not be that far from you. Secondly, you could be the head of Chinese Intelligence in the Middle East for all I know. I'd like to check you out."

More periods of glaciation and global warming passed as they weighed each other up.

"True, I could be anyone, but if you can come to the embassy, I'll arrange access, and we can chat freely. Also, please remember that I don't know who you are," he concluded.

"I worked for him a while back." She paused. "I'll contact you again with a time, but let's say that I'll come to the embassy late tomorrow afternoon."

"No problem. I'll be here."

"What's your surname and position?"

"Kevin Stenning. I'm the chargé d'affaires; you can look me up."

"I will, of course. I'm sure you'll look me up and find I'm not Leonard's daughter, but I am American, and I do have Leonard's phone."

"I know Leonard doesn't have a daughter, but that's no problem; you have his personal phone, which tells me a lot.

Leonard and I have been close friends for over ten years. As I said, it was he who phoned me when he arrived out here. Remember to bring your passport and leave all weapons at home." His English voice had a warm, if slightly world-weary, edge to it. "What's the surname on your passport? I need to tell security."

"Kingdom."

The call ended.

A member of staff tapped on Mike's door to ask if she needed clean towels and bedding, only to be politely turned away.

Mike immediately checked out Kevin Stenning's credentials – both the publicly available ones at the embassy and his position in the secret services. He was indeed the chargé d'affaires, if she had really been talking to him, and he was most definitely in intelligence.

How much can you gauge from someone's voice in a short telephone conversation? She wasn't sure, but he sounded genuine and concerned. What harm could come from turning up at the British Embassy in Doha to chat about a sick mutual friend? No rules had been broken.

————

Dinner at 7.00pm with the sons was fast approaching. Earlier, she had booked the flight from Dubai to Doha; it would take just over an hour. Firstly, she would have to get the Murchisons' chauffeur to take her back to the Royal Manta Hotel, where she would check out before going to the airport. The meeting with Chris Crippen had been set up, and she had texted Kevin Stenning to say she would be at the British Embassy at 4.30pm. Her Tuesday was now arranged.

However, something wasn't quite right. Of all the people Leonard could have phoned after he had failed to reach her, why did he choose Kevin Stenning (a Brit in Qatar)? Kevin had said that Leonard had phoned him when he arrived out here, and yet he was purposely travelling under the radar and hadn't even told his closest colleagues in London or Washington, DC.

Mike was going over all of this as she descended the stairs for dinner, feeling like something out of a Jane Austen novel: walking down a grand staircase to be served pre-dinner drinks by a young man waiting for her at the bottom. Harper was already in the anteroom, sitting on his own; he put down his phone as Mike entered. He was in a coral-pink linen shirt that rather clashed with his ginger hair and lounging on a white leather sofa.

"How was your day?" she asked.

"Good. I've dealt with all the paperwork and arrangements. I had to fly to Muscat from Khasab, but it only takes an hour. It's a domestic flight."

"That means your father can be flown out tomorrow?"

"Yes, he leaves Muscat at 11.00am, heading to Vancouver via Frankfurt. Callum and I fly out to London on Wednesday at midday. Hopefully, this crazy period is finished, and we can all get back to normal."

"Can your chauffeur take me back to the hotel in Dubai tomorrow morning after an early breakfast? I'm catching a 1.30pm flight to Doha and then back to London, hopefully."

The young man brought in her drink and placed another glass of beer in front of Harper. The servant turned and left the room, closing the door behind him. Harper picked up his phone and arranged for Mike to be picked up at 8.00am, for the driver to wait at the hotel while she checked out and then for him to take her to the airport.

"Thanks for coming here. It was great to learn a bit of history about Mother and Father. It must be obvious to you that Callum and I never knew anything about this; it explains a few things and why they were occasionally a bit distant. They were just protecting us."

"I'm glad the autopsy confirmed that your father died from natural causes. This gives you closure, I think." Mike was being unusually polite; after all, there was nothing more she could do for them or their father.

"Where's Callum? I'm getting hungry." Harper stood up, wanting to allow the staff to commence serving dinner.

The almost-silent air conditioning and subtle lighting cut out for a few seconds before resuming after a generator cut in. It was a quick reminder that they were near the top of a mountain many miles from any other human habitation. Harper smiled to himself.

"That doesn't happen in London," Mike said.

"No, that's true."

She had, however, completely misinterpreted why he was smiling, having no concept of the power station that the Murchisons owned to ensure that the quarry, cement works and related peripheral users continued to function under any circumstances.

There was a slight feeling in the room that the worst had passed, a feeling of being demob happy, as all the soldiers after World War II had felt after VE Day. They both relaxed, sipping their drinks.

"I know nothing about you apart from what's on the net," Mike unexpectedly expressed what was in her mind. "What do you do in London? What turns you on?" She was wearing her black wig and tight, black leather trousers, neither commonly seen in the Middle East or most other places, actually.

Harper smiled back. He had never met anyone like her, and he hadn't worked out what she actually did in the secret services or what her connection was with his father via the person he knew as Donald Reeve. "Gaming."

"Online gaming?"

"Yes, and with Callum, I write and develop software."

Mike was processing this when he said, "And American football. I support the Broncos."

For the first time since they'd met, there was the merest hint of sexual tension between them; they were only a few years apart and both single.

"I thought that you would have grown up a Vancouver Canucks fan?" she suggested.

"No, I'm not into hockey; I'm a mess. Denver Broncos, and I support Queens Park Rangers ... that's soccer – a London soccer club, in case you don't know."

"I know; I work," she corrected herself, "worked, in Chiswick for five years, which is probably three miles away from their ground."

"Wish I'd known; I could have parked the car on your drive. The parking at QPR is shit."

"Why not use the Tube?"

"No – I have claustrophobia. I don't use the Tube."

"But you get on planes?"

"Yes, but not enthusiastically and only first class, wearing headphones and drinking heavily in the lounge before I fly."

She smiled.

His phone rang. "Hi, Cal. Where are you? We're starving."

"They almost got me. We're fucked." He was speaking rapidly with a background noise of squealing tyres.

"What? What's the matter? What's happened?"

"We need some more security." He started to ramble and was becoming incoherent. "It must be the farm. If we don't give them the farm ... I know they'll kill us ..." His voice trailed off as if he didn't have the will or strength to continue.

"Who are they?"

The line went dead.

CHAPTER FOURTEEN

"We can't call the police," Harper answered Mike, who had asked the obvious question.

"Where's Mohammed? Can't he sort out some more security?" She was beginning to think about her own situation, trapped in what was rapidly becoming a gilded cage.

"He left an hour ago ... and I want to talk to Cal first."

"You don't trust Mohammed?"

"I don't really know him or who he's connected to."

A phone in Mike's pocket buzzed. "That's Callum coming through the gate."

"What? How?" But Harper was already on his way out of the room.

She followed him along the hall.

A minute later, Callum burst through the huge doors. He was clutching a bloody handkerchief in one hand, which he put back onto his left forearm. The brothers embraced and turned to look at Mike, almost in unison. No words were exchanged, but they had come to some sort of tacit agreement.

Callum spoke first. "Mike, we need to confide in you."

"Shall we patch you up first?" she suggested.

With that, they moved to a bathroom, where the wound was cleaned, dressed and a bandage applied. Harper gave instructions for dinner to be held back for half an hour but for strong drinks to be served. They retreated to the lounge; by which time, Callum had given a brief description of what had happened.

With a gin and tonic in his hand, he explained further. "They must have been parked among the lorries. You know the pull-in outside the entrance to the works?" he said to Harper.

"How many of them?" Mike asked.

"There were two in a white pickup that followed me, blocking the way back. A car – a yellow Toyota, I think – was parked ahead with its hazard lights flashing and a red triangle on the road. I presumed it had broken down. There was a local guy standing there waving us down."

"When did they shoot at you?" Harper was confused.

"I got out to speak to the man, and a shot came from behind. It skimmed my arm. I jumped back in the car and Jay – that's our driver, Mike – roared off and swerved around the Toyota. They didn't seem to follow us. Well, I didn't see any lights."

"It sounds to me more like a warning than an attempt to kill you." Mike was also trying to make some sense of the sequence of events.

While Callum described some more details, she was rapidly coming to the conclusion that Habib had been murdered, whatever the death certificate stated, and that the shooting was connected. Were Habib's killers in fact after Callum or Harper? Was Habib in the wrong place at the wrong time?

"Why would anyone want to shoot you or frighten you, Callum?" Mike was looking directly at him.

"Um, well, Harper and I have a business out here that's separate from Father's."

"Although it does depend massively on his works and port

for its power supply," his brother explained, beginning to fill in the gaps.

"It was his way of helping us."

"Well, what is it?" Mike in her wig could look intimidating when she stared directly at anyone – in this case, Harper.

"A crypto farm. We mine for Bitcoin. The power consumption is massive, which is why most farms – they're actually just warehouses – are located where there's cheap electricity, such as Iceland."

"And where's your ... farm?"

"It's a big industrial shed accessed only through the cement works down by the gulf. It's a perfect location. Apart from Father and Kamal Khalid, no one knows it's there. Oh, and the handful of people we employ, but even they don't know exactly what it's really all about."

"It's not illegal, though, is it?"

"No."

"Why did someone want to kill your father, if that's what happened, and shoot you?"

"They must want the Bitcoin we still own and to gain control of the farm."

"What are we talking about in US dollars?"

"Twenty million."

If the sons thought Mike would now ask a lot of questions about cryptocurrencies, money laundering or electricity generation, they were mistaken. She reverted to their current predicament.

"Right, we're all up shit creek. They've killed your father and shot at Callum, and we're all stuck in a villa halfway up a mountain, miles from anywhere. How many staff are here and are they trustworthy? How can we get to an airport without anyone knowing?"

It wasn't exactly a tableau, but for a few seconds, the three people froze in their positions as if they were stuffed animals in some Victorian drawing-room diorama.

Callum, with his right hand playing with the bandage on his left arm, was happy to talk practical solutions: "Aren't we safer here? If we leave the villa, they may be waiting for us."

"We can't stay here forever, Cal."

"Should we call in a helicopter? Is that safer?"

"That's a better idea, but they probably won't come here until morning; in the meantime, is there a panic room?" Mike asked.

"Cal, I'll organise a helicopter, and you show Mike the panic room."

Callum walked out and went through the villa with Mike. They came to a formal dining room that could have come straight out of a French chateau in the belle époque. In the corner, behind a triptych screen, there was a concealed door.

"We always wondered why Father had a panic room. There's no crime out here, and cement works don't tend to attract terrorists. I've only been in here once." He opened the door, stepped inside and turned on a light switch. Immediately, a battery power unit kicked in and the air conditioning began. It was baking hot and very oppressive due to its size and lack of windows.

"I don't know what your father – and mother, for that matter – actually did, but I'm guessing a room like this might be desirable." Mike was being honest.

"It didn't save him, though, did it?"

"No." Mike was already feeling uneasy about Habib's death, and this discussion wasn't allaying her fears.

The main item that took Mike's eye was the small fold-down desk. On it was a piece of encryption equipment that she recognised – this was presumably what Leonard had been referring to. Next to it was a pad, pen and a notebook with a distinctive pale-yellow cover. While Callum was speculating about the independent battery power, water and sewage systems, she was flicking through the notebook.

"May I keep this?" she asked as she put it in her pocket.

"Of course."

She picked up the pad as well, but she left the electronic gadgetry, which was of no use without the codes. "Let's hope we don't all have to sleep here tonight." She was thinking it would be a tight squeeze.

"Let's pack our bags and wait to fly out at first light. I'll make sure all the staff are on high alert."

"That would be good. I have to be in Doha by 3.00pm."

"Shall we go and eat? The chef has probably cooked it twice already."

———

In Doha, it was a beautiful evening, and three individuals in different parts of the city were about to have dinner.

The first person was Kevin Stenning from the British Embassy. He was in his black bow tie and dinner jacket at a formal reception hosted by his ambassador in the official residence. A small group of senior figures in the oil-and-gas sector were visiting, together with some people he knew from the Foreign and Commonwealth Office (FCO) and a woman from MI6 who was effectively Kevin's boss. He was sitting next to her, but any sensitive matters would have to be saved until they had a one-to-one meeting the next morning at 9.30am.

Her name was Yolanda, and she and Kevin had known each other a long time, but it was true to say that neither wanted to be at the dinner. She had wavy, blonde hair and a lazy left eye that made it difficult to hold her gaze.

"A penny for them," she said quietly while the others were talking about the servicing of gas platforms.

"Is that the most you can offer? I can see why you're not in charge of turning foreign assets."

She smiled. "Who says I'm not?"

"Congratulations on the demotion, then."

"Heard from our friend in Chiswick?"

Whether in business or in personal relationships, there are pivotal moments when you have to trust your instinct because you'll never have all the facts; you simply have to follow your gut feeling. Neither he nor Yolanda wanted to wait until tomorrow, and while the others around the table were busy, they could start to explore what was preoccupying them both.

"Does everything have to go back to London immediately?" he asked.

"No, there's nothing to send back. Our meeting is tomorrow anyway, and I'm nearly blind in my left eye and deaf in my right ear, so I don't pick up everything." Her smile widened. She was generally considered to be one of the sharpest minds in the secret services.

"He phoned me late evening the day before yesterday. He was in Dubai." Kevin stared at her while the others were laughing loudly.

Yolanda was looking confused; this wasn't what she was expecting to hear. "I thought he was being recalled to the USA?"

"He was out here unofficially ... on his way back to the USA."

"Strange route. Why did he call you?"

"He was in agony in his hotel room and couldn't call anyone else. He needed an ambulance to take him to the hospital."

Yolanda picked up her wine and sipped. "And you called for one from here?"

"Yes, of course. He was very ill and very nervous. We're all nervous, aren't we? Until the ... current tensions are sorted out."

"Where is he now?"

But before he could answer, the conversation around the table demanded their attention.

———

Chris Crippen was also at a formal dinner on a much larger scale, but one not four miles from the British Embassy. It was meant to be his last evening.

He was in a conference hall that defied description in terms of size and grandeur. No expense was being spared for this delegation as the Qataris really wanted the first Summer Olympics in a Middle Eastern country. The year 2040 was their opportunity, and nothing, including money, was going to stop them. An Italian opera singer and orchestra had been providing the music as everyone sat down for a sumptuous banquet.

There were kings and princes, PMs and Hollywood stars. Chris and the rest of the Olympic delegation were almost stunned into submission by the lengths that were being taken to impress the visitors.

Yet, despite feeling like he was in the box with King Charles at the *Royal Variety Performance*, Chris's mind was elsewhere: 300 miles away to be precise. As an operative who had had to exist at the sharp end of espionage, he didn't like it when things went well, ridiculously well – or perfectly. Habib Murchison's autopsy had provided the perfect result for everyone: natural causes. Tomorrow, after lunch, he would sit down with Mike and hear all the gossip from the villa.

He leant back as yet another athlete took a selfie of him and his colleagues.

———

The third person was Ahrun Yonan. He was at Hamad International Airport, sitting in a coffee shop, eating a salad from a plastic tray and drinking orange juice. He was trying to not display his nervousness to the world. At moments like this, everyone looks suspicious, but he was telling himself that every passenger had already been through security, and no one had a gun or knife. He was on his way to stay with friends in Iraq's ever-reducing Assyrian community. Here, they lived a very rural life completely under the radar, if one excludes the devastation by the Islamic State of Iraq and Syria (ISIS), or Daesh, as he knew it.

Habib Murchison's murder – and he knew it was murder – had shaken him to the core. Their lunchtime meeting at the restaurant was only the third time they had met. The fact that Habib had flown back to his villa and had been killed five or six hours after leaving Doha meant that his attackers must have known about their lunch appointment. Had they been monitoring the restaurant? Could they identify him, and was he next?

The decision to fly out to Iraq had quickly been agreed with his wife.

———

The dinner at the villa had been wonderful, even if none of them had really felt like a hot meal. Nobody had drunk wine, and the conversation had been muted. It had centred on cryptocurrency and how it was 'mined'. Mike, as a computer nerd, was well aware of the basics, especially about the encryption side of the system, but she tended to only know the headlines on the selling of Bitcoin, or parts thereof, rather than the actual mining.

"Let's keep this simple," Mike said, "How many Bitcoins are left to be found?"

"As you know, the limit is 21 million. Of these, 2.3 million are left to be mined." Harper was the one answering all her questions.

"And at what rate are they being found?"

"The first 18.6 million Bitcoins have been mined in just over ten years. It will take another 120 years to mine the remaining 2.4 million."

"That's because their release is slowed down?"

"Yes, every four years, the number of Bitcoins produced by the programme and made available is cut in half."

"How many are found each day?"

"Currently, about 900."

"How many do you find?"

"It varies, but we're averaging three."

"That's £70,000 a day?" she queried, exhaling.

"Yes, roughly."

"And how many searches, if I can call them that, do you do a day?"

"A day?" Harper was confused. "We do 255 million, million 'searches', as you call them, per second. Why do you think we use so much electricity?"

Mike rocked back in her chair and tried to take all this in. It took a few seconds. "So, who wants this valuable asset, if that's not a stupid question?"

"Most miners are American, Russian, Chinese or Kazakh. Oh, plus the Icelanders, who have the cheap electricity," Callum chipped in after Harper had answered Mike's barrage of questions.

"Have you been approached or threatened before?" she wondered.

"We were approached a month ago, but we don't know by whom," Callum said. "They wanted to buy the farm." It's possible Callum didn't know that 'buy the farm' also meant 'die horribly', but certainly any irony was lost on him. He continued, "For peanuts."

"We told them it wasn't for sale and that their price was derisory." Harper looked across at his brother.

"Will you give me their phone number? I'm presuming that they phoned you?"

"Sure," Callum said, and he proceeded to search for the number and ping it across to Mike.

There was an uncomfortable atmosphere in the lounge, not between the brothers and Mike but from a feeling of not knowing where the threat lay and what might happen before the helicopter arrived in the morning. Was there any point in them going to bed as no one was likely to sleep?

"Shall we have one more drink?" Harper was needing something to relax him.

"Why not?" Mike was completely on edge as her situation began to dawn on her.

"Sure." Callum joined the attempt to dial down the tension.

They heard an explosion at the villa gates that meant they never got to savour their gin and tonics.

CHAPTER FIFTEEN

What sounded like gunfire after the explosion was enough to send the sons running towards the panic room. Mike also set off in that direction, but she managed to ring Chris to ask for help as she ran. Unfortunately, she only reached his answerphone, but she left a message that told him what had happened and where they were going to be holed up. Her last words were for him to send help, but preferably not the local police.

The solid door to the panic room closed behind them and locked as innumerable bolts slid into place. However, the disguised outer façade was unlikely to fool any professional attacker for long.

The room was small, and this meant that the next few hours would be cosy. There was a desk and chair, a small sofa that folded out into a single bed, a portable toilet in the corner and a cabinet full of long-life food and water. A fridge-sized battery appeared to be the source of power, and a grille on the wall allowed the circulation of air from a concealed vent in the roof space. It was a prison cell – a prison cell for one person.

Ever practical, Mike suggested to the sons that they should

turn their phones off to conserve the batteries. She would leave her phone on to hear from Chris.

Callum opened a drawer in the desk and found a charger. "Harper, you turn yours off, and I'll keep mine on in case anyone tries to contact us." He fitted the charging cable.

Mike's mind was elsewhere as she stared at the box of tricks Habib had been using to communicate with Leonard in London. She picked up the notepad she had taken out of her pocket earlier and began to flick through it.

"Shouldn't we contact someone else before the internet or power dies?" Harper was the twitchiest of the three. "What if your colleague doesn't get the message?"

Mike looked up. "Who do you suggest? Do you have any friends in London or Canada who could act fast?"

They looked at each other, but no names were forthcoming.

"Give me a couple of minutes, I'm thinking through an idea," she told them.

Mike started to scroll through her phone, paused and began typing. She had been weighing up whether to trust Kevin Stenning. After all, he had the burner phone number and was Leonard's choice when he was desperate, and she had failed to answer his emergency call. How much did Kevin know about anything else? Habib, for example? Mike was thinking that the fact he was also not American or Canadian might be an advantage.

"I can't make tomorrow," she wrote. "I'm stuck in a villa in Oman. If things get worse, I may ask for your help. I prefer not to speak to my confederates, if you understand?"

She would await his reply, which should reveal whether Leonard had told him about Habib and whether he might help. All of this, it turned out, was a waste of time as the message failed to send. In fact, it dawned on everyone that there was no connection with the outside world from where they currently were. The mood inside their prison cell changed.

Callum was exploring their small room, although this was probably displacement activity. He was leaning over and looking down behind the three-foot-high battery unit that provided the power. "Aha!" he said, attracting everyone's attention instantly.

"You've found the escape tunnel, I'm guessing?" Mike was at her most cynical.

"Could be."

The two brothers began to walk the unit away from the wall as far as the cabling would allow.

"*There's something behind!*" Harper shouted.

There was much levering until a small door behind the unit appeared. Even the ever-dubious Mike stopped what she was doing. This was too good to be true.

"Is it a tunnel?" Harper asked as Callum leant over the power unit and peered into the void.

The silence that followed betrayed the unlikelihood that this was the case.

"No, I don't think so," was the more than disappointing response. "But there is what looks like a second power unit," he said with a rising voice.

"Great" – Harper wasn't enthused by this information – "so my phone will be fully charged, but I can't use it."

———

It wasn't until Chris had left the banquet and gala that he received Mike's message. He was completely thrown. What could he possibly do? Almost no scenario looked promising.

Chris knew where she was – in the panic room inside the Murchison villa – but even if he could get there in time, what could he do? Although actually getting there wasn't even a realistic possibility. He needed relatively local help and not the Omani police but someone in Dubai or Muscat; in fact, anyone within a couple of hours.

It was now 10pm and not a good time to organise any response. Could she survive through the night and make it to the helicopter that she had said one of the sons had ordered for 8.30am? He had no idea.

Back in his hotel room, the balancing of all the possibilities began to drain him. He still had a dozen or so contacts, some were in various ministries and embassies throughout the Middle East, from Kuwait and Bahrain to Riyadh and Cairo, but did he want them involved?

———

Kevin and Yolanda had also finished their dinner and were standing in the rear lounge of the ambassador's residence, looking out across the swimming pool and the three-dimensional patterns on the internal walls of the garden, illuminated from below for maximum effect. The palm trees were beautiful.

The other guests had left, and the need for complete discretion had disappeared. He was anticipating his meeting with Michaela Kingdom tomorrow afternoon, unaware of her predicament, and looking back at Yolanda, who was sipping an espresso from a small cup. She could see that he was deep in thought and that everything was not fine and dandy in his world – as if there ever was a time when it was. She was too experienced to ask; he would be more forthcoming when he had weighed up the options. Instead, she looked across at the dove-grey columns of the consular building.

"I have a feeling it's about to hit the fan," he said, "if it hasn't already."

She turned around to see that, in the distance, the ambassador was still chatting to other FCO staff. He was very senior indeed and was on his last posting, about to drive his beaten-up old German estate car back to the UK with his wife on a final road trip through dangerous countries and without complete support from the FCO, which would prefer that he flew back British Airways. Yolanda knew Kevin's problem was best kept to the smallest circle possible.

After an outburst of laughter from some of the people inside, she looked at Kevin. "Any particular reason?"

"Well ... I rang Leonard's phone to check on his health after I'd arranged an ambulance to take him to the USAF hospital in Dubai – his choice, by the way," he explained, smiling at her.

"He doesn't trust anyone, does he?"

"No. Would you?" he asked rhetorically.

"Everyone in the trade is looking over their shoulders to the extent that it's painful ... spook's neck? An occupational ailment not unlike housemaid's knee or tennis elbow, perhaps?"

"True. You were on the plane out here, I think, and missed some of this, but someone called Michaela Kingdom answered his phone when I called. You know how smart Leonard is, but why did an ex-employee have access to his phone, and why is she out in Dubai? I'm suspicious."

"In Dubai? What did she say?"

"Not much, we were both a bit guarded, but she agreed to come here, to the embassy, tomorrow afternoon."

"Do you think Leonard was on to something? Obviously, you're hoping you'll find out tomorrow afternoon."

"Yes, 'hoping' is the word, but I have that uneasy feeling in my bones."

The orange-and-blue glow of Doha at night graded upwards over the bombproof walls of the embassy compound to a perfect nocturnal blackness, broken only by a single grey lenticular cloud.

"We might only be 100 miles from Iran across the Arabian Gulf, but we might as well be on Mars. I don't think the tensions have ever been greater," he continued.

"Why was Leonard out here? Of all places?"

"He never told me, but I'm guessing he was trying to find out what Iran is going to do next ... and also to protect his legacy."

"You've checked out this Michaela Kingdom, I presume?"

"Yes, she was a CIA analyst under Leonard. She's now freelance, I think."

"And he chose her?"

"There has to be a reason. Let's hope she makes it to the meeting tomorrow."

———

The hours dragged and dragged beyond belief.

No one slept. Everyone was waiting for a noise or an explosion. They were trapped as if in a damaged submarine on the seabed, out of communication with the rest of the world. In fact, it was the complete lack of sound that began to take the biggest toll. Callum nodded off and knocked a small clock onto the floor. They all leapt and screamed before settling back down in an embarrassed silence. Why had there been no attempt to blow open the doors or poison them through the air vents?

They were also uncomfortable. The room wasn't designed for three people, and they took it in turns to be perched or propped up on the only bed or sitting on the only chair. The lack of phone and internet meant they had nothing to distract them and no feedback from the outside world.

Just after 6am, they were all wide awake. The air conditioning had kept the room at a reasonable temperature, but it was concerning them that it was draining the first battery unit.

Callum checked. "It's used about a quarter. That means that we have at least two days in total."

"God, I can't stand two days in here." Harper was becoming fractious.

"Are we going to wait until 8.30am and try to get to the helicopter?"

"Assuming it arrives." Callum didn't sound confident.

"Where are all the staff?" Mike asked. "Why hasn't one of them done something?"

"That's if they're alive and not part of the whole conspiracy." Harper was also not sounding confident.

"I think that we have to take a chance at 8.30am. What are we going to gain by staying in here any longer? Either they're sitting outside the door waiting or they aren't." Mike couldn't see how anyone, including Chris, could have organised anything. The gunmen had either made their point and disappeared, or they were in the villa and waiting for their targets to come out.

An hour later, they were to find out.

There was a hammering on the door. They all leapt up as a tinny voice came out of the entry-phone speaker.

"Harper! Callum! it's Mohammed. What's happening? I've just arrived, and the gates and doors are all open."

Mike grabbed Harper's arm as he moved to press the reply button, but it didn't stop him.

"Mohammed, what's happened?"

"I don't know. The night staff aren't here; the gatehouse is empty. The gates and front door are unlocked."

"Is anyone dead?"

"Not that I can see. There has been a small fire at the front gate, I think. Why are you in the panic room?"

"*Someone shot at me in the car,*" Callum shouted, but Harper wasn't pressing the button.

"Someone shot at Callum," Harper repeated, "and we heard an explosion."

"No one's here now. It's safe. You can come out. I've called my friends in the police."

Mike, Harper and Callum looked at each in silence, thinking the same thoughts.

Mike nodded and whispered, "We have to leave here at some point."

They looked like young barn owls about to leave the nest box for the first time.

Harper unbolted and unlocked the door. He stepped outside.

Mohammed walked up to him and gave him a hug. The others emerged, relieved to see everything appeared normal. In fact, they were all thinking, *Did that really happen?*

"Chief Inspector Saeed is coming personally. He's sent a team who will be here soon," Mohammed confirmed.

"That's very kind" – Callum looked at his watch – "but we have a helicopter booked in just over an hour."

"Why?" Mohammed asked.

"Mohammed, Father's body flies out this morning from Muscat, and we're flying out of Dubai tomorrow. We haven't got a clue what's happening here, but I'm not staying one minute longer in this villa. I don't appreciate being shot at."

"The police can sort this out while we're in London and in Canada for the funeral," Harper added.

"It would be better if you waited to talk to the chief inspector later this morning. He's on his way; he told me."

Mike looked at Mohammed, trying to weigh up whether she trusted him or not, she decided that she didn't and, if she were right, they needed to get out of Oman before the police team or the chief inspector arrived. However, she wanted to keep Mohammed on side for the next hour. "Are all the staff here?"

"No, but they're on their way. They were understandably nervous when they saw the front gate."

She was tempted to list a number of reasons why they might not have turned up this morning, including that they were involved. However, what she actually said was, "Great. I think we could all do with some breakfast."

"OK, I'll organise it." He turned and left the room.

Mike waited a few seconds and turned to the brothers. "I suggest we pack quickly, and you arrange for your chauffeur to drive us out of here. We need to get out of Oman, and this police jurisdiction before the chief inspector or his team arrive. Let's leave Mohammed thinking that we're departing by helicopter in an hour."

"I'll go and secretly organise the car," Harper said.

"Let's meet downstairs in fifteen minutes." Callum was already walking to the hall.

Mike turned and closed the panic room door before leaving herself.

Once back in her room, she packed in minutes while holding the phone to her ear. She was updating Chris in Doha.

"Be careful. Please, please be careful and get out of that villa," he was saying, "I was praying you got out of that room and into the helicopter. I didn't have much success with a couple of contacts. Sorry, I haven't been much support."

"Don't worry, I'm a seasoned operative," she said with a nervous laugh. "We'll catch up later. Fingers crossed, I'll be back in Dubai and on the Doha flight as planned."

Slightly breathless, she finished packing and went downstairs to meet the others.

Mike put her bag in the room that was just off the entrance hall and asked one of the friendly staff if she could have a quick coffee. Scrolling through her phone, it occurred to her that her message to Kevin Stenning, which had failed to send the previous evening, had gone as soon as she had stepped out of the panic room and her phone had reconnected with the villa Wi-Fi. "Damn," she whispered to herself. Perhaps it would have been better if that hadn't been sent, but it was too late now.

Ominously, Mohammed appeared in the doorway.

CHAPTER SIXTEEN

"I'm sorry," Mohammed said, shrugging his shoulders.

He was standing in front of all three of them in the room next to the hall. The brothers had just arrived, while Mike was already in a chair, drinking from a coffee cup and eating a Lebanese pastry.

"Father never mentioned it," Harper stated.

Mohammed was at his most apologetic. "I'm sorry, helicopters cannot land here at the villa. This is why your father used private jets from Ras Al Khaimah. There are restrictions on the airspace because of Iran and, I believe, the listening station up on the mountain."

"Who actually cancelled the helicopter?"

"I don't know. They must have checked the flight plan, maybe?"

There were several knowing stares between Mike and the brothers.

"Please enjoy breakfast; I see they've found some pastries, and I'll check when the police team will be here." He smiled and left the room. They were all stunned into silence.

"You have got to be ..." Callum didn't finish his statement. "Harper, let's get in that damn car and out of here!"

"I agree; I want to be anywhere but here. I have no idea if I'll ever come back here again. I told Jay to have the car outside and ready."

Mike stood up and grabbed her bag. She would be very happy to get out of this villa alive – whether that was on a bus or in a private jet really wasn't a priority.

Despite her misgivings that she was a crap operative, she managed to send a message to Chris saying that the helicopter had been cancelled, Mohammed was seriously suspect, and she hoped to be leaving in a car immediately before the police turned up.

They walked out of the large front doors and down the marble steps. There wasn't a cloud in the sky. Unusually, they were all carrying their small baggage themselves, as time was of the essence. The Mercedes with tinted windows pulled up, and Jay got out after opening the cavernous boot.

Loading the car didn't take long. It was patently obvious that everyone had packed the minimum in as little time as possible. The nightmare was almost over. They climbed in, and Jay drove off; the gentle buzz of the tyres on the paved drive was strangely reassuring.

The gates opened ahead of them, and Mike was waiting to see how big the explosion had been last night. Unfortunately, she never saw the outside of the gate or of the walls. Their way was blocked by two police Nissan Patrols.

"Shit," Harper whispered.

"They're Omani police. Where's the UAE border?" Mike asked.

"That white post," Callum answered, indicating a leaning metal pole that had lost its sign. It was about 100 yards down the road.

"Shit."

An officer got out of his vehicle and motioned for them to reverse back to the villa. The bonnet of the Mercedes had barely made it through the gate. The sound of the engine and tyres on the way back up to the villa wasn't quite so reassuring. Harper was the first out of the car, sweating on his forehead and shaking gently. One of the police vehicles had followed them up the drive.

"How may we help you officer? We're late for an appointment," Harper was tense.

"This won't take long, actually. We wanted to ask you about the explosion last night."

Mike and Callum had now joined Harper outside the Mercedes, but they said nothing.

"What explosion?" Harper asked.

"The one that damaged your gates and wall, actually." The officer had a black moustache and was wearing aviator sunglasses.

"We know nothing about this, Officer. Sorry we can't help."

The policeman said nothing.

"Who reported this explosion?"

"Your security guard, early this morning."

Harper knew that this was rubbish. The explosion had happened the evening before. "No, he didn't," he said, showing increased irritation.

"It might have been a member of the public; I'm not sure, actually."

"Officer, if I said that five vehicles pass this gate in a day, I would probably be exaggerating. This all sounds very unlikely."

Mike became aware that she, too, was becoming annoyed and that her pose – leaning her back against the car with her arms folded – wasn't helping. She opened the back door, got back inside and took out her phone.

"I'm sorry, but we need to investigate," the officer said.

"Then please investigate, but we can't help any further."

Harper turned towards Mohammed, who was coming down the steps from the front door. "Mohammed, here, will answer any of your questions. We have to leave now. Sorry."

"That is not possible. We must wait for Chief Inspector Saeed, who wishes to speak with you, actually."

"What about? We've told you that we know nothing about any explosion."

"I cannot say. Shall we go into the villa? He may be a few minutes."

Harper was about to say something, but he swivelled on the spot. He was wet with sweat and trembling; he looked like a drug addict undergoing cold turkey. This wasn't far off the mark.

Callum opened one of the car's rear doors and bent over to tell Mike that they needed to go back into the villa. She had just sent Chris a WhatsApp message, throwing caution to the wind:

"Police stopping us leaving villa. In case I don't make it, check out Ahrun Yonan aka BlueStar in Doha. He met Habib."

She put the phone in her pocket and pulled herself out of the car. Looking around as if seeing the mountain views for the first time, she walked calmly, not towards the villa but towards the police officer.

"Are you arresting me?" she said, her dark eyes under her black wig staring straight at him.

"No."

"Good. I'll sit in the car until the chief inspector arrives." With that, she started to turn.

"We should all go into the villa. He may be some time." The officer was clearly uncomfortable, but he was trying to encourage them all.

Mike rotated slowly back to the policeman. "Excellent. While I was sitting in the car, I've been speaking to the American ambassador about what's happening. I'll spend the additional time giving him an update. What's your name and rank?"

He told her, and she took two steps back, opened the door to the limousine and slid inside. Callum and Harper were halfway up the steps and not sure whether to get back into the car or proceed to the villa. Callum encouraged his older brother, who was clearly stressed, further up the flight of stone steps. They ended up standing under the portico in front of the door.

It was ten minutes later that a black-and-white, four-wheel-drive vehicle entered through the gates and drove up towards the villa's entrance.

A police officer walked over to the vehicle and spoke to the chief inspector as he got out.

Together, they walked towards the villa, while the policeman continued to update his boss. They stopped next to the Mercedes, and the chief inspector tapped at the rear window. Mike pressed a button and the tinted glass lowered.

"Would you step out, please?" he requested.

"Goodbye, Ambassador." Mike pressed a button on her phone and opened the door. She stepped out.

"Mike Kingdom," she said, extending a hand. "And you are?"

"Chief Inspector Saeed."

"Chief Inspector, I'm an American citizen, and you and your officers are preventing me from leaving the villa. I've just described all of this to the ambassador."

"I know Mr Raymond Allerton very well, Miss Kingdom. He is currently back in San Francisco."

"Quite possibly" – Mike didn't miss a beat – "but I was speaking to Doha ... where I need to be for an appointment with the chargé d'affaires at 5.30pm this afternoon." She was making all of this up on the hoof. "So, if you'll excuse me, Chief Inspector, I need to get back to Dubai for my flight."

"Miss Kingdom" – he removed his cap and placed it under his arm, perhaps to look less threatening – "you won't miss your flight, but there were reports of an explosion and gunshots at this villa last evening. However, before I can release you, I need five minutes of your valuable time inside first."

This gave Mike little choice and didn't sound that unreasonable.

"Mohammed, may we have some water? It's too hot to stand outside in this sun." The chief inspector even managed a disarming smile.

"OK, let's go inside for five minutes." Callum could see there was no alternative anyway.

In the nearest lounge, everyone except for Mohammed sat down in the armchairs while the requests for drinks were taken.

The questions from Chief Inspector Saeed, however, began immediately: "Where were you all when you heard or saw the explosion and the gunshots?"

Mike answered first to give Callum time to think: "I never heard any gunshots and was sitting in the other lounge when there was a bang ... but I thought it was a car backfiring. It was no big deal."

"I was also sitting in the other lounge, and it was just as Michaela says," Harper confirmed.

"I was returning from my last visit to the works before we leave this morning. The car was inside the gates and driving up to the villa when there was a noise. It could have been an explosion; I don't know," Callum stated.

"At what time was this?"

"About 7.30pm, I would say." Callum looked at the others

for confirmation. They nodded.

Like all good barristers, the policeman changed tack: "What's your relationship with the Murchison family, Miss Kingdom?"

"They knew my father. I'm visiting for a couple of days."

He changed direction again: "Why the urgent need to book a helicopter?"

Harper was becoming twitchier. "We decided it would be a quicker way to get to Dubai. We didn't know that they couldn't fly around here. That's why we now need to be driven to Dubai this morning. There's nothing sinister about any of this, Chief Inspector."

"I never said there was." The tension was increasing in the room as the water was brought in, and the conversation paused as glasses were filled.

"Why did you all spend the night in the panic room?" The chief inspector was asking in a quiet voice while looking each of them in the eye.

They were all completely thrown. Who had told the police? Mohammed? Another member of staff?

"Why does it matter? Why have you driven all the way over here?" Harper had now stood up.

"I'm simply trying to establish what happened last evening. I'm sure you want to be helpful?"

"Chief Inspector," Mike said, "I spent the night in the panic room because I do not feel safe in this villa or in Oman, for that matter. As I shall be explaining to the chargé d'affaires in ..." – she consulted her watch – "eight and half hours from now if I catch my flight." She didn't bother to explain that it was the British chargé d'affaires she was meeting.

"Miss Kingdom, you're free to leave whenever you wish and thank you for cooperating."

"*What about Callum and me?*" Harper was now shouting.

"Unfortunately, I need you to stay in Oman while we

continue our investigations."

"Into what?" Harper screamed.

"The death of your father."

"*What?*" the brothers exclaimed in unison.

"It was *you* who told *us* that he had died from natural causes. What has changed?" Callum asked as calmly as possible.

"You were shot at as you drove back from the cement works last night, and someone used explosives in an attempt to break down the gates."

The brothers were stunned into silence, mostly at the revelation that the chief inspector was aware that someone had shot at Callum last night.

"Your father's body isn't leaving Muscat this morning as planned, but it will be retained pending a further autopsy."

"What?" Harper could be barely heard as he sat back down in the armchair.

"Chief Inspector, we spent the night in the panic room because we don't feel safe here. Once we leave Oman, I cannot currently conceive that I or my brother will ever set foot here again. Why is us staying in Oman so important to you? We aren't suspects, surely?" Callum had also reduced his voice to more usual levels.

"You two are the common link in all of this, and I need to complete my investigations. However, if you feel threatened, I'll leave two armed police officers outside your gates, day and night, until the matter is resolved."

The chief inspector bent forwards to drink some water, and Mike used the temporary pause to stand up. She turned to the sons giving them both a quick wink before saying, "In that case, and with Callum's and Harper's permission, I would like to use their driver to take me to Dubai. They have my phone number if you need it, Chief Inspector."

He put down his glass and stood up. "It was a pleasure to

meet you, Miss Kingdom. Enjoy your trip to Doha."

"Thank you, it was also a pleasure. Goodbye, Callum. Goodbye, Harper. I'll be in touch."

She walked out of the room and past the study, inside which Mohammed was sitting at a desk on a call. He smiled at her – or at least she thought it was a smile.

It wasn't the heat that she felt first on stepping out through the two big doors but relief. In, perhaps, 150 yards, she would be out of Oman and in the UAE. Before her, the police cars were being reversed, having been given instructions from the chief inspector from inside the villa. Jay materialised from somewhere nearby and opened a rear door of the Mercedes. The interior was still cool from their earlier attempt to leave.

"To Dubai, please, Jay." She would probe him later as to whether he had been interviewed by the police. Apart from the people who had chased and shot at Callum, only Jay knew that this had happened on the way back from the works. This thought reminded her that she was about to be driven down towards the coastal plain and cement works in a few minutes. She no longer felt the initial relief.

It was time to check her messages and to contact Chris.

The first WhatsApp message was from Kevin Stenning. It simply said, "Sorry you can't make it. Hope you aren't stuck in Oman for long. Let me know when you're going to be in Doha. We should meet."

What did that last bit mean? Actually, what did he mean by "Hope you aren't stuck in Oman for too long?"

She was just sending a message to Chris to update him when she became conscious that Jay was looking in his rearview and wing mirrors a little more frequently. They were approaching a sharp bend with an almost vertical limestone face on the nearside and a rather inadequate barrier on the outside above the drop to the shoreline below. She really was between a rock and a hard place.

CHAPTER SEVENTEEN

Chris had been up early in his hotel room in Doha. It was Tuesday, and almost all his commitments to the Olympic delegation were now complete. He had only the swimming facility to check out later, and he had already told his colleagues that he was staying on for a couple of days, at his expense, for a bit of rest and recreation. Many of the committee were going back to Dubai where there was to be a high-level meeting.

Before going down for breakfast and with nothing better to do, he had spent some time checking for the name of the restaurant where BlueStar had met Habib. The photograph, forwarded by Mike, showed the view out of the window, which had modern skyscrapers in the background. Using this information for orientation, it took him less than ten minutes to establish what it was called, and he saved the details. He didn't expect that he would need them, but you never knew.

The basic details for Ahrun Yonan also didn't take long to find. As Mike had done, Chris established that he was an accountant working in the gas industry in Doha, was married to Shamiram and had two children. It wasn't difficult to find the address of their apartment on the edge of the city. He would go over there later, after he had completed his official duties. Firstly, he needed breakfast, after which he would spend some time searching Ahrun's history. Chris had an idea about his ethnicity and his past, but he needed to check if Ahrun was an Assyrian, an Arab or from a country further to the east.

Over eggs, hash browns and beans, he joined the general conversation with his colleagues about competitor accommodation, practice facilities, emergency procedures, etc. However, his mind was elsewhere, and after coffee and a Danish pastry, he made his way back to his room. Mike would land in Doha after lunch, and he wanted to be back at the hotel when she arrived. He was so relieved that she had successfully escaped from the villa, as he had felt very nervous at being unable to get there in time.

"I thought they were all Assyrian," he said out loud, as he sat in front of his laptop in his room, although this begged another suite of questions. He already knew that there were 5 million Assyrians in Iran, Iraq, Turkey and elsewhere and that there was a diaspora of 40,000 in Canada; a fact that had bothered him previously. Chris was suspicious and looking for reasons that Ahrun, using the code name BlueStar, was passing information to Habib Murchison, who – he surmised – had been passing it on to Leonard – information of sufficient value that Leonard would fly out to Dubai and Oman to collect it in person from Habib. Chris knew parts of the story, but how did this all fit in with Leonard asking Mike to investigate a potentially serious matter that had probably led to Leonard's suspension?

While Chris was no slouch at the computer, he couldn't wait for an analyst like Mike to arrive and research further. She would provide more leads for him to pursue. Before that, and having discovered where the Yonans lived, he needed to get a feel for the person.

———

Four hours later, with his official duties over, he was back in his room, changing out of his dark-blue blazer and white trousers. In a green linen shirt and tan chinos, he set off for the block in which the Yonans lived. In his pocket was one of the complimentary envelopes from the room in his hotel, sealed and sporting Yonan's name and address. Inside was a promotional leaflet from a Chinese restaurant. All meaningless and untraceable but offering a credible excuse for him attempting to deliver it, if stopped.

The taxi dropped him at an exhibition centre next to a park shaded by dark, spreading Ficus trees. He had no idea whether he would be ten minutes or an hour, so he made a note of the taxi company's details and set forth in the overpowering heat. His prosthetic limbs didn't really cause him a problem if he could walk at his own pace and stop when he wanted. They did, however, remind him of the old days when he could run anywhere and climb anything.

When he was two streets away, he approached a beige concrete block of apartments with dark-brown glass in the windows. He stood in the shade on the opposite side of the street and took out the free map from his hotel room. Always look like you're doing something, even if it's scrolling through your phone contacts, his CIA trainers had taught him. Never stand around aimlessly looking at nothing in particular.

It wasn't a surprise that no one was walking in this heat and that the traffic in the middle of the day was light.

He approached the block and walked into the cool of the hallway. The lift door was open, and he made his way to the fifth floor. He had only seen one camera inside the entrance. He made his way to apartment 503 and stood outside for a moment. He pressed the doorbell.

A short woman in a headscarf answered the door.

"I'm a friend of Habib Murchison," Chris said.

―――――

In London, the weather had turned cold and wet. It was exactly a week since Barbara Aumonier had made her first visit to the Chiswick office as the head of Five Eyes, and she had just entered her office. Her wet coat was hanging on a hook as even the boss didn't get a covered parking space, although where she had left her car was only a few paces from the staff entrance.

The activities of a large Chinese company that was paying MPs and their staff in the UK, Australia and Canada was at the top of her very large metaphorical in tray. The Five Eyes secretariat was ensuring that the information from the national counter-terrorism agencies was shared quickly and efficiently. It had been the Australians who had made the initial discovery after a major undercover operation in Canberra.

Tom was in his small office, distributing files to the five member nations as instructed by his boss. He was pleased things had calmed down after the turmoil of the previous week. Following the visit to his office by the two men, Leonard hadn't been mentioned again. Tom was hoping he was back in the USA and Mike was pursuing whatever she was pursuing out in the Middle East.

If Tom thought things had calmed down, he had come to this conclusion a little prematurely. There, on his screen, was a piece of intelligence from the CIA for circulation to the other agencies. It said that a key American asset had been killed by forces unknown in the Middle East and there was a credible suspicion that there had been a major breach of security.

Was this Habib Murchison? Surely not? Tom wondered, *He would be a Canadian asset not run by the Americans, wouldn't he?*

Tom broke with his routine and walked down the corridor to get a coffee from the machine; it was only 9.30am, but he already needed a change of scene. The steel-framed photographs of the likes of Toronto, Bath and Melbourne stood out from the white walls of the corridor. He had walked by them hundreds of times before. With a coffee in his hand, he paused by a window, delaying the return to his office. As he watched the planes on their flight path in and out of Heathrow, an Australian friend sidled over.

"Just seen a plane crash?" she asked.

"Oh, h-hello, Iona. No, I was thinking about the p-passengers on board."

"Relatives of yours?"

"More likely to be yours, don't you think?" Tom was from Herefordshire, and travel from there to London didn't involve aeroplanes.

"Quite possibly." She let the thought hang in the air. "Are you getting over a crap weekend or building up to a crap week ahead?"

He smiled. "I've just had a lovely weekend with my s-sister and her kids, so it would be a no on that front. As to this week, the jury's s-still out. It's only Tuesday, and I've b-been here for an hour and a half. How are you doing?"

Iona barely came up to his shoulder and always squeezed her eyes shut in embarrassment whenever she spoke to him. "Something's not right," she said quietly, and she looked rather beseechingly at him. "Do you know what I'm talking about?" She was breaking the unwritten golden rule: nobody talked shop or asked questions outside of set groups and certainly not in a communal space.

He took a sip as an Emirates A380 joined the procession into Heathrow. "Um, I'm n-not sure I understand."

"Why does the new boss keep deleting and redacting things? LDV never did that. Our job isn't to filter, is it?" She used the Australian contingent's nickname for Leonard de Vries – there were ruder alternatives.

"Um, is there a problem?" Tom was aware that this wasn't a conversation to be having in the coffee area, even if no one else was in earshot.

"Tom" – she was squeezing her eyes tight – "don't say anything; I understand, but why isn't she passing on some of the recent Chinese intel?"

"I d-don't know." Tom was feeling more and more uncomfortable, although he had worked with Iona for years, trusted her and thought they were both innocents who had found a niche environment. 'Nerds of a feather' Leonard had once called the two of them.

"You could check, couldn't you? It seems to be all relating to construction companies, as far as I'm allowed to see." She paused and relaxed her facial muscles. "I'm not trying to get you into trouble, Tom."

He said nothing while she looked out of the window and said, "Oh look, there's the Qantas from Sydney."

The sound of someone walking down the corridor put a stop to any other discussion, which was probably for the best. Tom threw his paper cup in the recycling bin.

"I'm t-t-twitchy, too," he said, his stuttering clearly showing this fact.

———

Mike grabbed the seatbelt with both hands. Jay, understandably nervous, had reacted to the loud bang by turning the steering wheel a little too enthusiastically while navigating a sharp bend. The rear of the car had slid towards the barrier, and Mike was being given an eagle's eye view of the steep, rugged rocks below. The car scraped along the galvanised metal for a few yards until Jay regained control.

"*Shit!*" she shouted.

"So sorry, so sorry."

"It's OK. We're all a bit on edge ... well, I am ... literally." Whether Jay understood this or not didn't matter, she was talking to herself. "What was that? An explosion?"

"I don't know," he hesitated, "but we're being followed."

"Really?" she spun around to see a yellow Toyota 100 yards behind.

"That's the same car that blocked the road last night," he said.

"Holy shit!"

In fact, the explosion was nothing sinister; it was the first blast of the day on the highest quarry rockface just the other side of the screen bank. Around 70,000 tons of rock had just collapsed onto the bench below in a cloud of dust. The car following them was, however, more sinister.

She took out her phone and managed to take a photograph of the car and its number plate. She sent it to Chris, Callum and Harper with the message "I'm being followed". The beautiful, rugged landscape now took on a hostile, Martian appearance, and she began to observe it in a heightened state of alarm. They would pass through a village very soon, she seemed to remember, and then they would join the major motorway that would take them back to Dubai. She tensed and relaxed her fingers several times while counting down from 100.

"Jay, how long until we get to civilisation?"

"Madam, that may be ten minutes. It is twenty minutes to the fast road." He sounded tense. Perhaps being the target of a shooting the day before and now being chased down a mountainside wasn't sufficiently offset by his minimal wages.

She looked over her shoulder, but the pursuing vehicle was staying a constant 100 yards behind them. The fact that she was in a large, well-built Mercedes reassured her, but there was no logic to this as no car on earth would survive a fall down into the ravine below; in fact, the manufacturer of the tangled metal scrap wouldn't even be discernible.

Jay had both his hands on the steering wheel as he navigated the ever-gentler bends. At moments like these, people are brought together in ways that aren't likely to happen otherwise.

"Jay, where are you from?"

"Tijuana, Mexico."

"That's a long way."

"The same as you?" He looked in the mirror and their eyes met.

"Well ... yes, I'm from Portland, Oregon."

"The same distance from here," he said, and his eyes went back to the road.

"Why do you say that?"

"I studied geography at the Universidad de Monterrey."

The normally ballsy Michaela Kingdom breathed in. "How did we both end up here?" She sounded fatalistic and resigned.

"Money," he said, pronouncing it 'Mon-ay' and sounding Mexican for the first time.

"Really?" she looked out at the acacia trees clinging on to the limestone crags.

———

In fact, the yellow Toyota didn't follow them onto the E611 main road to Dubai; instead, it turned off and stopped on the hard shoulder. Jay reported this news enthusiastically to Mike. Finally relaxing, she took in the arid landscape seen through a monotonous network of red-and-white electricity pylons and wires. An hour or so later, when the modern urban skyline of Dubai appeared through the orange smog, there was a realisation that she had escaped, but the brothers were still in serious danger. This was a subject for discussion with Chris that afternoon – if she made it on to the flight to Qatar.

Thankfully, the rest of the car journey turned out to be uneventful.

At the Royal Manta Hotel, the doorman stepped forwards, but he had to wait while Mike tapped Jay's telephone number into her own phone and sent him a quick text; she was learning fieldwork as she went along. She wanted Jay to have her number so that he could contact her in an emergency. They had established a respect for each other during the two-hour drive.

Rohan waved and beamed at her as she walked into the cool of the reception hall.

"I'm checking out," she said, "will you make up my bill? I'll go up to my room to pack."

"No problem."

Mike had begun to walk towards the lifts when he added, "Oh, Miss Kingdom, will you be taking your father's suitcase with you?"

"What? Oh yes, thank you."

"We've put everything into his one bag. I hope that this is all right?"

"Excellent."

"How is your father?"

"Stable," said Mike, although she wasn't sure that the word 'stable' had ever applied to Leonard.

She pivoted and headed for her room.

CHAPTER EIGHTEEN

Mike was collecting her luggage from the carousel at Doha airport when it dawned on her that she didn't know what was actually in Leonard's suitcase if she was stopped at customs. She prepared her story for that eventuality. As it happened, nobody took any notice. She decided, however, that she would open Leonard's bag later in her hotel room before flying back to London, even if the thought of going through Leonard's dirty underwear was not appealing. She left the airport and jumped into a taxi.

An hour later, she was sitting in the hotel restaurant about to have a very late lunch, with Chris ordering pizza margherita and a beer, which was obviously his favourite. He was wearing a pale-green linen shirt with sunglasses perched on the top of his head.

"Well, I'm sure glad to see you," he said. "Tell me what happened, from the beginning."

"I feel like I've been away for a year, not forty-eight hours. The first thing to say is that the Murchison villa is weird and gives off some pretty odd vibes. What sort of Canadian would build a mock White House high in the mountains on the

UAE–Oman border?" She was obviously reflecting on this before continuing, "It's absolutely not to my taste, but without a blink, I would like some of the artworks."

The waiter disturbed them with some ice-cold towels.

"A certain Chief Inspector Saeed rang up personally to deliver the sons the news that their father had died from natural causes. Really? I don't have the slightest doubt that he was murdered. Then we have Mohammed, Habib's Mr Fixit, who gives me the creeps."

Chris handed his used towel to a passing waiter. "I should never have let you go there alone."

"The sons seem tight, but they're very different. All was vaguely normal until Callum was held up on his way back from the cement works to the villa and shot at. The bullet grazed his arm, but his driver, Jay, got him back to the villa, where there was a small explosion at the gates, which sent us all into Habib's panic room for the night."

"*What?*"

"It was on the way to the panic room that I messaged you. While I was doing that, Harper booked a helicopter to get us out of that hellhole at 8.30am this morning. That never happened, because at … I don't know … 7.00am, Mohammed tapped on the door to the panic room, and we all emerged." She paused to eat some bread. "He told us that helicopters are banned from the area around the villa and that it had been cancelled. Along with the sons, we decided to get Jay to drive us back to Dubai."

She interrupted her flow, after checking the time on her phone, to tell Chris that Habib's body was meant to have left Muscat about four hours previously.

"We made it to the gate – well, halfway outside, to be precise – where we were miraculously met by two police cars and encouraged, and I use the term loosely, to go back inside until Chief Inspector Saeed turned up. You have to remember,

Chris, that this villa is in the middle of fricking nowhere near the top of a mountain. He told us that the body wasn't being released and that he had more questions about the shooting, but, luckily, he let me go."

"That's some forty-eight hours."

"I haven't finished yet!"

"I was followed all the way to the main road by the same car that attempted to hijack Callum."

"What's all this about, Mike?" The first course was being delivered, so he leant his large upper body back to give the waiter room to serve him.

"I think you'll be surprised," she said while running a finger under the fringe of her black wig. "This is all about Bitcoin."

"What? Who's trading in Bitcoin?"

"No one; well, a little bit, but this is all about a crypto mine, or farm, as the sons refer to it as. They've built a secret warehouse down on the coast, accessed only through the cement works. Their father has been supplying the electricity from the mini power station that he built to serve the two works and the port. They have 500 computers in this shed, which have generated $20 million worth of cryptocurrency." She took a swig from her glass.

"Who's after this facility? Do you have any idea?"

"The sons are a bit cagey about that, but someone has discovered relatively recently what they have over there – don't ask me how – and started to apply pressure. They had a threatening phone call offering to buy it for some ludicrously low price, which they rejected. Then, yesterday, they shot at Callum as he was being driven back from the works to the villa."

"And you think this Mohammed and the chief inspector are involved as well?"

"Well, it's all a bit of a coincidence, isn't it? And nobody in our business does coincidences, do they?"

"It doesn't sound like the shots and the explosion were serious attempts to kill the sons. If they had wanted to kill one or both of them, I can't believe it would be difficult. This was all about getting their message across, wasn't it?"

"You could be right. I'm not sure."

Chris pressed his large forearms on the table to shift his weight, almost tipping it over. "And what has this got to do with their father? Was he killed to put pressure on the sons? Presuming he was killed, that is."

"That's the odd bit, isn't it? Why do it so subtly that it's mistaken for a heart attack? Why did the chief inspector also ring the sons to confirm he had died from natural causes? Did they simply want Habib out of the way? Did they want the whole business enterprise to pass to the sons? This would make it easier for them to apply pressure."

"Odd," was all Chris said.

"What have you been up to, apart from worrying about me?"

"I've been very busy this morning. I located the person who was at the lunch in your photograph." Chris avoided mentioning his name or code name. "And I went to see him this morning; I've just got back. Sadly, he wasn't there, but I spoke to his wife and asked her to pass on a message to her husband. From what she said, I'm guessing he was back in Iraq … but as is to be expected, she wasn't very forthcoming."

"Who did you say you were?"

"I spoke to her in Arabic, and I think that helped, although Aramaic is probably her first language. I said that I was a good friend of Habib, who had given me her husband's name; that I was very sorry to hear Habib had died; and that I would like to help sort things out."

"What did she say?"

"Not much. There were voices somewhere in the flat, although that could have been a TV, and she apologised that she couldn't talk for long. I gave her my official IOC card and asked her to get her husband to call me. She did ask me how I knew Habib and what my business with him was. I told her I was an American who had been helping Habib with some of his more difficult projects. I didn't specify anything, and I said I was in Doha officially with the IOC. It's always best to give some checkable facts. She said she would pass on my message."

"Strange that our friend should suddenly feel the need to leave Qatar and go to Iraq or wherever. He must presume that his wife and family are safe in Doha?" She reached into the small bag that was over her shoulders and took out something small. "This is the half of the restaurant receipt that Habib had stuffed down the side of his chair. What's so special about this tiny bit of paper that our new friend and Habib needed to meet? There are just a few numbers written on it."

"Ha, I've already worked out which restaurant from the photograph you sent me."

"You would make a great analyst."

———

Kevin Stenning was looking out at the grey-green fronds and orange ripening fruit at the top of the Phoenix date palms that blocked his view of the rest of Doha. The air conditioning was on full, as it was a very hot day. Half an hour earlier, he had received a message from Mike asking if she could still come to see him as she had managed to catch the flight from Dubai. He had replied that he was at the embassy all afternoon.

On arrival, Mike showed her passport and handed over her bag and phone at security. Next came the tight squeeze through the airlock and scanner. A helpful girl accompanied her to a small meeting room where she needed to wait.

A short time later, the door opened to reveal a man in his forties with dark-brown hair, tortoiseshell-framed glasses and dimples on his cheeks, which appeared every time he smiled. "Miss Kingdom, welcome to the British Embassy. I'm Kevin. I expect you've checked my bona fides?"

"I have. I expect you've checked mine?"

"I have." There was an amount of cat and mouse necessarily taking place. "So now we're in a safe and secure environment, shall we speak frankly? I've known Leonard for a long time, and we've worked together on several ... projects. We're friends. He told me he was coming to Dubai, but that this was an unofficial visit. I only received one more call from him – the one asking me to call an ambulance to take him to the USAF hospital. After that, I heard nothing. I tried his phone, and you answered. That's it, really."

Mike looked around the small room, which was minimally furnished and, most likely, used to interview people for visas. "As you now know, I'm sure, I worked for the CIA in the US, then under Leonard in London and, finally, for Five Eyes. I was invalided out, and since that time I've led a quiet life. Occasionally, my peace has been disturbed by Leonard, who sees me as a private asset – particularly if he needs an analyst. You'll know that he's never really grasped the difference between an analyst and an operative. Every time I've freelanced for him, I've ended up in the field" – she waved a hand vaguely at the window – "hence, I'm out here."

"Do you know what Leonard was doing out here? I know he was – how shall we say? – being recalled to Washington. He told me."

"Kevin, you know the way it is. I do know, or thought that I knew, but it's probably best that I keep it to myself." She almost said that it didn't concern Qatar, and therefore he needn't worry, but she remembered BlueStar in Doha and bit her tongue. Kevin didn't press her further. He moved on.

"Do you know why he called me, a Brit in Doha, rather

than any of his US Embassy colleagues in Dubai? He sounded pretty ill and desperate."

There was a silence broken only by the sound of the air conditioning.

"No, and he never mentioned your name to me. He was … he was very nervous that what we should perhaps call 'the agencies' have been compromised. He had stopped trusting anyone much, and I think the trip out here was partly to do with trying to clear the problem up."

"Why do you say 'partly'?"

"Because I don't know. He never mentioned anyone in any of the US embassies out here to me. I'm as surprised as you are as to why he called you. I missed a call from him, which might explain this. But as to why he called you, it doesn't make any sense to me."

"How did you get his phone?"

"I went to his room. His phones, wallet, everything was as he left it. The hotel management were collecting it for safekeeping. I said I was his daughter and took his phones. I now have all his belongings, by the way. I've checked out of the Dubai hotel."

"Did you come to Doha just to see me?"

Mike hesitated a little too long. "Well, not exactly."

"Miss Kingdom, my remit is the—"

"Mike, please."

"Mike, my remit is the whole of the Arabian Peninsula. I may be able to help you if you can trust me enough."

"Trust is the most valuable currency in our business, isn't it?"

"It is." His dimples appeared. "Leonard trusted you enough to give you a vital project. Leonard trusted me enough to phone me, above everyone else, to get him to hospital. Doesn't that tell us both something?"

A critical moment had been reached.

"God, I could kill him. He's done this to me so many times. We both know he's no fool, and I wonder if he meant us to meet. Who knows?"

"He's not your conventional CIA director, that's for sure. I've known a few," Kevin said while trying to evaluate a young woman with a jet-black Cleopatra wig, uneven complexion and piercing, dark-brown eyes.

"Do you have to make our conversation official? In fact, do you have to report it to anyone? Can it be off the record?"

"I'll do my best to keep this between us, but I can't give you a cast-iron promise. I do give you my word that I'll do everything to protect Leonard."

Mike had decided not to start with BlueStar, but in Oman. "Have you had any dealings with the Murchison family in Oman?" She was watching him intently.

"No, not in the way you might mean, but I've been introduced to Habib socially at events here at the embassy and, of course, I know of his company – most people out here have. Murchison Arabco is such a massive supplier of construction materials to Qatar. I also know he's died and there was some controversy over his death."

"It was Habib who called Leonard out to his villa in Oman." She paused for effect. "He was killed a few hours before Leonard had gotten to the villa."

"Why do you say 'killed'?"

"Leonard told me he had been murdered and asked me to stir up trouble online to get an autopsy ... which – surprise, surprise – found he had died from natural causes. You may be interested to know that, only this morning, the Omanis have stopped his body from being repatriated to Canada so they can undertake a second autopsy."

"I couldn't understand why you'd sent that message saying you were stuck in Oman. Why did you send it?"

"I wanted you to know that I wouldn't make this meeting.

There were a few minutes when I thought that I wouldn't make it out of the villa. We spent the night in a panic room."

"Who's we?"

"The two Murchison brothers and me. Callum, the youngest, was shot at as he returned to the villa."

"How did you all escape?"

"They're still in the villa. The police won't let them leave until this is all cleared up. They let me go as I'm not involved ... but a car followed us all the way to the freeway."

"Do you know what the relationship was between Leonard and Habib?"

"You'll have to guess, like me."

"If Habib was a source, he was important enough that Leonard would fly out here himself when he had other things on his mind. I'm guessing that whatever they were talking about was as important as it gets."

Throughout the conversation, Mike had been considering whether to mention BlueStar or not. After all, having the code name would be of no use unless Kevin Stenning knew his real name. Chris had already found where Ahrun Yonan lived and knew he was in Iraq, probably in hiding. As things stood, no further progress was going to be made.

"If I said 'BlueStar' to you, would it mean anything?"

"Nothing. Why?"

"I'll let you know the next time we meet."

———

In the next room, Yolanda picked up her phone.

CHAPTER NINETEEN

That Yolanda Smith should end up working for the FCO or the secret services was no surprise, but only when viewed from her CV; her route to head of Middle East section had not, in reality, been straightforward.

Yes, she was the daughter of one of the late Queen Elizabeth II's ambassadors to Morocco: Sir Gerwyn Gruffydd, a pompous man who, in Victorian times, would have been described as 'clubbable'. She would still describe him as that, but with its more usual modern meaning. She hated him and despised everything formal about his position, to the extent that she took every opportunity to rebel or cause problems. Much to his chagrin, she chose to spend her four years in Rabat playing football with the sons of ambassadors from the Arab world or local children, some of whom were still her friends. She was a tomboy and a misfit who hated her appearance only slightly more than she hated her surname. The latter was happily changed by a now defunct marriage to a career civil servant; the former had never really gone away. Her thick, wavy hair had come from her father's Welsh ancestors, and its straw-blonde colour had come from – well, nobody knew. It was her lazy left eye that had drawn the most abuse as she grew up – first, at international schools, and then at Cheltenham Ladies College.

She had wanted to read history at university, but this hadn't happened – she had received no offers. Fortunately, her careers adviser at school had suggested that she put down geography and Arabic at Lampeter University as a safety-net choice. She hadn't the slightest intention of going there, but this proved to be unavoidable – it was Hobson's choice. That she found the course easy would be an understatement.

With fluent Arabic and a father who was an ambassador, one would be forgiven for thinking that this was why she ended up in the FCO. This wasn't the case – well, not at first. She fell in love with a boy who was applying for a civil service fast-track commission; his name was Roger Smith, and she applied as well. They were both accepted and headed for the bright lights of London – actually, the dim lights of London, as they ended up living in a dingy basement flat with central 60-watt ceiling lights and working in depressing offices with small windows and beige walls that hadn't been painted for twenty years.

The marriage hadn't lasted, but by then, people who were paid to notice such things had spotted she was wasted checking visa applications. For her part, she only stayed in London because she had begun training with the England ladies' football squad three times a week on a public playing field surrounded by poplars next to a gasometer in Hillingdon. She had to pay her own Tube fare to get there.

Absolutely none of this had anything to do with how she ended up head of Middle East at MI6.

After Lampeter, she had spent three weeks on a study tour of Egypt, ostensibly based at the University of Cairo. The local MI6 representative was an Arsenal supporter, and in an unlikely alignment of the planets, found himself talking to

Yolanda, one of the first players in their newish Arsenal ladies' team. Those conversations were the real reason that Yolanda had started on the journey to her current position.

No one person ever saw all of her many facets.

With red lipstick and wearing a black suit and ivory shirt, she could be the well-spoken daughter of a British ambassador, a lacrosse-playing Cheltenham Ladies College old girl who was happy to converse in English, Welsh, French and Arabic about world affairs. With greasy hair and wearing a sweatshirt and leggings, she could sink a pint in one go and talk football refereeing mistakes until well past closing time.

In Doha, she had just overheard Mike Kingdom in the next room mention BlueStar, and she had gone into full professional mode.

———

A hot wind was blowing up and over the Hajar Mountains, even as the faithful were attending prayers; as a katabatic wind, it became even hotter as it descended on the western side, heading down to the Persian Gulf.

The brothers were finally leaving the villa in the back of a Mercedes, though not quite as they had planned. They were sitting in a black-and-white, four-wheel-drive G-Wagon behind Chief Inspector Saeed and his driver. Their situation had gradually deteriorated from bad to worse.

After Mike had left, the sons had been questioned further on the shooting and the explosion. When it had become clear that the chief inspector knew Callum had been shot on his way back to the villa, he had admitted his deception and had described the whole incident without leaving out anything, and for a short while, this seemed to clear the air.

At this point, Mohammed had entered the lounge. The

chief inspector had turned in his chair to ask in English, "Where were you last evening, Mohammed?"

There's something strange about two people speaking to each other not in their mother tongue; there's always an important reason. The brothers were beginning to suspect that this wasn't politeness but was for show.

Mohammed answered, "I left early evening and went down to the works before I drove home. I came back at 7.00am this morning and noticed the damage to the wall and gate. When I came into the villa, I was surprised that there was no sign of Miss Kingdom, Mr Callum and Mr Harper. The chauffeur, Jay, told me he had brought Mr Callum back at about 7.30pm. I therefore searched the villa until there was only the panic room left." He looked at the brothers. "I then knocked on the door and told them the villa was safe."

"Mohammed, like last time, could you send me the CCTV footage from the gate and the villa?"

"Of course."

"We need to identify the vehicles that have been described and see who caused the explosion."

While Callum was thinking that it must have been Jay who told the police about the vehicles and the shooting, Harper was beginning to feel like he was stuck in the villa and would never actually leave; an earworm developed that took some time to disappear.

The chief inspector left the room to take a phone call.

Mohammed took the opportunity to talk to the sons. "I'm sorry" – he was speaking quickly and quietly – "There's nothing I can do. Trust me. The chief inspector is under a lot of pressure from above. Please cooperate with him. Tell him anything you know."

"Mohammed, we have nothing to hide. We don't understand any of this either," Callum also whispered.

"What will happen next, do you think?" his brother asked.

"The second autopsy should happen this morning. I hope it confirms the original result. Until he knows this, Chief Inspector Saeed has no choice – he will not let you leave. You understand?" Mohammed explained.

"And what if it doesn't confirm the result?"

The door opened and the policeman re-entered. Despite wearing black-tinted sunglasses, his face displayed the stress he was obviously under. "I am very sorry," he said, looking at the brothers, "I've just been given instructions by my superiors to take you into Muscat until the results of the autopsy are available."

"*What?*" Harper was not happy.

"We can stay here if you wish. There's no need to go to Muscat." Callum was quick to try to find some middle ground.

"I'm afraid that isn't possible."

"We haven't done anything wrong. We're not going to Muscat." Harper was sweating and shaking again.

"You have a choice. Come with me voluntarily in my car, or I'll arrest you and my officers can bring you in handcuffs." A new seriousness had entered the policeman's voice.

Everyone was standing very still.

"Mohammed?" Callum wanted his take on the situation.

"Please go with Chief Inspector Saeed in his car. I'm sure this will all be sorted out this morning. Would you like me to come with you or stay here?"

"Stay here for now, thank you. I'll call you if we need anything."

With that, they left the villa, but not before Callum had texted Mike to say they were effectively being arrested and going to Muscat.

As they sat together in the back of the black-and-white G-Wagon, the vehicle turned right out of the villa gates and not the more usual left towards the works, Dubai and the chance of flying back home – and freedom.

———

"... *because we've effectively been arrested and taken to a police station in Muscat ... in Oman!*" Harper was shouting down the phone to someone at the nearest Canadian Embassy in Abu Dhabi, across the border in the UAE. "Yes, of course I'll wait. Actually, come to think of it, would it be quicker if I called the emergency watch-and-response centre in Ottawa? I thought you were nearer." There was a pause. "Thank you; no, I got nowhere with the honorary consul in Muscat."

The brothers were sitting in a small office at police headquarters. They had been left alone with their phones and told that, if they attempted to leave, they would be put in a cell. Callum was busy cancelling the flight back to London for them and rescheduling the one to Vancouver via Germany for their father's body. He had already spoken to a firm of solicitors in London that had an associate office in Dubai. Harper was trying, unsuccessfully, to get someone from a Canadian Embassy or consulate to visit them and to start pulling strings. Unfortunately, progress had been slow so far.

Callum walked over to the water cooler and poured them both another drink into plastic cups. "Is it time to tell them about the farm and the threats?" he asked.

"No," Harper hissed, "Not until it's absolutely necessary. This may all blow over." He was the brother most invested in the crypto-mining business. His phone rang. It was from Dubai, telling him that a senior solicitor called Ali from the associate firm would be with them within the hour. "Thank goodness for that."

Almost immediately, Callum's phone rang. "Oh, hi Mike ... so you got my message?"

"What have they charged you with?" she asked.

"Nothing. They're waiting for the results of the second autopsy. These should be through soon."

"There's not much I can do from Doha to help you immediately, but I may be making some progress on other matters, which I'll communicate to you when you're free."

"We aren't interested in other matters at the moment. We just want to fly out of here ... for ever," he added, perhaps gratuitously.

———

Chris Crippen was about to meet Mike, who was keen to decide what they should do next or, if they had done all they could, whether to head back to London. It was Tuesday afternoon, and he knew she felt little progress had been made. However, for his part, the trip had revitalised him in a way he hadn't expected. He had become accustomed to playing international sport, but the games were infrequent, and most of the time, he was in the gym or in his flat. Similarly, he had accepted his official role with the IOC even if it was mind-numbing inspecting velodromes, swimming pools and tennis courts. There was nothing, he decided, that could replace the thrill of fieldwork. He was invigorated.

It was while he was chatting to Mike that his phone rang. He hadn't really expected to receive a call from the woman he believed to be BlueStar's wife.

"Oh, hello. Yes, of course, Mrs Yonan." He grabbed a pen and pulled a pad nearer to him.

"My husband has asked if it would be possible to meet you?" she asked in Arabic, their chosen common language.

"Of course, any time. Is he back from his travels?"

"Soon," she said rather vaguely.

"When and where would he like to meet me?"

"Would tomorrow afternoon be too soon?"

"No, that wouldn't be a problem. I'm presuming he means in Doha?"

"Yes. Do you know the Al Musar art gallery?"

"I'm sure I can find it."

"Would meeting after lunch be acceptable? Or possibly later?"

Chris was enjoying the thrill of not knowing what would happen next; apart from some work for Leonard, he had missed this for nearly three years. "After lunch would be no problem."

"There's a visiting Braque exhibition. The gallery opens at 1.30pm on Wednesdays. Could you meet my husband in front of the painting called *Violin and Candlestick* at 1.45pm?"

"How will I know it's him?"

"You'll be asked if it is meant to be a guitar."

Chris suppressed a smile. "Absolutely no problem, Mrs Yonan."

He took a few minutes in which to locate the gallery and to google the *Violin and Candlestick* painting; it wasn't to his taste.

"Oh, I love that painting," Mike said when they were catching up on the call. "I would love to see the exhibition. Can I come along?"

Chris had frowned.

"Not to interfere, honestly. I'll keep right out of the way and just enjoy the art."

"I thought you didn't like fieldwork?"

"Going to a Braque exhibition doesn't class as fieldwork. I would go anyway. I also want to see BlueStar in the flesh."

"You actually like cubist paintings? I would have thought that all those browns and greys were a bit dull for you. Speaking of which, I hope you aren't going to wear your red wig? You need to blend into the background."

"To blend into the background, I'll need to draw lines on my face and paint an extra eye on my cheek."

Chris put his head in his hands in a way that was more Munch than Picasso.

———

Chief Inspector Saeed opened the door without knocking. Callum and Harper put down their phones, on which they had been reading about yet another death of a music superstar by drowning after mistakenly taking enough drugs to kill a bull elephant. The policeman's face displayed no emotion and gave no indication of why he was back.

"I have the results of the second autopsy. It found that your father was poisoned. You were the ones who found the body and the ones who have inherited his fortune. I have no choice but to arrest you for his murder."

"*What?*" they screamed in unison.

"I understand that your Omani lawyer will be here within the hour. We'll speak again then."

He turned and left the room. The door was audibly locked.

CHAPTER TWENTY

The Al Musar was very modern, and like most other galleries built in the twenty-first century, it was a ridiculous combination of geometry and materials, as if the architect had been trying to outdo the pieces that it would ultimately contain. *Art galleries are no more than a group of flexible, rectilinear rooms, aren't they? Why do they have to look like spaceships?* This is what Chris was thinking as he walked up the ramp to the entrance doors. He was at the head of the very small queue waiting to enter at 1.30pm. He had already bought his ticket online and had his phone ready to show at the desk. A small brochure listed the works and gave the room numbers in brackets. *Violin and Candlestick* was listed as being in Salon 3. Wearing a set of headphones that provided an English commentary, he headed off to enter the correct room that was hosting the famous painting a couple of minutes before the arranged time.

Mike, meanwhile, had arrived earlier and was wandering in the formal gardens around which the gallery (or huge metal spaceship, if that's what it was meant to resemble) had been built. Ahrun Yonan hadn't yet shown up, and despite looking as if she were enjoying the shade and small sculptures, she was keeping the main entrance permanently in view. Mike had memorised his face from the photograph in the restaurant. There was no way he could enter without her seeing him. Time dragged. Patience, unless she was at a keyboard, was not her strong suit.

———

Earlier, before they had independently set off from the hotel, Mike had been giving her take on the situation. She had described one connection that Chris couldn't have made, given that he had never visited the Murchison villa: "Habib had some seriously expensive cubist paintings on his walls. Perhaps he and BlueStar shared a passion for Braque and Gris?"

"I've only really heard of Picasso," he had said in reply.

"But is this why he picked this venue?"

Now the tables had been turned, and the operator could explain the basics to the analyst: "I very much doubt it. This is fundamental fieldcraft. Let's remember that it's Wednesday, when most people are working, and the gallery doesn't open until lunchtime. In fact, he chose 1.45pm because the gallery will have only just opened, and there will probably be very few visitors – mostly Japanese tourists. It's unlikely that any of them will have made it through the other rooms to the specified painting by 1.45pm. It's perfectly normal for two strangers to stand next to each other in front of a picture and even exchange a few words. He chose this exhibition because he's worked out that no one in their right mind, except weirdos like you, goes to look at a load of garbage like this at lunchtime in Doha. My guess is that there will be very, very few people there, in case you're wondering."

She had folded her arms as some form of defence as Chris had continued, "I expect he'll sidle up to me, say the agreed words and suggest that we meet in a restaurant in twenty minutes. This will throw off any surveillance and give him a chance to monitor me as I walk from the gallery. It makes it difficult for any watchers." Chris had enjoyed explaining this. "He sounds professional to me."

Mike had given him a look from which most people would have recoiled, but he had merely smiled. Her phone pinged, and she read a message from Callum. Everything was becoming ever more urgent.

———

Back in the gallery, Chris had already seen enough of the paintings of tables, glasses, newspapers and stringed instruments after Salon 1. Even the word 'salon' was beginning to grate. As he expected, most genuine art lovers and visitors were moving slowly through the rooms, so when he walked into Salon 3, he was alone. There were only seven paintings on the white walls. A simple wooden box, centrally placed, provided a place to sit and contemplate the works; otherwise, the room was empty apart from a wire chair for the use of any gallery attendant. He took his time looking at each painting, reading the small descriptions next to each work and listening to the running commentary. Apparently, Georges Braque wanted everyone to look at these everyday objects from several perspectives at once. One was more than enough for Chris.

An attendant in a black jacket, trousers and headscarf walked into the room and sat down on the chair. Perhaps she wasn't used to visitors making it to Salon 3 so quickly at the start of the afternoon session. She was holding a small walkie-talkie and small bursts of Arabic crackled around the room until she reduced the volume. There was no acknowledgement that Chris's experience of the artworks had in any way been reduced by this intrusion.

He leant forwards, constrained only by the small bar at shin level that was there to prevent visitors getting too close. He took off his headphones and held them in his left hand after adjusting the slide to make them more comfortable.

Unexpectedly, the attendant appeared at his side. In Arabic, she said quietly, "Is that a guitar?" He turned towards her, and she continued, "Please follow me over to the door to the next salon." She pointed at his headphones and asked if he was having any trouble. He said that they were working fine and put them back on his head.

The attendant walked to the portal between the salons and paused.

It was as if Chris had never stopped being an agent – his years of training kicked back in. He bent down to read a small notice and moved off slowly to the next salon, like any other tourist. At the door, the attendant passed him a small card. This was a spot, well known to her, where there was no camera coverage; surveillance was, understandably, placed in the rooms to cover the art, not the transition between rooms. The visitors had already been checked on entering as thoroughly as if they were boarding a plane. The attendant walked off, speaking into her walkie-talkie and performing her duties without missing a beat.

He didn't hurry, but eventually, he asked another attendant a couple of salons later where he could find the toilets. He followed their directions and, sitting in a cubicle, he read the card.

"Come to an appointment at 5.30pm this afternoon." It gave an address of an optician's a couple of miles from BlueStar's apartment building.

Chris could feel that Ahrun Yonan was very nervous, and perhaps this was understandable, knowing what had happened to Habib and his sons after their lunch together. BlueStar wanted as many cut-outs as possible between him and anyone he might meet. Before leaving the cubicle, Chris sent Mike a brief message to update her.

———

Mike was frustrated that she hadn't seen BlueStar, despite having stared at the face of about 100 people queuing to buy tickets or milling about outside, and given her preoccupation, she couldn't even enjoy the outdoor sculpture exhibition, which was very much to her taste. She stayed for another twenty minutes and then headed back to the hotel.

When Chris made it back to his room, he waited for her text message, which asked him to meet her in the coffee bar next to reception.

———

The name 'Yonan' didn't appear on the odd-looking brass plate to the side of the sleek glass entrance.

Chris had arrived early and walked around the block, checking on where the doors, windows and fire escapes were; nothing seemed untoward, but he didn't expect it to. He had agreed with Mike that she shouldn't come, but she should be at the end of her phone back at the hotel.

Five minutes before his appointment, he had entered and been greeted by a receptionist behind a white desk. There was no one else visible.

"Chris Crippen," he had said, adding, "I have an appointment at 5.30pm."

The young girl hadn't bothered to check this on her system but had simply said, "Follow me."

After walking down an overly bright corridor, Chris was shown into a dimly lit room full of the usual equipment for testing eyes – the contrast with the glare outside was stark. He was told to take a seat, and the receptionist withdrew, closing the door behind her. He found himself memorising the graded letters on the eye chart even though he wasn't there for a test. It was an automatic response; everyone did it. A side door opened, and a woman was silhouetted before she stepped through and stood two paces in front of him. She was wearing a headscarf and blue-framed glasses. A light was flicked on, and Chris was confronted by Ahrun Yonan's wife, looking every inch the ophthalmologist.

"Thank you for coming, Mr Crippen." He hadn't expected her to speak English in an American accent.

"No problem," Chris replied, unsure whether to stand and greet her formally or to stay sitting.

"Apologies for the complicated arrangements, but they are necessary; I'm sure you understand," she said as she sat down behind a desk.

"I understand completely and would do the same myself."

"Who are you?" She spoke in a very direct manner.

"Chris Crippen; I'm sure you've checked. I'm looking forward to meeting your husband. I'm keen to talk to him."

"You're right; we have checked already. My husband, however, is still in Iraq. It's safer there, but you can talk to me. Again, who are you and why are you here?"

"I'm an ex-CIA operative, genuinely here for the International Olympic Committee visit. However, my boss at the CIA is – *was* – a very good friend of Habib Murchison." He paused to read her face, but it was inscrutable. "Habib asked him to visit his villa, but he – my boss, that is – arrived a day too late. He's had to leave the Middle East and asked me to investigate who killed his friend."

"Why does your boss need to use a former employee?" There was no emotion in her voice.

"Um ..." – Chris knew he couldn't make one false move or he would never get to meet BlueStar – "he was very nervous and didn't want to use the usual channels. I understand his relationship with Habib went back decades, and they were protective of their ... friendship."

They were dancing around each other, not mentioning Leonard de Vries or Sir Donald Reeve by name and certainly not mentioning BlueStar. She ran a little finger under her thin, beige scarf while Chris thought about how to convince her that she should give him access to her husband.

"Forgive me, I'm just a pawn like you," he said, "I think my boss doesn't want to lose all contact with your husband." Chris had leant forwards and was resting his large arms on his thighs. She said nothing, so he continued, "Habib had lunch in Doha with your husband hours before he was murdered at his villa. Their meeting was important enough that Habib had called my boss out here from London."

Her face had changed to the mildest of frowns. "How do you know my husband had lunch with this man?"

She was testing him and had put him in a position from which there was no escape. He could recognise and acknowledge the skills she was displaying, or not displaying. Was she, in reality, an ophthalmologist as well as an intermediary for her husband?

"My boss told me."

"That's highly unlikely."

The room, already cool, became colder.

Chris, who often rested his forearms on his thighs for comfort, sat back up and looked directly at her. "Would your husband like help from my boss?"

"What's he offering?" She was giving little away, and he was glad they weren't playing poker.

"I'm more interested in what your husband would like, but I'm guessing that everyone concerned wouldn't like the" – he reflected for a second – "connections ... that are now damaged

by Habib's death to put an end to a productive relationship ...
about which I know nothing."

For the first time, her face changed to a soft smile that
morphed into a slight sadness. "That would be a great shame
for everyone, I think."

This was the moment when Chris realised he needed to
play his trump card, if it indeed was a trump card and not
simply a piece of torn restaurant receipt.

"At the lunch in Doha, Habib tore a receipt in half. Possibly,
he needed to write something down for your husband. He
must have put the other half in his pocket just before he was
murdered; we think he wanted to hide the restaurant name
from his attackers. He didn't want them to check out the location and make the link to your husband. Could you help my
boss with what Habib wrote on the receipt?"

It was her turn to reflect and weigh up the possibilities.
Uppermost in her thoughts was how the young man before her
could know the essence of the meeting. She knew that her
husband and Habib had torn a receipt in half. The top half
would have made its way with him back to the villa. She didn't
know what Habib would have done with it. This threw up far
too many questions.

"Does your boss know about this piece of paper and what
was written on it?"

"Yes," Chris lied.

She looked around the room as if she were a client, not the
optician – perhaps this was the truth. Her face, when it
returned its focus to Chris, was enigmatic, but she said
nothing.

"Would you ask your husband what was written on the torn
receipt and what he wants my boss to do now we've lost Habib
as the middleman and translator?"

She picked up what looked like a slide rule from the desk
and played with it. When she spoke, it was in a slightly

lowered voice: "We all need to be extra careful, do you understand?" She did not elaborate.

With his massive upper body, he was a physically dominating presence in the room, but even with her diminutive size, her voice brooked no contradiction.

"You tell me what you know and what you want. I'll make sure every care is taken," he offered.

A device on her desk buzzed. She grabbed the mouse and rolled it to activate her computer screen. He could only see the back of the monitor, but the light on her face indicated that it had been powered back into life. After a couple of clicks, which may have been modifying what she was looking at, she looked up through her blue-framed glasses and said, "Do you know this person?"

She rotated the screen enough so that Chris could lean forwards, resting his hands on the back edge of her desk, and see it. He found himself looking at four views of the front and rear of the premises. There, looking at her phone while leaning on the wastepaper bin around the back of the building, was a woman in her mid-thirties in a black Cleopatra wig.

CHAPTER TWENTY-ONE

"What the ...?" Chris had walked out of the optician's and immediately phoned Mike. "I thought you were staying at the hotel? I'll meet you there in twenty minutes." He ended the call before she could speak.

The walk back may irritate his legs and fry his brains in the thirty-degree heat, but it was also an opportunity to let his anger subside. The truth was that he had barely spoken to an analyst when he had been active in the CIA; he almost exclusively dealt with handlers and intermediaries, protection and logistics, and embassy staff and administration. Information was fed to him or provided by him. Perhaps he liked it that way. He recognised that he would definitely make a useless analyst, so why did Mike think she could make an operative?

She was completely untrained and, patently, stubborn. Her idea of disguise was to change a stark red wig to a stark black wig, but she still betrayed her emotions on her expressive face, and her zest for life shone through her dark-brown eyes. She was attractive – everyone from young men to old women were drawn to look at her. He couldn't think of a person less suited to fieldwork – and she didn't stick to an agreed plan, which was the kiss of death to a team working at the sharp end of the secret-squirrel world.

At the entrance to an upmarket shopping mall built from white marble, he rested in the shade and leant on the chrome handrails that channelled anyone interested into the wide, cool and inviting void, which was like the gaping mouth of a basking shark. The shops inside sold only French or Italian designer labels and Swiss watches, as far as he could see.

"Didn't have you down as a Piaget man." Mike was seemingly unapologetic and unaware of the potential consequences of her actions earlier – or indeed now. Couldn't she have walked on by and met up in private at the hotel? Chris was dumbfounded.

"Mike, let's hope you're a good analyst because you are, sure as hell, shit out on the street."

She was unapologetic. "How did you spot me?"

"I didn't need to; our friendly optician has cameras on the front and back of the building. She asked me if I knew you and what your interest was in waste bins?"

The self-loathing that had always been inherent in Mike had only been exacerbated by the accident with Dylan. Her natural response was to lash out. "Was she bothered?"

"That's not the point. I had to reveal that we're a team. Now your cover is blown, and we've lost one of our options."

"So, she wasn't bothered?" Mike was in full 'attack as a form of defence' mode.

"No, she wasn't when I explained that we worked together, which reassured her as they had spotted you walking around the gardens at the gallery and followed you back to the hotel. Please, please don't break ranks again. Let's go back to the hotel and continue this conversation."

"Don't you want to hear my news?"

"Don't tell me that you checked what was in her bins while

you were blending into the background and found the other half of Habib's restaurant receipt?"

She ignored him. "Callum and Harper have been arrested for their father's murder."

"Well, that was always a likelihood. May we please go back to the hotel?" he said quietly.

"Do you want to hear my other news?"

"No," he interjected and pushed off from the bottom step, gradually falling into the rhythm that his prosthetics demanded.

She followed about four paces behind, but she gradually caught up with him. They were now next to a high wall with some overhanging acacia trees about ten minutes from the hotel. A white cat with ginger patches ran along the top and disappeared from view. The street wasn't busy.

"I could apologise," she said.

"Are you going to?"

"No, that's as close as you're going to get."

"Has anyone told you that you're truly infuriating?"

"I don't speak to anyone."

They walked on in silence until the building that housed their hotel came into view. Five minutes later, they were in his room; he was sitting on the bed, rubbing his thighs and bending his legs, and she was sitting in the smallest armchair in the world. They hadn't mentioned anything relevant to the case since the shopping mall, and Mike was about to explode if she didn't tell him her news. However, it was Chris who spoke first.

"Shall I update you?" he asked.

"Yeah, you go first." There was a smugness in her voice and a smile on her face.

"Her husband, our friend BlueStar, is flying back from Iraq this evening. I'll meet him tomorrow morning at the optician's. I can finally ask him what he was passing on to, or receiving from, Habib and establish a communication channel for the future."

Mike was shuffling in the chair, trying to find a comfortable position. "You already have a communication channel to BlueStar."

"True, but it's better to cut out the middleman ... middle-woman," he corrected himself.

"You don't get it, do you? Mrs Yonan, the optician, *is* BlueStar. It's the other way around; her husband is the courier and cut-out point."

He stared at her, waiting for an explanation.

"That's why I came to the optician's – to tell you that you were actually talking to BlueStar and to watch who came in and out of the building."

"How did you find out?" He sounded only mildly begrudging.

"Her middle name is Arbella, which is the same as Habib's wife, Mary. It took me a while this afternoon, but I managed to check, and they're cousins. Their mothers were sisters born in Ashur, Iraq, in 1958."

While Chris was processing all of this, he didn't speak.

"You know what this means, don't you?" she said as she stood up.

"Yes, you're a smart ass."

———

Someone being paid too much per hour had probably thought that the monumental sculpture in white concrete, melding the word 'Doha' in both Arabic and English, was clever. It sat like a set of false teeth, glaring at passers-by on The Corniche, the extremely long promenade that was built so residents, tourists and anybody else could escape the sterility of a life indoors listening to the thrumming of air conditioning while missing home. Qatar, without the gas field that provided the almost limitless money, wouldn't have been on anyone's bucket list as a place to work or visit; it had become a pastiche of a Disney attraction. It was a film studio mock-up of a desert fantasy located handily in a desert – a bit like Hollywood westerns.

It was Thursday morning, and Mike and Chris had walked a few hundred yards to find a bench under some palm trees, facing away from the grey-blue glass skyscrapers, which gave views of people walking and running against a backdrop of a grey-blue sea. There was nobody near them, and they could continue their conversation.

"I hate this place," Mike declared.

"Relax, you're not here for the authentic, old Bedouin experience of driving buggies in the sand dunes."

"Chris, why are we here? I don't mean this shithole or, specifically, this uncomfortable bench. Why did Leonard send us here ... because I know he did. I love and hate him in equal measure, but I've learnt that the sadder, fatter and more vulnerable he looks, the colder and more calculating he actually is. OK, forget the cold bit – no one can sweat that much and be cold."

"Walking here, I was thinking that he had asked you to find a traitor in the ranks, but everything he's led us to so far involves working out why Habib Murchison was murdered and who BlueStar is ... whether male or female."

"I still haven't quite sussed out why he put us together. We are the odd couple, aren't we?"

Two fit but, by the look of their taut faces, very unhappy runners bounced along The Corniche, counting the days until they could get back to Dallas or Frankfurt – they could only be investment managers.

"I'm guessing he didn't pick you for your sprinting," she said, staring at the runners.

"Or you for your tact?"

As some more people passed by, they sat in silence while looking at their watches in an oddly synchronised way.

"Time for me to go and meet BlueStar," Chris said.

Mike was having to suppress her excitement. He set off while she remained staring at the sea. For once she would behave – well, probably.

———

At 10.30am, he was back standing outside the optician's, checking his reflection in the window. Everything was a repeat of the previous day, and after following the receptionist along the corridor, he was shown into the dimly lit room again. While staring at the same letters on the electronic display through one eye, he was mentally prepared to play along with the charade that Mrs Yonan, if that was her name, had established.

The door opened, and she entered. He was immediately overwhelmed by her generously applied oud-based perfume.

"Mr Crippen, how are you today?" She sounded more relaxed now he had passed so many of her tests.

"Coming here twice has made me think that I might need glasses. I haven't been to an optician since I was a child."

"I'm sure good eyesight is useful in your profession."

"It's what you perceive rather than what you see, don't you think?"

"Certainly. I have a client who's a bird watcher. His eyesight is less than average, but he 'sees' more of them than anyone," she said in that soft yet confident voice of the medical professional.

Chris noted that she really was an ophthalmologist; it wasn't an act. He was experienced enough to keep quiet and to let her speak.

"My husband has asked me to tell you some things and to give you something. Shall I start?"

Chris splayed his large hands as a sign of his silent approval.

"My husband and Habib had arranged to meet in the restaurant. They never met in the same place twice. The purpose of the meeting was so Habib could hand over a key to my husband." Again, she didn't explain which of them was BlueStar. "It was a very quick lunch before Habib flew back to his villa. Unfortunately, the part of the receipt that you found in the chair next to Habib's body showed the restaurant's name, and I believe that, when Habib heard the intruders, he was trying to hide it; he didn't want them to know where he had been and with whom. It was a last-ditch attempt to protect my husband. The handwritten numbers on that piece aren't secret or sinister; they're the catalogue numbers of some pieces of art Habib was interested in buying. There you have it." Her shoulders relaxed.

Chris swivelled in his chair, more to make himself comfortable. "What does the key that was given to your husband open?"

She rested her arms on the desk and looked directly at him. "We don't know. Odd though it might sound, we don't know where he kept the strongbox or safe, but we presume it's in his villa. He was giving us a copy of the key and its attached code for safekeeping because he was beginning to suspect that he had been compromised in some way. There was to be a separate meeting in a month's time."

"Do you know what's in the strongbox?"

Her eyes were still evaluating him from behind her glasses. "We think so."

There was that royal 'we' again.

"Are you in a position to tell me?"

"We don't know exactly ourselves, but you can be assured that it won't be in the interests of Iran for us to find it."

Somebody walked along the corridor and past the closed door, but they didn't change pace.

"How may we help you?" Chris asked.

"Now Habib has been compromised, I fear we may be next. We need to regroup and relocate. My husband won't return to Qatar. So, Mr Crippen, I think it's better that we give the key and code to you. Please pass it on to Donald Reeve to use as he sees fit. Habib always trusted him, I believe." With that she stood up and unlocked a small medical cabinet on the wall. Inside, among some bottles and packets, was a key with an attached tag marked "DUPLI-CATE". She handed it to Chris with a slight sadness in her eyes.

"What's the code?" he asked.

"It's the word 'DUPLICATE'."

"Ah."

"I hope whatever you find inside was and is worth the life of Habib. I know you'll do your best."

Despite the solemnity of the situation, Chris was greatly relieved and, being ever practical, kept a cool head. "Who else knows about these?"

"Only my husband and me."

"Do you have any idea who compromised Habib?"

"No, he was – and we were – very careful. I believe it was something at his end not ours, but you never know."

"How can I get hold of you both? I may have future questions you can help me with."

"Leave messages on my phone. I'll keep it for the next few weeks, but don't be surprised if it's not often turned on. I won't return to my flat and" – she looked around her consulting room – "this is my last day here."

Chris knew better than to ask where she was going, but he could guess that she was intending to fly to join her husband in Iraq. He looked at the odd-looking and quite solid brass key with the beige-coloured paper tag before putting it into his wallet.

They were at the point where the conversation must end, and he must leave – neither wanted any awkwardness. They were unlikely ever to meet again.

He stood up, needing to use his arms to push down on the desk in front of him. "May I ask you what BlueStar means?"

"It's the centre of the Assyrian flag. Only Habib used it, but it seemed appropriate."

He started towards the door. "You knew Mary Murchison?"

There was a show of respect for his background research in her eyes when she eventually answered, "Mary was my cousin."

"I'm sorry. Ours is a difficult vocation."

"Indeed. Please stay safe."

"I will and thank you. I'll say goodbye."

She didn't stand, but she looked at him with a genuinely concerned expression. "May I ask how you lost your legs?"

"I was following someone too closely when they were blown up." He decided it was better not to mention that it was in Iraq, having been sent there by Leonard.

CHAPTER TWENTY-TWO

Mike watched an oil tanker fade over the horizon until only the wheelhouse was showing through a hazy mirage. A plane, leaving no contrail, joined the flight path into Doha airport as seen between the drooping fronds of palm trees. Through boredom, she used her phone to check it on Flightradar24; it was a Turkish Airlines flight from Istanbul. The runners had now thinned out in the heat of late morning, and she had little to occupy her fertile mind. Her promise to Chris that she would stay in the shade on The Corniche until he returned weighed heavily on her. BlueStar – whether it was the husband, the wife or the two of them – already knew she and Chris were a team, so what damage could be done if she wandered over to be nearer to their meeting place? It would reduce the time she had to wait to find out what BlueStar wanted to tell Chris.

Breaking her promise, she began the fifteen-minute walk, which took her along a busy highway and through a small park. She passed a group of small restaurants, which were coming to life as lunchtime began, and was now only a few streets away from the optician's. She suddenly felt the need to go to the toilet. Turning on her heels, Mike began to walk back to the first restaurant to ask if she could use their restroom. She would order a coffee so if they raised any issue, it wouldn't be a problem. In fact, the thought helped her decide to buy a take-away latte to drink as she waited for Chris before their journey back to the hotel. She would drink it in the shady entrance to the upmarket shopping mall – a good place to lie in wait.

Having turned back the way she had come towards the restaurant, she was aware of a couple walking towards her in running gear. Earlier, they had been jogging along The Corniche, hadn't they? The thought was fleeting. She smiled at them, but there was no reciprocation. The restaurant door beckoned and the need for the restroom became ever more pressing. None of the waiters, preoccupied with polishing glasses and folding napkins, asked her what she was doing, and the location of the ladies was clearly indicated. Inexplicably, something made her freeze as she walked down the short corridor at the back of the restaurant. What were the chances that a couple running along The Corniche should choose that exact moment to walk back along her exact route. She could feel the muscles in her body tense up. Unlike her previous unplanned forays into the field, this time she felt in control and able to analyse the situation. Spy films played in her head, and she imagined climbing out through a small restroom window, shaking off her pursuers. When she opened the door to the toilets, all such thoughts evaporated. Having never read the appropriate CIA manuals, she realised she had made a text-book error. There were no windows, there was no natural light, and the extractor fans were working noisily – there were no other exits from the corridor. She was in a cul-de-sac; she was a sitting duck, defenceless.

Sitting in one of the two cubicles, Mike was waiting to hear someone enter. Time passed slowly, during which all she could hear were the extractor fans and jumbled voices in the restaurant.

The click of the door opening made her crouch down even more and stop breathing. Having her underwear around her ankles didn't elevate her level of confidence, and with heightened senses, which is never a good thing in a restaurant toilet, she waited. As there were only the two cubicles, the next sound should be the opening of the door next to her, but there was nothing.

Bang! The noise shocked her into action. There was no point dying while sitting on the toilet – just ask Elvis. She pulled up her underwear and trousers and opened the door.

The cleaner, who had dropped the yellow cone proclaiming "Caution – slippery when wet" onto the tiled floor, was standing over the small basin. The bang had been very frightening in such a confined space. Mike was now conscious of the blood pumping loudly in her ears. Neither party said anything.

The woman had one hand on the mirror above the basin and was just beginning to throw up – noisily. Mike decided not to wash her hands and left rather guiltily, wondering how many of the male staff knew their colleague was pregnant.

Having collected her coffee in a polystyrene cup, Mike was on high alert for the joggers, but they weren't to be seen anywhere. A quick glance in the CIA manual would have told her that their cover had been blown and a new team would be in place by now. Out of the cool restaurant and into the almost midday heat, she shielded her eyes. The episode had served a purpose; she had relaxed too much and had forgotten she was dealing with life and death. Analysts aren't fools, but they aren't likely to die every day as a consequence of some small mistake made while sitting at their keyboards – operatives are. She was muttering and chastising herself as she walked with added purpose to the shopping mall. A middle-aged woman in Arab dress was trying to tempt the white-and-ginger cat down from the high wall. Mike smiled, walked on by and took no notice.

As the CIA manual on surveillance states: "Always be doing something." Don't simply stand around. Tempting cats down from a wall wasn't mentioned specifically.

———

"Do you know anything about Afonso de Albuquerque?"

Tom was in Barbara Aumonier's office, expecting to be given a load of new tasks for the day ahead. She appeared to be in a friendly mood.

"W-was he a conquistador?"

"No, Tom, he was a Portuguese explorer who was the first governor of Goa in India. On his way back and forth, in 1507, he managed to take control of Hormuz, which is between modern-day Oman and Iran."

Tom was looking blank, but his boss obviously had something on her mind. He wisely stayed silent.

"Even in 1507, they knew how important the Strait of Hormuz was, and this was way before the discovery of oil and gas."

"That's ... uh ... interesting."

"Will you do me a search of the files in our systems? Anything in the last three months that has the word 'Hormuz' in it. Will you cross-reference this with any mention of the Murchisons – Habib, Callum and Harper? Give me the top fifty results that combine any or most of these." She handed him a note with these words, and a few more, written on in an elegant hand.

"No p-problem. I'll do it straight away."

One of her phones buzzed, and he took the opportunity to leave.

He had only entered the building a few minutes earlier and hadn't even reached his office and logged in. At least the instructions were clear. The quiet of his own space beckoned.

He headed to his office, sat at his desk and put his lunchbox into the drawer next to him, but not before taking out a Yorkie bar and breaking off a single chunk. This was a routine he followed every day because he needed a sugar intake before he started his work. Every day, it was a long walk from his rented room in Mrs McFerran's house to catch the Tube to Chiswick and trudge to the office, especially in winter. He was logging in when the phone on his desk rang. It was his boss calling him back into her office. He traipsed back there as requested.

"Tom, will you do me a search of all files and communications mentioning BlueStar?" She spelt it for him. "In fact, will you also add it to the Hormuz/Murchison search, please?"

Tom managed to control his expression in order that he didn't betray any recognition on his face. It seemed like no time since Mike had mentioned that name to him. Barbara was obviously following the same route as Mike; he would have to be careful.

Once he'd returned to his office, the results came up very quickly; this wasn't surprising if one knew the computing power available to the secret services. Tom's level of clearance meant he could open the majority of the files, but not all. However, none of the files in the top fifty results were marked above his security level. He saw that not one contained the word 'BlueStar'. Whether this was a good thing for Mike or bad, he could only speculate. Either way, he needed to let her know. Involuntarily, his hand opened the drawer next to him and took out the chocolate bar before breaking off another chunk. This would completely mess him up as there were exactly five chunks, which usually lasted him the whole week.

It was almost 10.00am in London and 1.00pm in Doha or Dubai, so he couldn't leave the office to phone Mike for another two and a half hours.

For five minutes, he perused the fifty files and communications, finding nothing controversial or really, to his eyes, of interest to any agency. Many appeared to concern the Murchison company's interest in a project to build an underground canal and parallel pipelines to transport minerals, oil and gas from near Dubai to the Omani coast. This would bypass the Strait of Hormuz.

It sounded industrial and, at best, of commercial interest. Most of it was already in the public domain. He sent the findings to his boss and, finally, began the tasks he had expected to be undertaking that morning.

———

Mike Kingdom's heart was still racing when she reached the relative cool of the mall entrance; most of the relief came not from the cold air escaping every time the sliding doors opened but because there was some shade from the burning sun. She let her eyes adjust while leaning against a handrail. This was uncomfortable, so she sat on one of the steps and scrolled through her phone messages. Chris shouldn't be long.

The explosion was deafening.

Car alarms were screaming, as were several women on the pavement approaching the mall. A cloud of red dust wafted down the road, revealing scraps of paper that settled gradually to earth. A mass exodus through the sliding doors and down the flight of steps made her stand up and try to move outside, away from the building. In the chaos, it took her a few moments to realise that the billowing, black smoke was coming from the optician's. She began to run in that direction, scanning all the faces ahead, trying to see Chris. There was no sign of him. A glance down the side road that gave access to the back of the shops only served as a reminder that she had been standing at that exact spot yesterday. If it was a bomb, who was the target? Her? Chris? Mrs Yonan? All of them? She was only a few yards from the front door of the optician's, and the first police car or ambulance could be heard approaching, so it must have been nearby. Water was spraying out into the street from some fractured pipe high above where the whole shopfront had disappeared.

The thought that Chris may have survived a bomb in Iraq only to be killed in the relative safety of Doha overwhelmed her. Thoughts of her own survival and Dylan's death added to her growing panic.

Dylan's voice was in her head, telling her to get a grip and to get away. She shouldn't be seen or spotted anywhere near the crime scene, if that's what it was.

"Mike!" The voice came from behind her, back towards the mall, and she was temporarily disorientated.

"Chris!" She ran towards him and threw her arms around him.

"Let's get away from here," he whispered in her ear. "There's nothing we can do."

They walked back towards the hotel.

In the small park, they stopped and sat on a bench under a tent-like structure. Chris stretched out his legs, and Mike leant back in an exaggerated pose. They didn't speak straight away.

"Do you think she's dead?" Mike enquired.

"I don't know, but it doesn't look good, does it? I had left her no more than five minutes earlier and was on my way back to the hotel.

"You were so lucky."

"I know. I ..." He didn't finish the sentence.

"Who were they after? Her, presumably?"

"I would think so" – he was looking around, checking out anyone within fifty paces – "and I think we should be very careful, get back to the hotel and get out of Doha."

"Do you think we're at risk?"

"Possibly, but I think she was the target. We should stay out of the limelight and get out of Qatar."

"But who did this?"

"The same people who killed Habib, I would think. Come on, let's go."

They began walking again, but they hadn't gone far when Mike asked, "What did she say when you met? Was she on her own or was her husband there?"

"Just her. She gave me a key. It's in my pocket. It was given to her husband by Habib. It's why he came to Doha and probably why he was killed." He was back to speaking in staccato sentences. Perhaps it was a nervous reaction.

"The key to what?"

"A safe or strongbox in his villa."

"What's inside?"

"She had no idea, but so far, two people have been killed." He paused but kept walking in his distinctive rhythmical, rolling gait. "After I said goodbye, she was going to leave the shop and Doha for good. I think she was going to regroup with her husband in Iraq. Shame she didn't make it."

"How do you guys do this every day? I'm scared shitless. I'm now suspicious of everyone."

"Stay suspicious; it will keep you alive."

"I think I was followed from The Corniche this morning ... but I could be being neurotic."

"Who by?"

"A pair of joggers. No, I'm being neurotic."

They walked a little further and stepped into the hotel foyer, visibly relaxing in what they subconsciously felt to be a relatively secure environment. The cool air on their sweaty skin felt much colder; their hands were clammy and grubby from the dust following the explosion. They summoned the lift and stepped inside.

"Now what? You're the operative." Mike had regained her

normal spiky demeanour and made the decision, for the umpteenth time, that she really should sit at home in front of a computer where the biggest risk was breaking a nail while opening a can of drink.

"We go to the villa, of course."

"*What?* Are you mad?"

The lift doors opened, and they were forced to suspend the discussion as a couple were coming towards them along the corridor. They were trying to cram a jacket into a bag while walking and looked as if they were late for an appointment.

What was it that the CIA manual suggested?

CHAPTER TWENTY-THREE

They had agreed to go to their rooms to pack, then have something to eat in the hotel and leave for the airport very early in the morning. Mike still wasn't sure if flying to Ras Al Khaimah airport and going to the villa was a great idea, but Chris had tried to convince her by saying that Habib was dead, and the sons weren't there.

"We'll be in and out in half an hour," he had said, "and you know the villa and staff, whereas I don't."

"You sound confident."

"We've both invested a lot in this now. Let's get the contents of the strongbox and fly back to the UK. We'll arrange for Leonard to pick it up. He'll be happy with that. As to finding traitors, I think we're at a dead end out here."

In her room, she was packing the bright-red wig into her case, she hadn't really worn it much so far. It was, without question, not a colour to wear while trying to recede into the background. Part of her wished she'd kept the mousey-brown wig she'd bought in Morocco, which would have been ideal for this sort of thing. Thinking back to her polystyrene heads on the shelf in her cabin, she could visualise the name Atropos written in black felt tip on the head on which the red wig sat. After Clotho had begun your life and Lachesis had decided how long it should be, it was Atropos who decided how you should die. No, it definitely wasn't the wig to wear today.

Before leaving England, and not knowing how long she was going to be in Dubai, she hadn't known what to pack. As a consequence, she had thrown everything into her suitcase, which after several unexpected flights and hotel or villa stays, no longer fitted into her luggage quite so easily. It was while packing her gizmos and Leonard's phones that she decided her days of what she laughably called 'fieldwork' were over. Habib was dead, BlueStar was also most likely dead, Leonard was safely in a USAF hospital, and the two Murchison sons were locked up, but they had enough millions in the bank that some deal would no doubt be struck and they would resume their lives in London, possibly never to return to Oman. Why put her head back in the noose?

Her phone lit up. It was Kevin Stenning.

"Hello, are you still in Doha?" he asked.

"Not for long."

"Oh, that's a shame. I was going to invite you over to the embassy this afternoon."

"Thank you, but I'm not feeling entirely safe in Doha. I don't know if you've heard, but opticians seem to blow up unexpectedly."

"Not a problem unless you were buying glasses at the time."

"I didn't need to buy them; I could pick them up off the sidewalk."

"Could we continue this conversation here at the embassy ... where I believe you'll be quite safe?"

"At what time?"

"Well, it's 1.00pm now. Would 3.00pm suit you?"

"OK, but I need to be back at the hotel for dinner with a work colleague."

With her minimal packing completed apart from her wash-bag, she went downstairs to find Chris and to grab a light lunch; there was nothing else to do.

"I think you're crazy, but then I noticed that quite early on. Personally, I really wouldn't take unnecessary risks. I would stay in the hotel until we get a taxi to the airport tomorrow," he said on hearing about her plans.

"I sort of understand, but, honestly, I'm only going in a taxi to the British Embassy and back. If security at the embassy isn't at a higher level than here, we all have a problem."

"Why did he invite you? Did he say?"

"He didn't say anything much on the phone, as you'd expect, but he doesn't know what we've been up to, of course. I may find out what he's been doing, which could be useful."

"I don't think you should tell him about the key and our planned trip. He doesn't fall in the need-to-know category, even if Leonard seems to have trusted him."

"You're probably right, but I haven't even told him about you. He may have heard about how Leonard is; who knows? I might learn something."

"From someone who's streetwise, please be careful. You'll be my eyes and ears." He looked genuinely concerned.

"And your legs?"

"Ha! You are unbelievable." His face broke into a broad smile.

———

The journey to the embassy was short – for which she was thankful. Unsure whether to book the taxi using her own phone, she had decided to do it via reception. Even when she had walked the five steps from the sliding doors to the taxi in the sunshine, her nerves were on edge. Everything around her looked suspicious: the driver, the blacked-out windows of the car, and even the teenage boy on an electric scooter enjoying the ramps and slopes of the car park.

The taxi journey proved uneventful, even though she remained on high alert the whole time until they arrived at the embassy. After getting out next to the embassy's entrance, she walked quickly to the visitor's entrance. The woman behind the glass recognised her, but the routine didn't change; it never did.

This time, Kevin met her under a picture of King Charles III on the wall alongside a large *Ficus benjamina* with slender, plaited trunks in a stainless-steel pot. There was a smell of cleaning fluid or polish, or possibly both.

He shook her hand in a reassuring way and, at the top of the flight of stairs, he said, "Come on in."

It may have been his office or a version of hot-desking, she couldn't tell. There were no photographs of the kids, no dive equipment piled in the corner and no antique brass coffee pot on the single shelf.

"Have you come far?" he asked, breaking the ice.

"Metaphorically, light years."

He put his hand behind an ear and tilted his glasses up like Eric Morecambe. There was a natural chemistry evident between them that rather defied definition. "Have you heard from Leonard?" he asked.

"No, I've been busy. Have you?"

"No; well, not directly, but through the network. I understand that his operation was successful."

Several suitably rude responses came into her mind, but she never voiced them, perhaps out of some respect for Leonard's pain or, more likely, because she didn't really know her audience. "Where is he?"

"I believe he's in hospital recovering. Someone I know at the US Embassy said they hadn't flown him to Langley but had sent him to Germany instead. It was nearer."

She nodded.

"What have you been doing apart from picking up Gucci glasses from the pavement?" he queried.

"It was a sort of BOGOF: bomb optician's, get one free. What have you heard? Anybody killed?" She was looking directly at him from under her black wig; Lachesis would be proud.

"Well, such events are rare here, and in the neighbouring countries. They don't do 'bad press'; the jungle telegraph would be very busy if there were any jungle. As it is, we just have a few whispering palms, or perhaps that should be 'whispering behind palms'."

Mike put both her hands behind her head and slouched back slightly in her chair, feeling the safest since she had left the embassy the last time. "Anybody killed?" she repeated.

"Not to my knowledge. A gas-bottle explosion, I've heard," he said. "Official sources are saying it's just an unfortunate accident. Nothing to see here."

"Well, it was an optician's shop."

"Were you out jogging or shopping or ...?"

"The latter," she said enigmatically. The two small plastic bottles of water on the desk between them suddenly took precedence.

"Shopping?"

"No, I meant the 'or ...', if you get my meaning?"

"Not really. Who blows up an optician's shop? Nobody is making any connections. Are there any?"

However much you prepare what you're going to say, Mike was realising that, in the field, your plan evolves to the point where there's no reason to formulate a plan in the first place. As Field Marshall Helmuth von Moltke said, "No plan survives first contact with the enemy." It was much like the negotiations to buy a house you've fallen head-over-heels in love with.

What's the point of starting with a low figure – you're going to buy it at the asking price anyway, aren't you?

If she told him about BlueStar, what could Kevin do? She – if it was indeed she who was BlueStar – was either dead or on her way to Iraq, and her husband was already there. Mike decided she would hold back only some of the details. "You remember that I mentioned BlueStar to you when I was here last?"

"I do."

"Did you check it out?"

"Of course; it came up with nothing." He meant on the Brits' system.

"BlueStar is – and by which I mean 'was' after today's explosion – Leonard's primary source in the Middle East. He never knew her, as she only dealt with him through Habib Murchison."

"Really? Who was she?"

"She was the optician. Her name was Shamiram Yonan. Her husband Ahrun acted as an intermediary with Habib. It was why he flew to Doha just before he was murdered."

Kevin leant back, mimicking Mike. "I've never heard any mention of them. I'm guessing from their names that they were/are Assyrians? Working against Iran?"

"I'm guessing so. I was trying to contact her. That was why I was near the optician's when the bomb went off." Mike conveniently left out Chris's involvement, the brass key and their plans to go to the villa tomorrow morning.

He rocked backwards and forwards in his chair, shuffling the questions in his head. She was spiky and inexperienced. If he pressed too hard, she would either clam up, leave or tell him to go swivel – probably all three. And so the dance began.

"How did you identify BlueStar?" he asked gently.

"From a photograph on Habib's phone of him meeting her husband at lunch here in Doha."

He parked the question of how she had gained access to Habib's phone and decided to proceed with a slow waltz. "Do you know why they met for this lunch?"

Her arms were folded. "Yes."

"That's very impressive." There was no follow-up question; he had plenty of time. He took another swig from the small bottle of water.

"Not really, Habib's dead. She needs a new ... route to Leonard."

So, you've spoken to or met her already, was what went through his mind and stayed there. "I'm sure Leonard will recover, and you can pass on all this information."

"I hope so."

The real reason she had agreed to this meeting lay in her apprehension at travelling back to the villa. The fear she had felt in the panic room and the generally hostile reception from Mohammed and the chief inspector were still raw. If anything were to happen to Chris and her, all of this, well, *escapade* would have been in vain. Oh, and she would probably be dead or worse. She knew she was building up to telling him where she would be tomorrow. Not about Chris and not about the key, just where she would be if she suddenly disappeared off the radar. Where was that annoying Leonard when she needed him?

"Tomorrow, I'm—" Her phone rang.

It was Tom. "Hi M-Mike."

Slightly startled, she put her hand over her phone as if she were on a landline. "Kevin, where may I take this call?" This was a polite way of asking him to disappear.

"You stay here; I'll organise some tea." He stood up, smiling, and left the room.

"Tom, it's good to speak to you."

"M-Mike, my b-boss has just asked me to g-give her a list of files that link H-Hormuz with the M-Murchisons." He sounded stressed.

"Tom, relax. Thanks for letting me know. Did you discover anything interesting?"

"No, nothing too unexpected, but she then asked me to f-factor in the p-person in the photograph you sent me." He swallowed audibly.

"Really? Oh shit. And what did you find?"

"Nothing. There's no m-mention of him, but I thought you needed to know that she's aware of him." Tom still thought that BlueStar was Ahrun Yonan.

"Tom, that's so useful." She paused weighing up what to say. "Please be careful; things are getting a bit, let's just say 'hot'." Mike might never be described as maternal, but she knew the risks that Tom was taking and felt like an older sister.

"Have you heard from our old b-boss?" he asked.

"Only second-hand, but I understand he's recovering in hospital."

"G-good. I'd better g-go."

"Hopefully, the next time we speak, I'll be back in London."

The time from when the call ended until Kevin Stenning stepped back into his office would tell her whether he had been listening. He knew this and waited three minutes before tapping on the door. The office was bugged anyway.

He had heard the words "Tom, that's so useful." Now he wanted to know what this was.

"Here's some tea. One's black and one's with milk. The sugar's on the side. I drink either." He put the small tray down on the desk in front of her. He said nothing else, tempting her to fill the gap.

She was buzzing and couldn't control herself. "Shit! All I can say is that 'optician' must be trending on social media at the moment."

"The news has got out?"

She sucked in some air and tried to restrain her raging emotions. "I wish Leonard were here."

He sat back down rather clumsily behind his desk. "Mike, I could go down on bended knee and ask you to trust me, but I've been in this business long enough to know that you would run away and never speak to me again."

Mike's wigs did not define her, but they did frame an expressive face. They just tended to emphasise what you already knew before she opened her mouth. The jet-black curtain of hair and dark-brown eyes, the colour of tourmaline, may be what you saw first, but once she spoke, you were in no doubt.

"Do you have an indirect route to Leonard?" she questioned. "I don't know what to do." Oddly, this didn't sound weak but rather positive.

"I only have the numbers for the telephones you have ... and all of the official lines, which won't go directly to him, as you know."

She didn't speak but looked at the cup of tea before her as if it were poison. Mike was gradually coming to a decision. "I think I do trust you ... but that's a luxury I cannot afford."

"I understand. No, I really do understand." He sounded like your favourite teacher at school when you'd decided to drop a key subject at A level.

"If I leave everything turned on – on my phone – such as location services, you can track me, can't you?" She already knew the answer and was merely encouraging him to do this.

"I personally can't, but I know a man who can; in fact, a whole department that does nothing else. Any particular reason?"

"I'm going into the mountains tomorrow, and I might get lost."

CHAPTER TWENTY-FOUR

It was Friday morning, and Harper – along with his brother, Callum – had spent two nights in a police cell. The heavy door to the cell was opened by an officer accompanied by an elegant, tall Arab in a pale-grey suit. The Murchison brothers leapt up.

"Ali, thank God. We were losing hope," Callum declared excitedly.

"Come with me to somewhere we can talk," Ali had said, striding off along the corridor ahead of the policeman.

They went into an interview room, in which the brothers were finally free to talk to their new solicitor again.

"They've taken our phones." Harper wasn't in a good place mentally; he looked drained and pale.

"Things will improve now," Ali stated in immaculate English, which came from years at public school and completing a law degree at Durham University.

"They can't get any worse." Callum had clearly not read the situation, which could get very much worse: the death penalty for murder was enshrined in Omani law.

Ali let that pass and continued, "Since my visit yesterday,

I've come to an agreement with the chief inspector – actually, with him and a senior minister, but please don't ask me questions about that. You're still charged with murder, but they've agreed you can be placed under house arrest. You will have to surrender your passports."

"What about our phones?" Harper asked.

"Where?" his brother was ever practical.

Neither thought to thank Ali for his work behind the scenes, which was well beyond the call of duty.

"You can keep your phones, but you cannot leave your father's villa. Please appreciate that this is a big concession,"

They did not.

"What's to stop us going to Dubai, buying a couple of false passports and flying away?" Harper was repeating what he had been thinking back in the villa. It was an automatic response.

"Nothing, but if, at any time, you were caught outside the villa or escaping, the courts would see this as a clear admission of guilt. I can't recommend it." Ali sounded so reasonable.

Callum put his head in his hands, then looked up. "Have they found any evidence or motive or ...?"

"No, they're still investigating, but you found your father dead, he had been poisoned and you're the only two people who stand to gain ... and very substantially. That's enough for the authorities here." *And most other authorities around the world*, he didn't bother to add.

"But what can we do? How can we be proactive? Otherwise, we're just in their hands," Callum asked.

"We work behind the scenes, putting pressure on the authorities from the top down. The Canadian government is now involved, and the Omani authorities will not want this to escalate into an international incident."

"But can't we hire people, private detectives, I don't know, but someone to try to find out who killed our father, if he was killed? And what about an independent autopsy to prove he died of a heart attack or whatever?" Harper was rambling.

"We want to be proactive, whatever the financial cost, is what my brother and I are saying," confirmed Callum.

"This isn't Canada or London. An independent autopsy, even if it were to be allowed, would only annoy the authorities and turn them against you. At the moment, please remember that the authorities are being reasonable, although I know it doesn't look like it from your perspective. As to a private investigation, this is possible, but with the same risk of upsetting the police."

"Have they found the two men who turned up in that pickup or van, whatever it was?" Callum was trying to find something they could pursue.

"No, the vehicle was registered in the UAE, and the two men haven't been identified. They aren't on any Omani database."

"Well, isn't that suspicious? Are the UAE police trying to find them? Can *we* find them?" Harper's voice was getting louder with each question.

"Yes, they're trying to locate them. I'm not sure what anyone else could do that the UAE police aren't doing already ... but if you want me to appoint somebody, I can?"

"Yes, Ali, please get someone – and fast."

"What about the staff at the villa?" Callum was looking at all possibilities.

"All the staff have been interviewed and all the CCTV footage examined. The only person with any serious financial interest would be Mohammed, and he wasn't at the villa."

"It must be those two men from the UAE; it's obvious." Harper could see no alternative.

"When and how do we get to the villa?" Callum brought the conversation back to logistical matters.

"After completing some paperwork, a police officer will

drive you. He'll also stay at the villa. I'm sure you'll have no problem with this; I've already agreed to it."

"Great," Harper said ironically, appearing to have quickly forgotten his two nights in a police cell.

———

Kevin had a visitor in his office.

Yolanda was sitting opposite him in a black suit, but with her white blouse undone perhaps one button too far, making her look like a barrister who had just lost a case and was having a large white wine in Ye Olde Cheshire Cheese on Fleet Street.

"How was your trip?" he asked.

"Not as productive as I'd hoped." She sounded like she needed a white wine. "The man I met was not as described on the packet."

"May contain nuts?"

"Something like that. Possibly more like 'Best before 1980'. However, despite his age, he does have a brother who could be very useful."

"In a ministry?"

"No, but he has the Minister of Security's ear."

"What? In a little box? Is he a blackmailer?" Kevin was having fun.

She smiled. "No, he's a senior *fonctionnaire*, but as you know, civil servants can be useful."

Yolanda's quick trip to Kuwait yesterday had been part of her remit covering the whole of the Middle East. It wasn't all white wines with the ambassador. "Anything new here?" she asked.

A calendar displaying a snowy scene chose that moment to fall off the wall, causing them both to jump. "How time flies," he said. He got up and retrieved it, but he decided quickly that it needed a new nail in the wall. He put it on a small table and sat back down. "Mike Kingdom came in yesterday afternoon."

"Oh, really." She did up the top button on her blouse. "Your invite or hers?"

"Mine, but she was willing. I've given her enough time to investigate on Leonard's behalf. I wanted to see what progress she had made."

"Any?"

"Lots. She's identified Leonard's contact, via Habib, out here. Her code name, or at least Habib's codename for her, was BlueStar. She is, or probably *was*, Shamiram Yonan, an optician here in Doha."

Yolanda's eyes had already started to open wider, or at least her right eye did, as she had heard the news while travelling.

"The explosion yesterday was an attempt to take her out. It was probably successful," he continued.

"Iran?"

He just shrugged. "Probably; she's Assyrian, so I'd guess you're right."

"What's Mike Kingdom going to do now?"

"She's not exactly normal by any standard and I mean even including our world. I think she might be following a hunch. She's very loyal to Leonard, her ex-boss."

"There has to be one, I suppose. Personally, I can't imagine working for him. His idea of manners is not lifting his arse when he farts."

"Effective, though?"

"I've no idea; I've rarely sat next to him at dinner, thankfully."

"I meant ..."

She smiled. "So what's her hunch?"

"No idea, she didn't say, but she's clearly nervous about it. She joked about wanting me to track her phone because she was going off into the mountains."

Someone knocked on the door and, when invited, leant inside. "Anyone order a taxi to the airport?"

They both said no, and the door was closed.

"Heard from Leonard?"

"No," Kevin replied, "but Leanne in the US Embassy tells me that he wasn't sent to Washington, but to the military hospital in Germany instead."

"Because the beer's better?"

"More than likely. She said that he was recovering."

"Recovering alcoholic?"

"All of the above. But it's left his protégé a little exposed out here."

"She seems to be wary of the US Embassy. I think we should get the usual suspects to monitor the situation. I have a feeling deep down inside about this."

"So do I."

———

Hamad International Airport in Doha resembles what the Eden Project would have been if it hadn't been paid for by the Lottery Fund. Mike and Chris were gazing up at the sinuous, geodesic roof and marvelling at the palm trees. They were on their way to check in.

"If we ask for assistance for you, can we board ahead of first class?"

He turned towards her, lost for words. "What?" He then looked up at the palm fronds and said, "There's no first class; it's an A320 that takes an hour. Who travels first class for an hour?"

"But we could board first? I've never done that."

"It's overrated. You understand that we then have to get off last, don't you?"

"There's always a catch, isn't there?"

"Be careful what you wish for."

"A coffee," she said, and they moved off towards a café.

A pedant might have questioned the word 'coffee'. Her large cardboard cup had many ingredients of which coffee was indeed one, but at best, it was a secondary or tertiary component. She was happy, although that might have been because of the slice of chocolate cake.

"Your life revolves around food and drink, I've just realised," Chris observed.

"No, it doesn't."

With that, he knew unwittingly that he had touched a raw nerve. It was part of her regime for handling the traumas that had occurred in her life. She needed structure. Unexpectedly, the discovery of her soft underbelly affected him. He was so used to being detached emotionally from what he was doing and who he was with. Operatives were trained to pick up on nuance and emotion, weakness and bravado; it was a big part of his skill set.

"What are we doing once we land at Ras Al Khaimah?" he asked.

"Have lunch?" she said with a rather bitter edge.

"After that."

She had been weighing up whether it was better to turn up unexpectedly in a taxi and talk her way into the villa or ring Mohammed and face it head on. Mike settled on turning up unannounced; she was still very wary of Habib's Mr Fixit. "We'll hire a car, and I'll drive to the villa. I'll ring the bell and talk my way in. Simple. Perhaps I left an earring behind, who knows?"

"You don't wear earrings, do you?"

"Good of you to notice, but who cares? I'll get us inside ... and then, what's the plan of action?"

"We find the strongbox, as BlueStar called it. Firstly, I want to try the safe you mentioned – the one in the study next to where Habib was murdered."

"I never saw it, but Callum said it was behind a panel. It was where they retrieved his will from."

"It sounds the most likely place to me if it's where he kept important papers."

The thought of Callum made her look at her phone, not to phone him, but to check when he was last online. Wednesday evening at 7.42pm. They must still be under arrest. She looked back at Chris in his white tracksuit jacket. "And if the key doesn't fit?"

"We do a systematic search. You do upstairs, and I'll do downstairs. We ought to try the panic room. I know you didn't see a box or safe from what you've said, but you did tell me that his communication equipment, as provided by Leonard, was in there, together with the codebooks. I'm guessing he contacted Leonard in the privacy of the panic room, where he would never be disturbed and that members of staff rarely entered."

"Good plan, Superspook. What do you think is in this darn box?"

"Well, it'd better be worth it. Habib and BlueStar are dead, the sons have been attacked, and Leonard flew out here to get it."

"It must be something to do with Iran." She was speaking quietly, but there was no one in earshot.

"Or his late wife's earrings? Who knows?"

"You do know that the box, safe, whatever, may not be in the villa at all?"

"Where else could it be? Not in the gardens. What do you mean?"

"It could be down at the cement works or the port buildings or even in the sons' crypto farm. I bet Habib has his own office down there somewhere. Nobody has ever mentioned it, but it sounds likely, don't you think?"

"We'll have real difficulty finding it if you're correct." He looked slightly crestfallen, and his black eyebrows lowered as he thought about this.

"Don't worry, it's not ideal, but we would probably have to involve the sons to gain access."

"I wonder how they're doing?"

"Still locked up in Muscat, judging by their phones. Do you like travelling?" She had let her mind wander.

"Not when I'm playing basketball."

She looked at him sideways, frowning.

"'Travelling' is a basketball term. You get penalised if you do it."

"Whatever."

"No, seriously, I find travelling bittersweet. Even now, I get excited by flying, even though I've done it a hundred times. Now, though, I have to put up with the pain of going through security and the physical pain from sitting for hours in a plane seat."

They finished their drinks and made their way slowly along the corridors. She watched him waddle along with a rucksack on his back, too proud to be pushed in a wheelchair through an airport or ask for a buggy to take him to the plane.

When they reached the gate, they sat in the only two available seats that were next to each other. Chris filled his chair and overlapped with Mike. She was glad it was only going to be a one-hour flight, as he was sitting next to her on the plane. It made her realise just how well-built he was. They were busy joking about this when boarding began. In the row behind them, two men stood up, one putting away a book he had been reading and the other pulling out one white earphone, allowing it to dangle as he listened to the announcements.

CHAPTER TWENTY-FIVE

Kevin Stenning was rubbing his glasses using a small squirt of lens cleaner and a tissue. His eyes were tired from reading the Middle East papers online and watching the Arabic TV news reports simultaneously. He had been in the embassy early because he had a queasy feeling in his stomach that wasn't caused by the Thai meal he had eaten the previous evening but by the attempt on Shamiram Yonan's life. Some quick research had established that she had practised as an ophthalmologist in Doha for some years. If, as Mike Kingdom had said, she had been Leonard's main source in the Middle East via Habib, this amounted to a huge investment of time and resources in spying terms. The caution and techniques that had been deployed told him she was professional but perhaps nervous; all of which would be understandable. Using her husband as a cut-out and going through an elaborate vetting procedure at the gallery before meeting Mike were all textbook mechanisms. Of course, Kevin had assumed it was Mike who had undertaken all of this as she had chosen not to tell him about Chris Crippen.

Something was bugging him, but he couldn't put his finger

on it. *What's the time?* He looked up at the clock on the wall – it was 9.30am. Timing, that was it – timing.

After years in Doha supported, he assumed, by an under-cover Assyrian network, it was during the week or so when Leonard came out to see Habib that her cover had most likely been blown. What had happened? Was it that Habib had been exposed somehow, and the killers had traced his movements back to discover her husband and her own role? After all, this was a version of what Mike had done.

He, and Yolanda with her wider brief, had heard nothing of an anti-Iranian Assyrian network working out of Qatar. He would love to have been involved. What had blown its cover? He was only speculating, but it seemed to him that Habib's half-hour meeting in Doha had triggered everything. That meeting was extremely important. What was it about? Here, he went through the same thought process as Mike and concluded that something physical had been exchanged, other-wise it could have been dealt with more safely and more easily by encoded electronic communication.

He asked himself what he thought about Mike Kingdom. Any fool could see she wasn't an agent, but she was probably a good analyst. She had about as much chance of hiding in the background as Coco the Clown. And where was she now? *In the mountains.* What did that mean, and why tell him? Unless she had gone skiing in the Alps, he had to assume she was still in the Middle East. He prayed she wasn't going to Iran, although he could see no way she could get there, so that left the UAE and Oman. Logically, she was going back to the villa or that general area, but what would she return for? Habib was dead and the sons were under arrest in Muscat, this he knew. Again, it must be important, and the need to return had only developed after she had met the now infamous BlueStar.

What was the reason for going into the mountains and so urgently?

There was another odd piece of timing. Mike Kingdom was outside or near the shop when it exploded. Kevin, like everyone in the secret-squirrel community, knew that only planets aligned – and then rarely.

He looked back at the papers and news programmes on his screens. Many articles and reports mentioned the explosion, but all had repeated the official line that it was most likely caused by a faulty gas cylinder, and all said there was only one casualty – a young Jordanian woman who was the receptionist. There was absolutely no mention of Shamiram Yonan. This style of reporting was not atypical in Kevin's long experience of Qatar.

So, he asked himself, *did she die? Was she injured? Did she escape?* While Yolanda and her contacts in all the Middle Eastern countries were trying to establish the extent of the BlueStar network, he decided to find Shamiram Yonan.

He would start by going to the optician's shop and seeing the damage for himself. While he was doing this, a female colleague could contact the local hospitals to see if she had been brought in yesterday.

———

Chris liked Ras Al Khaimah International Airport; it was on a smaller scale than Doha or Dubai, such that all the distances were much shorter, and for him, this was a huge bonus. He could see only five planes, and one of those was a Boeing 737 being pushed back from the gate to fly back to somewhere like Mumbai. The terminal was of a more human scale and didn't feel as if the architect was trying to create the world's largest greenhouse. Happily, it didn't take an eternity for their bags to arrive on the carousel, and there was nobody interested in them at customs.

They hired a silver Volvo S90 as they had no idea where

they would end up and how long it all might take. Mike moaned that she preferred motorbikes to cars, but one look from Chris had quashed any stupid fantasies she might have had. In preparation for the journey, it took him a minute to move the passenger seat backwards. The complimentary small bottles of water that had been pointed out to them before leaving seemed unimportant until they realised the air conditioning only worked within a very narrow definition of the term. The most efficient and quietest option proved to be opening the rear windows an inch.

The two of them set off under a cloudless sky on the one-and-a-half-hour drive to the villa. With the orange sand dunes extending westwards to the sea and the rugged, grey mountains to the east, they headed for the E11. This was the main highway through the UAE, which took them most of the way towards their destination.

On leaving the main road, they followed the winding route up into the Hajar Mountains, with a mixture of yellow lines, alternate black and white painted kerbstones, and the occasional metal barrier being the only items separating them from frightening drops. Mike was carefully retracing her previous journey in the taxi to the villa, inwardly regretting that she wasn't leaning over on the bends as she rode her bike – alone. Chris, for his part, was marvelling at the landscape and rehearsing the plan of action for once they were in the villa.

As they drove the last five miles, Mike became ever twitchier as memories of the explosion, the panic room and being followed on the return journey towards Dubai flooded back. They approached the leaning white post that represented the boundary with the small outlier of Oman, and the villa walls came into view. She pulled up outside the gates and got out of the car.

"Hello," came a voice she didn't recognise over the intercom when she pressed the button.

"Hello, I'm Mike Kingdom. I was here earlier this week with Callum and Harper. Would you let me in, please?"

"Wait," the voice said, and she began to turn back towards the Volvo.

"Hello? May I help?" This was a different voice, which she recognised as the butler or house manager. Unfortunately, she couldn't remember his name.

"Hi, hello again, this is Mike Kingdom; I was staying here three days ago. Do you remember? May I come in please?"

"Mr Callum and Mr Harper aren't here, unfortunately."

"I know that, but I was wondering if I could come in anyway. I think I left some jewellery in my bedroom."

"Hmm." He hesitated, trying to put something into English. "Mr Mohammed has told me not to allow any persons into the villa until he returns."

"Yes, but it's me, Mike."

"Hmm, I know."

"When will Mohammed return?"

"I do not know. He is in Muscat. Maybe this evening, maybe tomorrow."

This was not going well.

"It will only take ten minutes, and I've driven for two hours to come here."

"I am very sorry. Please telephone Mr Mohammed. You have his number?"

"Yes, I do."

"I'm sorry."

She returned to the car to escape the blistering heat.

Chris had heard the conversation through his open window. "Now what?"

"I'll phone Callum. I don't really trust Mohammed, but at least we know he's in Muscat."

With that, she started dialling. Nothing happened, so she

redialled, and after that, she tried Harper's number. "Shit! Their phones are still off."

"Their phones have probably been removed by the police if they've been arrested, don't you think? It's probably why Mohammed is in Muscat, if it's not all been sorted yet."

"I'll have to call Mohammed. This will be more difficult. I'll put the phone on speaker so you can hear."

Sitting in the driver's seat, she reflected for a few moments before dialling. "Hi, Mohammed. Yes, it's Mike. How are you?"

"I'm in Khasab on my way back from Muscat. Unfortunately, Mr Callum and Mr Harper are still under arrest, but they now have a good solicitor. I'm working with him to get them released."

"Oh, well done. I've been trying to call them."

"Unfortunately, they've been in the police cells for two nights; their phones have been taken away. They should be on their way back and at the villa by evening."

"Send them my regards, please."

"Of course."

"Mohammed, I'm at the villa. Would you tell the gate man to let me in?"

"I know; I saw you on my phone."

Chris turned sharply to look at Mike and put a finger to his lips. Mentioning him would only complicate matters.

"Excellent." She didn't miss a beat. "I came to see them both and pick up some earrings that I left in the bedroom."

"No problem. I'll get them to open the gates. Please stay for lunch. I hope we'll be back by late afternoon, and we can meet again."

"Thank you, Mohammed. That would be nice."

The call ended, and a minute later, the gates opened.

———

There was a strange smell of burnt plastic in the street. Black smoke had created swirling patterns up the concrete façade of the two floors above the optician's shop, and there were now wooden sheets instead of the large panes of glass. There was no 'Police – Do Not Cross' tape. Instead, there was an aggressive-looking police officer on his phone, pacing up and down outside; nobody was likely to approach him. Kevin Stenning walked slowly forwards, assessing the damage to the shopfront, which was extensive. At the corner, he turned down the side road and looked at the back of the parade of shops. The damage here was minimal; in fact, all he could see was broken glass in the rear windows and a waste bin on its side. He strolled by and decided that, should Shamiram's consulting room be at the back, she may well have survived. If the rear of the shop had looked like the front, she wouldn't have had a chance, and he could have crossed her off his list of potential sources.

A man was standing on the street, smoking a cigarette. Kevin tested the waters with him by making some bland and undeniable statements of surprise at what had happened. The man turned out to be a fellow Brit who worked in an accountant's office facing the rear of the optician's shop. He said he knew Shamiram, as she had been his optician for two years, and he had seen her get into her car after the blast. The accountant said that she looked distressed but not obviously injured.

"She drove?" Kevin asked.

"Yes, she drove her little Toyota Camry most days. It only just fitted next to the bins."

"Well, I hope she's safe."

Kevin walked away, surmising that she wouldn't seek medical attention unless she absolutely needed it. It was time for him to set off back towards the embassy.

Just then, Martha, who had been checking the medical

facilities in Doha, rang his phone. "No luck with the hospitals," she said.

"Thanks for trying," he replied.

Now what? Kevin thought there was a very small chance she may have gone home. It was worth a try. He collected his car and made his way the relatively short distance to her suburb. There was some visitor parking behind the low block of apartments, and this gave him a chance to check out if her car was in evidence beneath the covered parking bays. Much to his surprise, there was a white Toyota Camry in front of a helpful sign displaying "Apartment No. 503". This matched the number from his earlier research. Unfastening his seatbelt, he reached across and opened the glove compartment on the passenger side, taking out an envelope containing a visa application form. Knowing that it was unlikely she would still be in her flat after her office had been blown up, he set off for the entrance.

Once inside the lobby, he was faced by the lift, but he took the stairs instead; this was a basic precaution. Lifts announce your arrival to all and sundry. Lifts trap you inside with no alternative route of escape. Lift doors open to reveal you as a soft target. At her floor, he stepped out through the fire doors, looking for CCTV cameras and checking for any sounds of activity. Along the carpeted corridor there were only five flats evident.

At 503, he paused, listened and tapped on the door. Before there was any response, he could see the small marks where it had been professionally jemmied open. He stepped back a pace, moved to the side and gently pushed on the door. It opened slowly.

"Mrs Yonan," he called out before entering, holding his envelope prominently in front of him. This was what the manual called 'a percentage decision'. If you barge in and surprise someone, they will most probably attack you as an automatic response. If you announce your presence in some prosaic way, they still might shoot you, but most likely, they'll explore the circumstances first. It gives you a chance to talk your way out of danger.

All the internal doors were open, and from the hallway, there were no immediate signs of further destruction. On entering the lounge, Kevin could see that the room had systematically been searched. This meant every drawer had been removed and emptied, every mat rolled back, and every picture removed from the walls. He was pleased not to find any bodies. In the bathroom, he looked for any signs that Shamiram had returned and cleaned herself up. In her bedroom, he came to the conclusion that she had come back to the flat, grabbed everything that was important and left quickly, not using her own car.

The hen had flown the coop.

CHAPTER TWENTY-SIX

Chris suggested to Mike that she should turn the car around so it was ready to leave once they had found the box. She furrowed her brow and made a point of parking right at the bottom of the steps to the imposing entrance.

"Mike, let's assume we have twenty minutes or less. If Mohammed isn't on our side, it doesn't matter whether he's in Muscat or Manhattan, he'll have his friends come here before you can say, 'Double cheeseburger and fries.'"

Chris got out, leant on the roof of the car to stretch his back and made his way up the steps of the villa. They were shown inside, and Mike explained to the butler that she was looking for her earrings and made up some weak excuse as to why Chris was with her. Eagerly, she accepted the invitation of iced water and anything else that would occupy the staff for the next few minutes. She suggested that they sat in the small lounge, which was where she believed Habib's safe was located. It had contained his will and was behind a bookcase, according to the sons.

As soon as the butler had left, she jumped up and began feeling for a switch or button underneath each shelf. This didn't take long to find, and she pulled the panel open to reveal a large, black built-in safe. Chris took the key from a zipped pocket and prepared himself, looking for the hole in the safe door. There wasn't one. It needed a code not a key. He quickly shut the panel.

It took the two of them only a couple of minutes to check out the rest of the study. Mike explained that the connecting room was where Habib had been found dead, and Chris went in to check it out while Mike waited for the water. The adjoining study also revealed nothing after the various paintings had been lifted from the walls and the expensive rugs had quickly been rolled back.

Chris returned and grabbed a swig of the iced water that had been served while he had been next door. "Where now?"

"Let me check his bedroom while pretending to check mine. Give me the key."

"I really think it will be down here. Why don't you search upstairs? And if you find it, I'll bring the key up. I'll go on looking downstairs. Which room are you putting your money on?" He had naturally assumed the role of organiser in anything operational; she, however, wasn't used to being told what to do.

"It will be upstairs; I have a feeling. Give me the key. I'm not running back down here for it."

Rather ungraciously, he handed her the brass key. She held it in her hand and looked at the tag with the word 'DUPLI-CATE' on it. It suddenly struck her that this was the same as the one – which was now in her cabin – that Leonard had given her in The Greedy Pelican for safekeeping. Knowing that it must have been sent by Habib to Leonard, but it was never to be of use, almost broke her heart.

"No problem." He turned away. "I'll check out the dining room and the lounges. How many damn rooms are there in this place anyway?"

Mike made her way up the grand staircase to the upper floor. At the end of the long corridor, the double doors to Habib's bedroom came into view. She had searched this once before when looking for the piece of paper in his pockets. No safe had been apparent, but that wasn't what she had been looking for. She remembered that Mohammed had been suspicious of her; his face came into her mind, and as it did, she thought he could be watching her again via the internal security system. They needed to speed up, as he could telephone his friends or the police or worse.

Habib's master bedroom was vast. There was no time to admire the paintings; either they concealed a safe or they didn't. There was fitted carpet, which, thankfully, removed the need to lift up rugs. She assumed his secret safe wouldn't be in some ridiculously complicated and awkward location but would be simply and neatly concealed. The back and top of the wardrobes drew a blank, as did behind the dressing table and chest of drawers. She moved quickly into his en suite bathroom.

For a few seconds, she was mesmerised, having never seen marble of such exquisite green, mauve and white. The taps on the basins and bath were gold and looked ostentatious. Did he ever take a bath? She wasted no time and checked out the back of the cabinets and a recess in the walk-in shower. Nothing.

By now, her heart rate was becoming unhealthy, and she moved through the adjoining bedrooms with little enthusiasm.

———

Downstairs, Chris thought that the safe wouldn't be in any of the rooms where staff were heavily active; it wouldn't be in the kitchen, for example, or in the hallways and corridors. Unlike Mike, he had realised from the outset that they would be monitored and had a few minutes at best. It was these thoughts that made him think Habib might have located the safe or strongbox where there weren't CCTV cameras. He paid attention to these places and, in particular, to blind spots. The dining room piqued his interest as there were no visible cameras.

There were no cupboards and no likely looking places. He was moving as quickly as possible, but he lost his balance and grabbed a heavy curtain in a desperate attempt at saving himself, only to bring the poles, pelmets and yards of fabric down, knocking a vase onto the floor.

Mike, having come back downstairs by then, already pale and shaking, ran into the room. "Are you OK?"

———

Undoubtedly, experienced operatives had been at work. Kevin could appreciate that the team had been efficient in checking out the apartment, but now, with his freshly pressed handkerchief in his hand to leave no prints, he could see that Shamiram had removed everything of consequence as well. Yachtsmen often have 'grab bags'; these have everything important inside and aren't down inside the boat but are placed up top near the wheelhouse or cabin, ready to be picked up as one abandons ship. He had the feeling she'd had her equivalent prepared, which had enabled her to walk in and walk out in minutes. Her professionalism continued to amaze him. It took one to know one.

The flat had reasonably large rooms, and the lounge with a balcony had a panoramic view across the rooftops to the sea.

He could only risk spending a short time in the flat, but he knew that searching under the mattress for secret papers or a diary was a complete waste of time. She had prepared for this event from her first minute in Qatar. Equally experienced, he knew what he was looking for.

It was stuck to the fridge door alongside a souvenir magnet from Ölüdeniz in Turkey and a plastic palm tree of indeterminate provenance. His eye had fallen on a kid's A4 drawing in crayon. It was probably meant to portray a camel, but it had an additional leg that may have kept Darwin awake at night. He looked at the young child's handwriting and saw that it said in Aramaic "To Auntie, from Ishtar".

Leaving everything untouched and the front door as he had found it, he left as quietly as possible and retraced his steps down the lifts and out into the road. While walking to his car, he rang Martha back at the embassy, asking her to check on Shamiram's sister's or brother's kids, looking for one named Ishtar.

He knew that the Assyrians were a tight community and it was unlikely that a leader such as BlueStar would be acting alone without support, however minor the role they actively or innocently played. Kevin had been looking for an indication of someone who might be in Doha and to whom Shamiram might have turned for short-term protection before escaping back to Iraq. It was the fact that the child's sketch was on an uncreased A4 sheet that made him think this had been handed to an aunt in person, not folded, placed in an envelope and posted. It shouldn't take Martha long to check this out as she had already been tasked with drawing up a Yonan family tree, backed up by help from London and Cheltenham.

Irritatingly, he had already made it back into the embassy compound when she phoned. Running through the door into the main building, he told her to wait and come to his office in a couple of minutes. She was happy to oblige.

"You said the child's name was Ishtar. Her mother's name is Ghezalle. She's Shamiram's sister. They live here." Martha handed Kevin a print-out of the incomplete family tree and a map of Doha.

"Has Shamiram used her phone?"

"Cheltenham says she hasn't used it since the explosion."

"She's a cautious lady. Will you get them to monitor her sister's phone? I'll head straight back out. I have a feeling she's there until they can get her out of Qatar ... and, of course, she may be injured."

"Will do."

Kevin grabbed a bottle of water, left his office, and went back down the steps and out to his car. He set off following an almost identical route to the one he had taken earlier.

———

Ghezalle lived in the same district as her sister, only in a large villa that probably had four bedrooms. He drove past twice and found somewhere to park; unfortunately, in direct sunlight. He walked on the shady side of the street and crossed over when he was opposite the door in the boundary wall. There were two names on the entry phone, and he guessed there were two related families living there. He pressed the top button and waited.

"Hello?" a female voice answered in Arabic.

"Hello. Is that Ghezalle?"

"Who is this?" This probably confirmed that it was her, as anybody else would have said no.

"I am Kevin from the British Embassy," he said slowly and clearly, "I am looking for your sister Shamiram. I have just been to her flat, and the door was open. I have brought your daughter's drawing of a camel. It was on the fridge door."

"What? I am sorry, but I do not understand. You have the wrong address, I think."

"Please tell Shamiram that I know what happened at her shop, and I am here to help. I am on my own, and I will stand out here while you ask her. Thank you."

"What? My sister is not here."

"Can you phone her and tell her that I am here?"

"No, sorry."

"I will stand here for ten minutes. Thank you, Ghezalle."

The entry phone clicked off, and Kevin moved back so he could be clearly seen through the lenses of both the gate camera and the one on the corner of the roof. He purposely didn't get out his phone and stood still, looking as disinterested as possible at anything around him.

It was a long five minutes when absolutely nothing happened in any of the villas or on the street, apart from two doves building a nest above his head.

Breaking the stillness, a Filipino man of about thirty appeared around the end of the road and walked along the pavement in his direction. Drawing level, he passed a piece of paper to Kevin and kept on walking. He said nothing.

Kevin opened it to find a telephone number handwritten in pencil.

———

"Shit! Chris, you frightened me."

"I'm OK, I'm OK." He pulled himself up using a dining chair.

"Have you found anything?" Mike asked.

"Yes, that my legs don't work."

"There was nothing obvious upstairs."

"I've found nothing down here either."

"Chris, I'm worried about the internal security cameras. Anyone could be watching us and on their way. We really don't have time. Should we go?

"Five minutes more. I want to try the downstairs bathrooms. They have doors that lock and no cameras, so they're good for hiding small safes." He walked off quickly, staring at the silk rugs beneath his prosthetic limbs as if they had evil intent. "You check the panic room," he added.

Mike went into the hall and walked to the far end. It brought back unpleasant memories that flashed through her mind. She entered the large formal dining room with the belle époque furniture and drapes. In the corner behind the triptych screen, she approached the concealed entrance.

Way behind her, she heard a door slam and a lot of shouting in Arabic from several unknown male voices. In among this, she heard Chris say in a loud voice, "Mike isn't here; she's gone!"

Confused about what to do, she pulled the triptych screen back in place and put her back against the hidden door.

Someone was asking Chris in broken English how she could have left if the car was still outside.

"*I don't know where she is,*" he shouted back, "*We have permission to be here, Officer; we are guests.*"

With Habib having been murdered in the villa and the two sons on their way back from Muscat, Mike decided she could do nothing to help Chris and she had no idea if the police were real or fake. With a feeling of déjà vu, she sent Kevin the message "In the panic room at the villa" and opened the door.

The relief from locking the steel door behind her was huge.

Nothing had changed since her last visit. This time, however, she was on her own. Chris would guess where she was, but no one else would be able to work this out, surely? The 'police officers' wouldn't know about the panic room, and Mohammed and perhaps Chief Inspector Saeed would still be an hour away, even if they had made good progress. Was it Mohammed who had called the police, having seen live footage from the cameras? She could think of no one else unless the butler had got suspicious. Sitting at the small desk, she thought it was likely to be only a short time before all hell let loose. There was, as before, no internet, which seemed odd, but she didn't have time to worry about it or attempt to sort it out. The air conditioning was on twenty-three degrees Celsius, and the small room smelt stuffy. She turned the temperature down and the fan up.

As always happened when she found herself in stressful situations, she heard Dylan's voice in her head. This time it was saying, "*You should have read the manuals.*" "Yeah, all right!" she said out loud, realising she was talking to herself. A cold shiver passed over her skin and not from the cool air blowing from the vent. "Pull yourself together, Mike. What are you going to do?"

Did she have an hour before they rapped at the door? Then what? Resistance would be futile; she couldn't stay in the room. They could simply wait until she ran out of food and water, which reminded her that she should check if the reserves had been restocked since her last visit. They had not. *Who, under normal circumstances, has access to the unlocked room anyway?* she wondered.

Not knowing what was happening to Chris made her even more uneasy.

CHAPTER TWENTY-SEVEN

Kevin moved his car across the road to a parking space under the shade of a feathery Casuarina tree. He started the engine and left it running. The air conditioning blasted out for a couple of minutes, which gave him time to think and to prepare. He grabbed a pen and pad from the glove compartment and turned off the engine. He wiped his tortoiseshell glasses with his handkerchief and was ready to dial the telephone number.

"Who is this?" a female voice asked in Arabic when he made the call.

"Kevin Stenning from the British Embassy."

"I know, Mr Stenning; I have checked your credentials."

"And who are you?"

"I think you know who I am. Perhaps we should be careful what we say in this conversation?"

"I think that would be wise."

"You'll understand that I'm nervous at the moment?"

"Of course, I do understand, are you ... physically in one piece?" His gentle voice was one of his most useful assets.

"I'm fine and will live a few more years, I hope, by the grace of any god who's listening."

A message flashed up on his phone from Mike Kingdom: "In the panic room at the villa."

He didn't miss a beat and his voice betrayed nothing: "That's good to hear. I wanted you to know that I share with you a passionate desire to find the person who yesterday so rudely turned up at your place without an appointment."

"It is one of the downsides of my profession." She didn't specify which of her professions she was referring to or perhaps she meant both of them. "May I ask you how you got my address?"

"I think we have mutual friends?"

"Well, I hope that they are *friends*." Her emphasis on the last word implying 'Americans' to any Brit in intelligence, which Kevin Stenning clearly was.

Me too, he thought, mulling over his brief couple of meetings with Mike. "Do you have any idea who visited your place of work and home?"

"No ... well, yes, in the sense of ultimately who it was, but not specifically. Do you know?"

"I won't lie to you. No, I don't ... but I'm in the process of finding out. I would love to meet you, but I wouldn't advise it. You have my number and know where I'm based. May I assume I can call you on this number for the foreseeable future?"

"Yes, this number will be active for a few days." Rather cryptically she added, "Should our mutual friends prove to be not so friendly, then I may be glad that you made contact."

"I wish we'd met each other some time ago. I should have seen this coming."

"Me too, but we don't all have twenty-twenty vision, sadly."

"No ... and I wear rather inadequate glasses."

"Sadly, I cannot help you with that."

The call ended.

He pulled his seatbelt across and restarted the engine. Even in the partial shade, the temperature inside the car had started to increase. On his hands-free, he phoned Martha and asked her to invite the usual suspects to his office; he would be back in twenty-five minutes, if the traffic was normal.

Invigorated and frustrated in equal measure, he drove back to the embassy through the searing heat of the desert, entered the building and bounded up the stairs. At the top, he poured himself a plastic cup of ice-cold water and made for his office. Martha came in before he had taken a second swig.

"The usual suspects will be here in five minutes," she said.

"Perfect."

'The usual suspects' was the office nickname for Yolanda, who used the expression enough that it had been noticed. On one occasion, she had worn a patch after an operation on her left eye, which had led to the creation of less-favourable nicknames, but 'the usual suspects' had stuck.

"Martha, this is the number on which I've just spoken to Shamiram Yonan. I don't want it listed or recorded in the files yet. Will you, without attribution, ask for Level 5 monitoring of the number? It's important. I want to know everything as well as geo-locations."

"I'll set it up before Yolanda comes." Martha spun on her heels and left.

In the few minutes on his own, Kevin tried to make sense of what had happened over the last twenty-four hours. What had been passed between Habib and BlueStar was top of his list. It was probably something physical, Kevin was now certain of that. Habib was so sure of what he would receive, exchange or give that he had called Leonard out from London at least the day before. Even if Leonard had dropped everything, it would have taken him the best part of a day to travel out to the villa (and Leonard had one or two pressing matters of his own that would need to be shelved). Habib also wanted Leonard to be given it personally. Whatever it was, everyone was avoiding communicating it by phone or electronic means. It must be of critical value.

Yolanda – wearing a long, turquoise shirt over loose, black trousers – walked into his office followed by Martha. "Well, this is all very exciting. What happened?"

Kevin gave a potted version of the events and asked Yolanda what she had established about the Assyrian network, if there was one worth talking about, from her various sources around the Middle East.

"I think everybody's chasing us and not the other way around. It's only since the bombing of the optician's place that everyone has cottoned on to the fact that she was Assyrian, and this might be the reason. No one has linked it to Leonard, and no one had heard of BlueStar."

"Really?" Kevin's voice wasn't revealing what this was telling him. He had hoped there was another party guilty of betrayal, other than the one now foremost in his head.

"What did BlueStar say to you?" Yolanda was staring at him with her good eye.

"Well, her cover is blown in Qatar. Her place of work has been bombed and her flat ransacked. Her husband is hiding in deepest Iraq, and Habib – her route to the Iran-hating, Western world – is dead. Leonard, a contact she had never met, is in hospital in Germany." He stopped to drink. "I expect she'll be in the northern plains of coldest Iraq within twenty-four hours, if she isn't there already, or at least in some halfway house in Bahrain or Saudi."

"So, we've missed the boat?"

"Not necessarily." But for some reason, he didn't tell her about Mike's message.

Mike took off her black wig and balanced it on a bottle of water. Wearing it for so long when she was hot and agitated made her scalp itch. Waiting for someone to knock on the door – or, worse, blast their way through it – was doing nothing for her blood pressure. Like a prisoner in a new cell, she touched every wall, explored every object as if she had never seen one like it before and peered behind anything that could be moved. She was keeping herself busy so she didn't start rerunning the bad moments in her life, which tended to come to the fore at times like these.

Remembering the phone cable in the drawer, she put her phone on charge and picked up the small communication unit provided by the CIA. She had never operated one, and the codebook and jotter pad were in her luggage in the back of the rental car, together with Leonard's phones and his suitcase. Who would she contact even if she could get it to work? It was utterly useless and just sat in front of her eyes reminding her of the futility of the situation. She had a phone and a secure communication unit, both not usable.

Bored after five minutes, she began to inch the battery unit away from the wall in order to see for herself what Callum had found. It was indeed a back-up battery unit of the same type built into the space behind; there was no way she, or any individual, would be able to manoeuvre it out into the room without tools and mechanical help. Her hopes of moving it to reveal a handy escape tunnel were firmly dashed. She sat back on the floor and concluded that it was time to re-enter the villa and face the consequences.

It was at that moment when her eyes fell on one subtle difference between the two battery units; there was a small, thin flap on the door of the one at the back. Did it slide? Did it rotate? She disconnected her phone and used the torch. It rotated to reveal a keyhole. She leant to the side to retrieve the brass key from her pocket and inserted it. There was a loud clunk as the internal bolts moved. The door opened an inch. With childlike glee, she clawed at the heavy door and pulled it open.

Mike was faced not by the shelves of a safe or the way through to a tunnel. There, only two inches inside, was another door or panel with a keypad located centrally. It didn't have numbers, but there were the letters of the alphabet from A to Y in five rows of five. Under these keys were three buttons: Open, Lock and Clear.

To be cheated at this point, having found the safe, was almost too much to bear and tears began to roll down her cheeks.

"Close the safe and put the first battery unit back in place!" she heard Dylan's voice say in her ear.

She jumped up and, in the confined space, moved the central table to make the manoeuvring easier. This, in turn, moved the rug on which the table stood. It revealed the corners of a small trapdoor, flush with the floor.

Her hopes had been raised too many times before. This could be a drain or access to utilities. Using a knife from the desk drawer, she levered it open and gasped as a shaft with a ladder on one side became evident. Now what to do?

She quickly put all the small items, such as chargers and the knife, back in place and closed the safe door, pocketing the key. The big battery unit posed the biggest dilemma. Yes, she could expend a lot of effort putting it back, but was it good use of the ever-decreasing time she had left? Initially, she decided to leave it out in the room, then changed her mind and spent several minutes walking it back into position. Perhaps, ten minutes had passed since she had entered. It was time to leave.

She positioned the table on the mat in the centre of the room as best she could, leaving enough freedom for her to enter the shaft. She rolled up part of the mat ready to cover her escape. The shaft was narrow and would have been a tight squeeze for a man like Habib. In a fiddly manoeuvre, she went down five rungs and reached back up to unroll the rug over the trapdoor which shut to leave her in total darkness.

Using her phone in one hand and with the other holding the bottle of water, she somehow grabbed the ladder and descended. The shaft had perhaps reached eighteen feet deep before it revealed a side tunnel. Her three-dimensional awareness wasn't her strong point, but she knew that the villa was approached by a flight of steps and that the general floor level was elevated above the surrounding gardens and paved areas. She had no idea in which direction she was heading or what she might face at the end.

It was hot and the tunnel was festooned with dusty cobwebs, but thankfully for her, only cockroaches were present, scurrying from the light of her phone. She never saw the big, grey scorpion.

Her knees were sore from crawling and her trousers torn. At one point, her wig was pulled off by some projection from the ceiling. A graze produced a small trickle of blood, but this went unnoticed under the replaced wig. A wall appeared at the end after a total distance of something like 100 yards.

A shaft with a shorter ladder than at the other end led upwards. She paused to regain her breath and rearrange her wig, which had slipped on her sweaty, bloody head; she then rubbed her hands as if she were about to meet a bank of paparazzi once she exited this hellhole. Pointing the light upwards revealed a single, very narrow hatch connected to a framework that held a metal ratchet system. Her heart sank.

Where would this tunnel exit? Outside the perimeter wall, in the ancillary buildings or in the gardens? She climbed up the short ladder, held herself steady and examined the contraption in front of her. There was a handle connected to an arc of metal. She pulled it down to its full extent. There was a clang and a creaking sound above her. By moving the handle up and down, the ratchet was made to do its job, and the sound of soil or stones could be heard sliding from the hatch as it lifted up. As soon as daylight appeared, Mike altered her position to squint outside. There was blue sky, a rocky landscape and no sign of the villa or its perimeter walls.

After a couple of dozen heaves up and down on the handle, the hatch was open enough to let her climb out. Firstly, she wiped the grit and dust from her eyes and the sweat from her brow. With her eyes adjusted to the light, she pulled herself up and out of the hole to find herself on the far side of a small, rocky outcrop about twenty yards beyond the perimeter wall. Were there security cameras or alarms? She needed to keep low and out of sight until she had worked out where she was and, frighteningly, what she was going to do as evening approached, high in the mountains and miles from anywhere that might be guaranteed to be friendly.

Having connected to the network, Mike's phone buzzed.

CHAPTER TWENTY-EIGHT

"I'm a guest." Chris was trying to explain this in Arabic to the four policemen who had turned up in two vehicles with blue and red lights flashing, which were currently blocking the rental car in case it was used to escape.

"We've had a call that there are intruders in the villa,"

"Who called you?" Chris was trying not to be aggressive, given what he and Mike were trying to do in the villa.

"That doesn't matter."

Well, it does actually! But Chris kept that thought to himself.

"Now you know I'm a guest, I'm sure you can leave and deal with more important matters."

"We need to check."

"Check what?"

"The villa."

"No problem." He moved across the impressive entrance hall and sat on a chair that cost more than he had ever earnt in a year.

This was the first time since the explosion in Iraq that he had properly been in the field; he felt helpless. Not because he was likely to run away and jump over the gate, but because he felt weak, emasculated and as if his gun had been taken away; this was psychological not physical, but it hurt all the more for that.

He wondered where Mike was and assumed she had heard the noise; he had spoken as loudly as possible, hoping that she could, as a minimum, prepare herself or possibly find somewhere to hide, such as the panic room.

"Where is your friend?"

"What friend?" he asked as calmly as possible.

"The woman."

"No idea."

The police officer, who may have been a sergeant, stared at him fiercely.

"I hope you have authority from very high up to do all of this?" Chris queried.

"We do." The man's stare had hardened further.

Chris looked away as benignly as possible and gazed at some tapestry on the wall opposite.

As if reacting to this nonchalance and needing to assert his authority, the sergeant said, "Stay here. Do not try to leave."

Chris bent forwards and rolled up his trousers. "That won't be a problem."

A junior policeman, fascinated by the prosthetics, was instructed in Arabic to watch over him. They were aware he spoke fluent Arabic, so they made no snide comments. The other three police officers proceeded to search the villa. With at least thirty rooms, this would take a while and give Chris time to think.

After ten minutes, he was relieved that they had yet to find Mike, wherever she had found to hide. In the meantime, he had balanced all the options and knew it was only a matter of time. Then what? They had done nothing wrong. They were guests. They were looking for lost earrings. Whether the police believed that or not didn't really matter. What were they going to be charged with? And this was before Mike phoned Callum and Harper asking why the police were in their villa. Here, Chris was assuming it was Mohammed who had seen them searching and had called his friends in the police. The only slight problem was that the sons were currently incommunicado and under arrest, but in all likelihood, this would soon change.

While passing the time, he went over what he and Mike had in their car and bags. He had nothing except all his IOC clothes and paperwork; perhaps it was time to point out exactly who he was. As for Mike, he didn't know specifically what she had; however, she did have Leonard's suitcase and his phones, but these could be easily explained. His mind went back to his first time in the field on a dangerous mission, when he was obsessed with checking that he had nothing on him or in his belongings that might be compromising.

The sergeant was talking to members of the household, which indicated to Chris that she hadn't been found yet. He would have guessed she was in the panic room, but he would never have imagined her crawling along an underground tunnel, scraping her knees and head, having discovered the safe that was at the centre of this whole BlueStar–Habib–Leonard affair.

On hearing the sergeant returning, he rolled a trouser leg up further and removed a prosthetic limb. He was rubbing the stump as the policeman re-entered the hall. In fieldwork, you use whatever cards you're dealt – all the manuals say that. No policeman anywhere in the world would think he was involved in some burglary or robbery.

"Mr Crippen, we cannot find your friend, but we will." He was staring at the prosthetic limb on the floor.

"I'm sure you will; she probably went to the bathroom after she had checked her bedroom for the earring."

The sergeant ignored this. "Chief Inspector Saeed is on his way from Muscat; he'll be here within the hour."

Chris was about to play the 'I need to get back to Doha for official Olympic business' card, but he knew now that it would be useless. The sergeant wouldn't release him before his superior arrived. Again, he was left alone with his guard and continued to massage the stump of his left leg.

It was obvious to him now that Mike had probably gone back into the panic room, having used it before with the sons. *Perhaps, she found a strongbox or safe inside?* He considered this, but he then dismissed the thought as she had described it as a tiny space with no room for one inside. She would have to come out eventually, of course, but she could say she felt threatened by the arrival of the police. After some face-saving interrogation, they would be released. Then, the sooner she drove them both back to Ras Al Khaimah, the better.

He cursed Leonard under his breath for dragging him into this, but then again, it had almost worked out. If only he had found the safe.

———

"Kevin?" Mike whispered as she scrambled as quietly as possible between rocky outcrops across the scattered scree; the loose stones and gravel were difficult to cross, and she didn't want any of it to create a mini avalanche. The sun was still blinding to her right, and the heat was radiating from the surface of the limestone all around her.

"Mike, I got your message. I've been trying to call. Are you OK?"

She only had two friends who could help her: Chris, who was trapped in the villa, and Kevin, who was 300 miles away. She had no choice any more; it wasn't the time to hold back. She could be caught at any time. "Kevin, Habib gave BlueStar a key. It opens a sort of safe in the panic room at his villa. I opened it, but the police have turned up. I've escaped down a tunnel and I'm now out in the mountains. I have no idea where to go. By the way, inside this built-in safe is another door with a keypad. It has all the letters from A to Y arranged five by five. I don't have the code. BlueStar only gave us the key. Can you ask her if she knows the code?"

"What? Yes, I'll try. How can I help you? Shall I ring my friends at your embassy in the UAE or Oman?"

"No, no, no; please don't contact anyone and keep this to yourself at the moment. I can't explain over the phone. Trust me."

"What are you going to do?"

"I haven't thought yet; I've just escaped ... I'll follow a goat track down to the road, probably."

"Then what?"

"No idea, but if anything happens to me, tell Leonard I hate him and the answer is in that bloody safe. I must go."

"Look after yourself."

Then there was silence apart from the occasional crack of a rifle shot that turned out to be layers of rock peeling off in the heat.

Her mouth was dry, but she only took the smallest sip from the bottle she had brought with her from the panic room; it needed to last. Apart from that, she had her phone and the safe key. If only she had read the manuals.

A narrow goat track barely a foot wide rather decided the route for her. She marched off, wondering about Mohammed. She was guessing he was the only person who might know there was an escape tunnel. But would Habib have told any of the existing staff? If he hadn't, it would be a very long time – probably tomorrow – before they could break in through that thick metal door. It would require specialist equipment, surely?

She was now walking along a defile with high sides that

would be the perfect place for an ambush, but nothing happened; in fact, there was little sign of life other than a lone acacia tree in the distance, shaped over the years by the munching of goats. There was no wind apart from the occasional convection current from the heat in the rocks. At the tree, she was about to stop and take stock, but she changed her mind when a swarm of flies rose from the goat shit on the bare ground beneath.

Time passed slowly, and she must have only walked about a three-quarters of a mile, but it was difficult to judge in this mountainous terrain.

Where am I going? Mike was asking herself at the point where escaping from the villa was no longer uppermost in her mind, but what comes next was beginning to take precedence. She needed to find somewhere to sleep before it got dark, and she knew that, in the Middle East, night fell quickly at about 7.00pm; if it was like the previous night, the sky would be clear and starry, causing temperatures to drop rapidly. There was a chance she might make it down to a road, but equally, at any time, her route may be blocked by a ravine or cliff.

The time to make a decision was cut short when the goat track led directly to a pillar of grey limestone. The path bifurcated: to the left, it headed down towards the sea, way below her in the distance, and to the right, it followed the contours around the mountainside, where it looked as if it joined a rough road that rose up towards the white ball that was the listening post on the next summit. This was an option she hadn't even considered.

Mike needed to choose.

———

Kevin knew he had to act fast. There was no time for subtlety or tradecraft. He picked up his phone and dialled BlueStar's number. She didn't answer until his fourth attempt, perhaps half an hour later.

"This is Kevin." He waited for this to register.

"Good afternoon, I wasn't expecting you to call again so soon."

"There's no time to explain or for any pleasantries, I'm afraid. I'll keep this as vague as possible. The good news is that we've found the safe and opened it. The bad news is that we don't have the access code. We have a small window of opportunity." He was speaking calmly but leaving no doubt that this was critical.

She paused while she thought about this. "I see. I'm confused because I gave the code when I handed over the key."

Kevin was also confused, not knowing anything about Chris Crippen or that he was, at that moment, separated from Mike and sitting under police guard in the villa.

"Who has gained access, if I may ask ... in general terms, colleagues from your organisation?" She was trying to work out who now had the key.

"No, our friend from the west."

"I'm nervous about who now has the key."

"I don't know how to reassure you, but I can vouch for the person. Please be assured that whatever we find will be communicated to you. I give you my word."

There was a very long pause before she spoke. "You realise this is the end for me, either way? I'll have to disappear from the scene, possibly forever."

"I'm sorry – genuinely sorry. I wish we could have met earlier and under different circumstances."

"Me too."

"Perhaps the contents of the safe will be worth all your effort?"

"I sincerely hope so." Another pause. "The code word is written on the key tag, if it's still attached."

"That I don't know."

"I look forward to having a lot of night-time reading. The code word is 'DUPLICATE'." She spelt it out for the avoidance of any doubt.

The call ended, and he immediately called Mike – who was, at that moment, walking on a flat track that hugged the mountain to her right. The listening post may be manned twenty-four seven, and in any case, it was a facility run by the Brits. Might it be safer to head there rather than down to the coast road where any passing vehicle might be hostile?

Her phone rang, and she answered it.

"Mike, the code word is written on the key tag, if it's still attached. It's 'DUPLICATE'." He also spelt it out.

"Shit! I'm forty minutes away from the villa. Do we know what's inside?"

"No, but our friend is staking her life on it."

"OK, I'll go back."

"She said she gave you the password."

"She gave it to an intermediary."

He didn't ask further. "Be careful."

"Wait, do you know if the listening post here is manned? It's one of yours, isn't it? There's a chance I might be able to get there by nightfall. Send me a message."

———

While retracing her steps, she was glad she hadn't descended into the valley. Exhaustion was making her feel giddy, which wasn't helpful on loose stones and next to scree slopes. Trying to keep up a brisk pace made her sweat, especially under the wig. However, it did give her some protection from the sun, which was now quite low in the sky ahead of her.

On passing the acacia tree with its cloud of flies, she was cursing herself for not trying the word 'DUPLICATE'. Habib was very clever if it was him who had thought of hiding the code word in plain sight. The bottle of water was too inviting, and a large gulp washed the taste of the desert from her mouth. She would pick up another in the panic room for the return journey, if she managed to get in and out alive.

As she went round the last rocky outcrop, the villa perimeter wall came into view.

Moving on all fours to avoid any cameras, she scrambled her way towards the entrance to the shaft. The small door was standing up vertically, revealing the ratchet mechanism. She was glad she hadn't closed it, but she wasn't sure how that was done anyway. Putting her hand into her pocket, she checked for the key. Perhaps, this was something she should have done earlier. It was with great relief that her fingers found it.

With the torch on her phone ready in one hand, Mike began her descent of the ladder.

CHAPTER TWENTY-NINE

It was 2.07pm in Cheltenham, and Kevin was telephoning, on a secure line, someone known as 'Von Trapp' because he used to spend his life up mountains and was obsessed with Julie Andrews. They had known each other for many years, and they had actually shared accommodation in Cyprus for three months. His real name was Samuel Onions, and this might be why he saw Von Trapp as an improvement.

"Sam, how's life in the Cotswolds?"

"I've moved to a flat in Gloucester, so I have no idea. I would guess it's still full of fat blokes in red jackets, one size too small, chasing foxes. You know I'm a city boy at heart. How's the desert?"

"It's a massive building site. It'll soon be concreted over. I don't know how the cranes don't crash into each other, there are so many of them."

"Not like Blighty, then? Here, cranes are like steam trains – something to be pointed out to the kids; that's if I had any."

They quickly caught up on a mutual friend who was ill, and then Kevin cut to the chase: "Sam, I have a weird question about something that might very soon be a serious problem for me. Your listening post in Oman up on the Musandam Peninsula – do you have many people on-site at the moment? I mean twenty-four seven."

"A few, but it's basically controlled from here, as you know. What do you need?"

"This isn't about intel. This is about an asset. If I had a … person who turned up there in the next hour or two, is there someone to let them in?"

"What are they? A mountaineer?"

"No."

"We're not a bloody hotel. What's wrong with Dubai?"

"Bizarrely, your place might be the closest refuge. This person could be there any time from, let's say, in an hour until, I don't know, late tonight."

"What time is it there now? … Just past 5.00pm; it will be dark by 7.00pm."

"This wasn't planned, as you might guess."

"I'll contact someone called Andy; he's a good chap, but they don't have a lot of visitors – by which I mean they don't have any visitors. How will they know he's kosher?"

"It's a 'she', and shall we use the word 'duplicate' as the password to mean that all's well?"

"I'll get Andy and his local security guy to look out for her. As you well know, we don't have a doorbell and welcome mat."

"Sam, this is as important as anything we've been involved in. So, thanks for the help, and will you keep this quiet?"

"No name, no pack drill. Will someone pick her up in the morning?"

"I'm on to that next."

Kevin took the phone from his ear to see Yolanda standing at his office door.

"Important operations afoot?" She pushed the door open and stepped inside.

"Let's call it a 'walk-in'." He was being less than precise with that term, which normally refers to locals who turn up at the embassy unannounced and offer to sell their grandmother for a packet of cigarettes.

"Unusual?"

"It's been a strange day. How has yours been?" He was keen for Yolanda to leave so he could send Mike Kingdom a message as soon as possible, just in case her plans changed.

"Unusual, as well. I've just been speaking to Barbara Aumonier."

"How is she?" He had always found her workmanlike but not overly helpful, which had made him wonder more than once about her new role at Five Eyes. Yolanda and Barbara had known each other a long time.

"She wanted to tell me that the Canadian PM has got involved with the arrest of the two Murchison brothers. He's been making calls to all and sundry. He must see it as a vote-winner because he's gone in hard."

"Are they being released?"

"Yes, they will be, as will their father's body. It won't be public knowledge for a while yet. All charges are to be dropped. No more action. Nothing to see here. Please move along. The Omanis will say they were detained to protect them from 'forces unknown' who were trying to kidnap them or extort money from them, particularly cryptocurrency."

"And why was their father killed?"

"Apparently, the two autopsies were inconclusive. No more action. Nothing to see here. Please move along." Her repetition was driving home the point that the Omanis wanted the world to forget this episode.

"I'm a bit slow today, but am I beginning to see a pattern here?"

"Barbara was asking me what we knew. She's already asked the others." By 'the others' she meant the USA, Canada, Australia and New Zealand.

"Where are the sons now?" Kevin was keen to know how this might interface with Mike's activities.

"On their way from Muscat to their father's villa, I believe, and then I expect them to fly out and never to return. Have we ever established what Habib Murchison was up to, apart from making millions – sorry, billions?"

"No, we haven't" – which wasn't a lie – "I expect all his secrets died with him" – which was a lie.

"You look as though you need to deal with your walk-in, so I'll leave you to it. Let me know if anything happens in Oman." She turned and left the room, quietly singing the chorus from a catchy song.

He grabbed his phone and sent Mike a message, knowing that she was, at that moment, most likely incommunicado while she bravely re-entered the villa. It said: "Your overnight accommodation is good and ready. If asked, the password the same as today's code word."

———

Chris Crippen was getting very frustrated. He had been sitting in the hallway for over an hour and a half, and the unproductive conversations with the more senior of the policemen were wearing thin. Having replaced his prosthetic leg, he stood up and began to walk across the room.

The sergeant appeared from one of the doors. "Where are you going?"

"To the bathroom."

"Leave the door unlocked."

"What? No." He opened a door, stepped inside and loudly turned the lock. Sitting on the toilet, he stared at the phone in his hand. If things went wrong, his phone may be examined. He needed to be careful. He cleared the history, but he knew this was only a temporary solution. Apart from his IOC calls, of which there were hundreds, he had only spoken to Mike and to BlueStar. It would take them a long time to find any of this – by which time, he hoped to be miles away. But why make it easy for them?

He debated for a few seconds and could only think of one person who might help. He sent an innocent-looking coded text.

Rubbing his hands together, he was halfway across the hall when the large front doors opened and in walked two men, one in a black uniform, carrying his cap under his arm.

"I hope you've been treated well by my officers. I'm Chief Inspector Saeed," he said in English, offering his hand to Chris.

"I'm not sure why I'm being detained. I'm a guest here," Chris answered in Arabic.

"You speak Arabic?"

"I'm an American over here in Doha with the IOC on their inspection visit. I need to get back there, you'll understand."

"I'm sure you won't be detained for long."

The other man who had entered didn't say a word or introduce himself. Instead, he walked to the back of the hall and disappeared through a door.

"I hope not. I spoke with your Crown Prince and Minister for Culture, Sports and Youth on Monday evening at a dinner hosted by the Qataris." Chris's implied threat was left hanging.

"As I said, I'm sure you won't be detained long. Where is Miss Kingdom?"

"I have no idea. She asked me to come with her to look for an earring she had lost when she was a guest of the Murchisons a few days ago. I was checking the rooms downstairs, and she was doing the same upstairs, particularly in her bedroom. Then, your four officers burst in and detained me. I've been sitting in this hall since."

"How do you know Miss Kingdom?" The chief inspector

was still wearing his sunglasses and so betrayed nothing with his eyes.

"We're old friends. We met up again in Doha during my official visit there. My duties are almost finished in Qatar, and I was happy to give her some company on a short break here via Ras Al Khaimah. May I ask you what the problem is?"

"It's a long way to come to look for an earring, don't you think?"

"And this is a concern warranting the attention of a chief inspector and four officers of the Royal Oman Police?" He paused. "She understood that the Murchison brothers weren't here, and she's soon leaving the Middle East. It seems perfectly logical to me, especially as I believe the earrings are of sentimental value and irreplaceable."

"Who drove here?"

"What?" Chris was having to use all his personal and professional restraint. "We hired a car from Ras Al Khaimah airport, and she drove here." He bent over and pulled up his trousers. "I have two artificial limbs; I'm a Paralympian in the US basketball team, if you're interested."

The chief inspector seemed to have about exhausted his questions. "Will you wait here while I see where Miss Kingdom is?"

"I'm not likely to run off, am I? I'm not bloody Oscar Pistorius."

"I hope not, Mr Crippen; he was jailed for shooting his partner, wasn't he?" And with that, he walked off into the villa.

Chris turned around and sat back down again on an ornate, quilted chair. He looked at his phone and saw a single thumbs-up emoji. Help may be on the way.

Over the next ten minutes, there was much activity in and out of rooms and up and down the grand staircase. Chief Inspector Saeed and the other man walked over to him.

The policeman spoke first: "Mr Crippen, we cannot find Miss Kingdom. This is worrying."

"Well, she can't have disappeared; she's here in the villa somewhere. The car keys and her bag are over there on that table; I'm presuming the car is still outside?"

The chief inspector walked over and looked into her very small bag, but there was clearly nothing of interest. Perhaps he was looking for her phone. "This is Mohammed," he introduced the other man. "He knows this villa inside out."

Chris stood up, "Hello, Mohammed. I was with Mike outside the gates when she spoke to you about gaining access. Perhaps, you could tell the chief inspector that we're not burglars."

Mohammed's frown, above his sunken eyes, deepened. "There's only one place left to search, Mr Crippen, and that's the panic room. Why would she go in there?"

"I don't have the faintest idea, but she did tell me she had been in it during her last visit ... with the Murchisons, as I understand. There was some explosion outside. Perhaps that's where she dropped her earring. I don't know."

"Would you mind coming with us to check, Mr Crippen? If she's inside, she may not come out unless she receives reassurance from you." The chief inspector rotated his body and extended an arm like a waiter escorting guests to a table.

"Please lead the way." Chris allowed the two men to turn, and as he walked by the Louis XV side table, he put the car keys in his pocket. They walked along the corridor into a formal dining room. Mohammed moved a tapestried triptych screen to the side and revealed a door.

———

Most of the dust-laden cobwebs had been cleared when she had crawled through the tunnel the first time. Mike's knees, however, did not enjoy being scraped over the uneven floor again, and her back hurt from arching while trying to shine the torch forwards. Knowing the length of the tunnel helped, and as she passed a pipe crossing the tunnel ceiling that she had noticed previously, she reassured herself that, in fifteen minutes, she would be back and passing it for the third time. Her nerves were as frayed as her trousers.

At the end, she gripped the ladder with one hand and began to climb. The cooler air descending into the tunnel was her first indication that she was re-entering the villa. Using a combination of her head and hands, she pushed the rug out of the way and used the torch to check out the room. There were no policemen, or anyone worse, waiting for her as she flopped onto the floor and ignominiously hauled herself up using the table. There was no time to lose.

Seeing the battery unit, she cursed herself and began to walk it out from the wall a second time. Kneeling hurt, but in order to gain access to the safe, she had to arrange her aching bones into a configuration that allowed her to open it and type in the code word. The brass key turned easily in the lock and revealed the keypad beyond. The word 'DUPLICATE' on the brown tag at the end of the string mocked her.

Nervously, and with ridiculous precision, she tapped in the nine letters, followed by pressing the Open button. The lock sprang instantly.

Pulling the inner door open while holding the torch took some dexterity. Was the safe going to be empty, like some Egyptian tomb sacked by grave robbers? She peered inside and saw quickly that there wasn't much within: three blue A4-size files, each filled to a half-inch thickness with papers, and an A4-size notebook with a hard, green cover. After removing them, she ran her fingers over the shelf and side walls, but there was nothing else.

She closed the inner door and locked the safe, pocketing

the key. Anyone coming in after her still wouldn't know if there was a safe and whether it had been opened. Now she was faced with a logistics problem: how to get the four items down the escape tunnel. The phone charger cable was back in the drawer of the little desk. She took it out, and after tying a few crude knots, the three files and notebook were bound together and became a little more manageable.

Was there time to push the battery unit back in front of the safe? She decided there wasn't, and she didn't have the strength anyway. After a quick check of the room, she arranged the table and carpet so she could disguise the trapdoor again once she was on the ladder.

There was a hammering on the door and raised voices.

CHAPTER THIRTY

With her phone in her pocket, Mike gripped both the ladder and her makeshift sling in her left hand. Using her right hand, she closed the trapdoor while reaching through to roll the carpet back over the top. It would have to do. Now seriously tired, both physically and mentally, she descended the ladder, only turning on her phone torch once she had reached the bottom of the shaft.

"Damn!" she said out loud. She had forgotten to pick up another bottle of water. Her spirits dropped, and for one second, she thought about going back, but she ditched the idea as they were now aware she had gone into the panic room. All that mattered was that, whoever they were, they were actively in pursuit and only on the other side of the door – hopefully, a virtually impregnable door.

Her knees were seriously grazed and bleeding. Cockroaches scurried as previously, caught in the beam from the phone torch, but she was too preoccupied to bother about them. She ducked under the small pipe that crossed the ceiling and swore to herself that this was the last time she was passing through this or any other tunnel. Staring out of her cabin at the forest edge, swigging an ice-cold beer, was where she wanted to be, not imitating a seventeenth-century tin miner in Cornwall.

The end of the tunnel came into view, and she reorganised everything she was carrying. The daylight streaming down from the opening above her head looked very inviting. Climbing out, the air smelt of aromatic plants. She gave no thought to the open hatch; there was no need to close it. Before her, the stony track wound away into the distance, and like a marathon runner hitting the psychological wall, she plodded along, concentrating on each step and not the daunting prospect ahead. The temperature was now pleasantly warm out of the sun, which was throwing her shadow onto the goat track.

The flies under the acacia tree didn't swarm up as enthusiastically this time as they had done on the previous two occasions she had passed them – perhaps they had found a safe place to spend the approaching night. Now running on an almost empty tank, Mike stumbled along the path until she reached the point where it divided, heading down towards the sea and veering off towards the summit with the listening station at the top. Once she had dismissed nightmare thoughts about police dogs tracking her or special forces dropping down from helicopters, she took stock.

Nobody had been murdered in the villa; well, OK, Habib had been murdered, but she was thinking about her visit with Chris. All they had done was ask for access and look for an imaginary lost earring. These weren't crimes of the century. Everyone might be twitchy, but there was a limit to what they – whoever they were – would do. "They probably think I've been taken ill or I escaped to the panic room when I heard the police enter the villa. Nothing more," she said out loud to no one – not even a lizard basking on the rock and about to hide away in a crack.

It was only symbolic, but she had passed the furthest

point that had been reached before. The rough access road up to the listening post was perhaps twenty minutes further along the contour, as long as there were no hidden obstacles – here, she was thinking of barriers to her progress and not what any goats might climb. The setting sun was beginning to cast very long, sharp shadows that accentuated the valleys and the vertigo-inducing views down towards the Persian Gulf.

The contents of Habib's safe were tucked firmly under her left arm, causing her to sweat more and to have to balance on the loose gravel without the benefit of extending her arms. She hoped it was worth it – by which she meant that she hoped it was worth Habib's life and everything she had personally gone through so far. The terrain became ever more testing, and at one point, the path had been eroded. It no longer existed, and she was confronted by a gully where the water had torrented down the mountainside during one of the infrequent but dramatic tropical storms. It was one full pace across the void, but the drop to the left turned it into a challenge of Olympic proportions. If she fell, the contents of the files and notebook would go with her, possibly never to be found or read. And what was in them? Her curiosity was off the scale, but self-preservation had taken priority. *Hopefully, it's all worth it,* she kept repeating.

She took a deep breath, relaxed her taut and tired muscles, and took the stride across the gap. The relief of crossing it reinvigorated her.

The limestone beds were deeply folded, which meant that the path was sometimes smooth, sometimes jagged and often thrown up at odd angles every few yards. From a particularly shiny, almost-smooth rock surface, she stepped across onto the track that had been blasted and bulldozed up the other side of the ravine to allow construction of, and to give access to, the listening post. The latter consisted of a white geodesic dome, resembling a golf ball when viewed from afar, and some tall aerials.

The danger of falling or twisting an ankle had gone, only to be replaced with the fear of being spotted. She wasn't exactly back at home on Interstate 5 in Oregon; this was a track with passing bays wide enough for a vehicle. There could be some traffic up and down, and there would also be cameras. More than all of this, it was uphill. She cursed herself for not taking a bottle of water out of the fridge. Why had she been so twitchy? It was obvious that no one was going to come after her once she had moved that triptych and locked the panic room door behind her.

And how was Chris doing? She had no idea why she was worrying about him. He was a big, grown man with years at the Agency – and he could speak Arabic. Yes, he had prosthetic limbs, but it didn't stop him being on the IOC panel and playing wheelchair basketball. Like her, he had done nothing wrong and had nothing incriminating on him, so she had faith that he would talk his way out of anything.

She had so few friends. At the moment, her life revolved around – for which, read 'depended on' – Leonard de Vries, Chris Crippen and Kevin Stenning at the British Embassy in Doha. "I need to get out more," she said out loud, "No, I don't; for fuck's sake, I need to stay in more! And I need to stop talking to myself." Thoughts of Kevin Stenning and the need to pause and get her breath combined to halt her progress. She took out her phone and sent a message: "Got everything. On my way up the hill to your place."

Tiredness ate away at her, and her inquisitiveness began to get the better of her. What was in the files and notebook? Just when she might have sat down and started browsing her prized possessions, a small but sudden rockfall happened behind her, and this spurred her into action. She stepped forwards with a new sense of urgency.

The track snaked, climbing at a gradient of one in ten, which had been chosen as the maximum a vehicle could sustain for any distance on the uneven surface. This meant she was walking at a fair rate, but she had a long way to go. To her right, the sun had dropped below the horizon formed by the mountains. She was now walking under a darkening sky that graded from a rich, deep blue down to an orange glow as nightfall approached. The temperature had dropped noticeably.

Her phone buzzed. It was from Kevin: "Did you get my message? My friends are looking out for you. Password the same as your code word, if needed."

She sent back a thumbs-up emoji, not having received his first message for some reason.

It looked like there was another mile to go, with the last stretch consisting of a series of steep hairpin bends uphill. Below and behind, the lights of the port and cement works began to twinkle. There was no sound. Where the track had been cut through a shoulder of rock, she found a convenient spot to sit. Curiosity had won. Using her teeth and fingernails to undo a knot, the phone charger cable released the files and book onto her lap.

The contents of the first blue file, illuminated by her phone torch, were in Arabic and Farsi. She couldn't read anything, but she didn't need to: it was made up of specifications for military ships with diagrams and photographs. Hopefully, it was of use to someone at the CIA. The second and third files revealed similar contents but with correspondence printouts and detailed maps that she also couldn't read or recognise.

The book with the green cover was different: it was handwritten in English. She flicked through it to get a flavour. An A4 sheet fell out. It was a letter in Farsi with an English translation written in between each pair of lines. When the full implications sank in, she was stunned. Habib may not have fully appreciated what he had discovered.

A pair of headlights appeared some way below her. The beam swung back and forth as the vehicle navigated the hairpin bends on the way up. It could be friend or foe, but what were the chances that a vehicle was coming up to a secret facility in the mountains just at that moment. She had maybe five minutes before it reached her, which was nowhere near enough for her to run up to the listening post. There was no time for thinking.

She quickly messaged Kevin about what she had read, that the files were hidden behind a rock to the left of the track around 500 yards from the gate and that a vehicle was approaching; that's all there was time for. She found only one suitable location, but at least there was no need to worry about rain; a small slab of stone on top would weigh down the book and files in case of winds ripping through the valley.

"Go back down the track," Dylan's voice echoed in her ear, or it might have been that she was developing her own skills. If hostile, the car's occupants would assume she had hidden anything where she was or where she had just passed. They wouldn't expect her to have backtracked. The anticipation was unbearable.

The noise of the car's engine grew louder. Now in twilight, the headlights seemed bright and dazzling. She was standing still with her arms by her side, having walked back downhill, perhaps 100 yards. There was nowhere for her to hide, and either side of the track offered very steep slopes up or down, which definitely weren't to be tackled in the disappearing light. The car began to slow down as it approached her.

———

Chief Inspector Saeed hammered on the door. "Miss Kingdom, you are quite safe; please come out." He was depressing the speaker button on the partially concealed entry phone.

There was no response, and the policeman turned around to Chris. "Would you please reassure her?"

Chris stepped forwards and said in a loud voice, "Mike, I'm here with Chief Inspector Saeed and Mohammed; we're all safe. Please unlock the door."

Again, there was silence.

"Is there any way to open this door? You know, an override system?" the chief inspector asked Mohammed in Arabic.

"No, not to my knowledge. I think it was built eight years ago. I've been here only four, and I've only been inside the room twice."

"Is there another door? Is there any other communication system?"

"Not that I know of; I could ask the butler. His duties include making sure the water and supplies are kept up to date, but this is a once-every-two-months task. There really isn't much in the room – a desk, a chair, a table, a battery unit, a fridge ... not much else. It's very small."

The chief inspector was pensive for a moment. "There must be another door – an escape hatch onto the roof or a tunnel, surely?"

"Again, I don't know."

"Mohammed, would you tell one of my officers to come here? I want them to walk around outside and have a look."

"No problem," he turned and left the formal dining room.

Chris pressed the button again. "Mike, can you hear us? If you can, please bang on the door."

Silence.

"I'm worried she's in there but is in difficulty. Perhaps she can't get out, or there's some other problem." Chris sounded concerned.

"Can you think why she might have gone in there in the first place?"

"Well, I presume she was looking for her earring. I'm

guessing she had looked everywhere else in the villa ... and thought she had dropped it when she had been in the panic room during her last visit, after the explosion by the gates. Maybe the door shut behind her? I don't know, Chief Inspector." Chris was sweating slightly despite the air conditioning; this was all very stressful.

The policeman spent a few seconds looking at the door and its surrounds. "Mr Crippen, if you'll forgive me, I'm having a little trouble with this 'looking for an earring' story. Perhaps, I'm too old and too cynical, but I don't see Miss Kingdom flying from Doha to Ras Al Khaimah, hiring a car and driving for an hour and a half to look for an earring. She doesn't look like someone who spends thousands on diamonds, and her ears aren't even pierced, I think."

"Why else would she have come back?"

"That's what's bothering me. Why come back to a villa where you've previously had to hide in a panic room after people have shot at your friend and there has been an explosion at the gates? Oh, and after someone has poisoned their father. I don't get it."

"Does everything have to be connected?"

"Possibly not, but after a life in the military and the police, I've found that, yes, things generally are."

There was a noise outside the dining room further down the hall.

"Ah, perhaps Mohammed and my officers have found her?"

There were raised voices and the sound of banging. They had barely made it into the hall when the front door burst open, and Chris and the chief inspector were confronted by Callum Murchison, closely followed by his brother, running up the steps.

CHAPTER THIRTY-ONE

"What's going on, Chief Inspector?" Callum was looking around the large atrium at a group of people that included police officers, Mohammed and a broad-shouldered man with black hair standing with one hand on a table that appeared to be supporting him.

"We're still investigating the murder of your father and had reports of two suspicious characters entering your villa. It turns out that one was your family friend, Miss Kingdom, together with this gentleman, Mr Crippen."

"Who are you?" Callum asked Chris.

"I'm a friend of Mike; she came here to find an earring she had left behind. I came with her. She was under the impression that you were in Muscat and there was no one here, so she telephoned Mohammed to ask if it was all right to come in."

Both brothers turned towards Mohammed.

"This is true. I was on my way back from Muscat, as you know, when Miss Kingdom called. I gave instructions to let her in," Mohammed confirmed.

"Where's Mike?" Harper asked in a nervy voice.

"We can't find her," the chief inspector replied. "We

presumed that she became frightened and locked herself in the panic room. We can't get an answer, however."

"What frightened her?" Harper continued, trying to make sense of, well, anything.

"Probably the four police officers who burst in. I was looking for the earring in the downstairs rooms while she was doing the same upstairs. She must have heard the commotion and was thinking it was a repeat of what happened before." Chris was looking across at the brothers.

"Obviously, you've tried the intercom with the panic room?" Callum was checking they hadn't just banged on the door. He was remembering his own night inside.

"Yes, and I'm about to send police officers to search outside the villa." This reminded him. "Do you know if there's another way into the panic room? A door? A shaft? A tunnel?"

"Not to our knowledge. Father never mentioned one, but why would he? When we were in there, all we found was a second battery unit behind the first one, but there was no tunnel behind it. The room isn't big." Harper sounded dismissive.

"What happens next?" Callum asked.

"We go on looking. As for the two of you, as you know, I've been instructed to keep you under house arrest here in the villa until the matter of your father's death is resolved. You may have your phones back, but please don't leave the villa or you'll be taken back to a police cell in Muscat ... without your phones."

Mohammed was staring at the sons, willing them not to say anything provocative. It had taken a lot of behind-the-scenes activity by him, as well as the solicitor and the Canadian diplomatic corps, to get this dispensation.

"We're hoping this is cleared up very quickly, Chief Inspector." Harper was getting nervous again.

"So am I," he replied.

"Shall we try to regain some sort of normality? Mohammed, please call Basem and arrange for some refreshments in the lounge." Callum was keen to leave the hall, sit down on a comfortable chair and collect his thoughts.

They had long finished their tea, and after consuming a tray of sandwiches, they had moved on to ordering some more food from the butler while the chief inspector came and went, checking if his officers had found Mike. Almost an hour had passed when there was a further noise outside the front door.

It opened, and a policeman entered, followed closely by a young woman in a dirty black wig and filthy, torn clothes, with blood on her forehead and both knees.

"Ah, Miss Kingdom, you've been found. We were all getting very concerned. Where were you?" The chief inspector stepped towards her from the lounge door.

"I went into the panic room as I thought that the villa was under attack again. I left by a tunnel that I discovered, and I ended up walking through the mountains to a road. These police officers found me and brought me back here."

"Well, as you can see, there's no attack, and everyone is safe."

"Mike, good to see you. We've just been brought back from Muscat and are under house arrest. We'll update you later," Callum said.

"That will be great after I've washed and tidied myself up. May I get some fresh clothes from my suitcase in the car?" She was looking at the chief inspector.

"Of course. I'll see you in the lounge."

Chris walked over and gave her the car keys that he had put in his pocket in case they had needed to make a quick escape. "Do you need help?"

"No, Chris, I'm fine. I'll be back in two minutes." She turned to leave and was accompanied by one of the police officers who had found her walking down the track. While his colleague had searched the gardens inside the perimeter wall, he had walked around the outside and discovered the open hatch. He had walked along the path for five minutes, but he had turned around, deciding that she was heading for the rough road that led up from the coast to the British listening post. It had taken some time to rejoin his colleague, drive down towards the sea and back up the track. Fortunately, she wasn't lost in the mountains but walking down the road towards them.

Mike had collected some clothes and had gone to freshen up in the bedroom she had previously used. In the shower, it became apparent just how dirty and dusty she was. Her knees looked a little better when the blood had been washed off, and after her shower, she luxuriated in the warm, white towels. There was, however, no time to waste. Staring into the large mirror, she knew she could trust no one and should get back to Doha, where Kevin would be waiting for her. She straightened her bright-red wig, the first one she had grabbed from her bag, and prepared to go downstairs. Hopefully, Atropos wasn't going to end somebody's life any time soon. She decided that, when she got back to her cabin in the woods, she would change the three polystyrene heads. Perhaps naming them after the three Fates had been a stupid idea.

———

Shamiram Yonan was still in a safe house in Doha when her phone rang. "Hello?"

"Hello, this is Kevin Stenning. I promised to call you if we discovered anything."

"Hello, Mr Stenning."

"I'm not sure if you're still in Qatar, but I wanted to tell you that the *duplicate* key worked" – he said the word 'duplicate' slowly – "I hope to have the contents here in Doha within twenty-four hours. Perhaps I could give you a *duplicate* set of the documents?" He said the word slowly again.

"Thank you, that would be very kind. What's in them?"

Kevin didn't want to be too specific on the phone, but he wanted to give her an idea of what was inside, if he had understood Mike's message. "I believe it has lots of information about cruises, facilities available on board the ships and where they were built. It also has a letter that's very useful to me in that it includes a name, although it may not be of interest to you." He mentioned the name, but then said no more about that person.

"May I ask you who found this ... these things? Was it a young lady?"

"Yes, it was. She has been most helpful."

"Does she know her life is in danger?"

"She does, and I'm waiting to hear if she's safe. There may be nothing we can do, sadly."

The call ended. Kevin had previously made two other calls after receiving Mike's message. Of these, the second was to Sam Onions at GCHQ on a secure link from the embassy.

"Hello, Kevin."

"I understand that Julie Andrews didn't make an appearance?"

"Oh, fuck off! But you're right, no one turned up as far as I've been told."

"No, I believe she didn't make it. She got close, though. In fact, she's hidden three blue A4 files and an A4 notebook behind a rock just down from the listening post. Gerry from Muscat is on his way now to pick them up, but he'll be five hours or more. Will you send Andy down to collect them urgently and keep them until Gerry turns up? I want them inside our fence ASAP. These are precious, and I don't want to risk anyone else finding them. The local coppers might be getting interested."

"Will do."

The first call had been, not surprisingly, to Kevin's counterpart at the British Embassy in Muscat. Gerry had been standing by the strange water feature in the atrium, which resembled an oversized shower head suspended from the ceiling and discharging into a basin. He walked up to his room while exchanging pleasantries with Kevin on the phone. Once inside, he stood looking out at the manicured gardens illuminated by concealed uplighters under a starry sky while Kevin described the message from Mike and that he needed the files and notebook collected as a top priority and only by Gerry; the contents were too secret to be dealt with by the fifty or so Omanis who worked for the embassy. He explained that he was about to phone Sam Onions, and that Andy should have collected them by the time Gerry got there, but he should check with Andy on the way over. Gerry might have to help find the cache, given that it was night and Kevin had no precise details of where Mike had actually hidden it.

Ten minutes later, Gerry was being driven out of the compound by a colleague in a white four-wheel drive Land Rover Discovery displaying CD (*corps diplomatique*) number plates.

Kevin, having made his calls, was sitting back in his chair. He was thinking about how to contact Leonard without going through any official channels. The man was a complete legend in the secret-squirrel community, but he was also unpredictable. Firstly, Kevin needed to find out where he was after his successful operation in Germany. Leonard's personal phones were now with Mike Kingdom, so that route of communication to him was closed.

Kevin picked up the phone and spoke to one of his counterparts in the US Embassy, seven miles away on 22nd February Street. "This a friendly call to see how Leonard is doing." There was no need to specify which Leonard, everyone assumed you were talking about Leonard de Vries.

"His operation was successful. I don't know the details, but I hear he's left Germany and is recovering at his house in rainy London."

"Great news! I'll send my regards through the usual channels. Are you going to the conference?"

"Sure am. You offering to buy me a beer?"

"Always happy to buy you poor Americans a beer."

After a few more pieces of gentle banter, Kevin was again left in his office mulling over why Leonard was in London and not Washington, DC, and how he might get a personal message to him.

———

To say that the telephone lines between Canada and Oman were humming, metaphorically speaking, would have been an understatement. The Canadian PM had made two calls himself and made it very clear he was being advised that no murder had taken place and that two prominent Canadians were being held against their will; indeed, they were suffering the ignominy of being arrested. The Omanis, for their part, were trying to explain that they suspected a murder had taken place and their procedures needed to be followed. The transfer from the police station cell in Muscat to house arrest in their father's villa had been the first concession; there was about to be a second.

In the villa, the sons, Chris, Mohammed and the chief inspector were taken aback as Mike walked into the lounge in her red Cleopatra wig. Most of them hadn't seen her in anything other than the black one. The fact that it was so geometrically cropped and so vivid stopped all conversation. She had even put moisturising cream on her face, not as a concession to vanity but from a need to rub something soothing into her dry skin. She hadn't really wanted to put on the red wig, but now she had, she was hoping this wasn't a bad omen.

Mohammed stood up. "Would you like some tea?"

She nodded, and he poured. She tried to read the atmosphere in the room, but she couldn't feel anything other than tension.

The chief inspector's phone rang, breaking the silence. He spoke in Arabic, which meant that Mike and the Murchison sons couldn't follow the conversation. Chris, however, could understand, and he burst out smiling and swivelled in his chair to do an understated thumbs up to all three of them.

The call ended.

"That was the Deputy PM. All charges are dropped, and you and your father's body can leave Oman immediately, without restriction. I'm genuinely sorry for any inconvenience caused."

"Chief Inspector, you were only doing your job; we fully understand." Callum was quick to smooth over any cracks and to do anything that eased their departure.

Harper, meanwhile, was on the phone to Jay, asking him to bring the car around ready to take them to Ras Al Khaimah airport, which was the nearest airport *not* in Oman from which they could fly. He wanted to be under any another jurisdiction as fast as possible.

"I presume that Chris and I can leave as well?" Mike enquired.

"Yes, Miss Kingdom. I'm sorry you haven't found your earring. I'm sure that Mohammed will arrange to have it forwarded, if it's ever located." He had a sardonic look on his face. "I must inform the officers and release them from their duties. And, Miss Kingdom, I'm so pleased that my officers found you in one piece this evening; I was personally very worried about your safety." His demeanour had changed subtly as he stood up and left the room.

"I'm leaving Oman never to return," Harper addressed no one in particular. "I don't care how many millions the lawyers cost us, they can sell the lot ... and I mean *the lot*." He looked pointedly at his brother.

"Mike, maybe we can speak another day or meet in London? Now doesn't seem the right moment, but thanks for all you told us and tried to do for us. I'm guessing that you and Chris don't need a lift to the airport as you have a car?" Callum's face had lost some of its tension.

"Thank you. I'll drive us to the airport, and we'll be back in the UK via Doha before you can say, 'Abracadabra.'"

Everyone stood up.

Mohammed looked slightly disgruntled. "May I help any of you with anything?"

"No, thank you, Mohammed; you've been wonderful and without you, I'm sure we would still be in Muscat. Will you liaise with our lawyers and do whatever's needed to get Father's body on the next plane to Vancouver?" Callum requested.

"Of course."

"Let's pick up our few personal things and get in that car within five minutes," Harper said to his brother, and then he left the room.

"Are you ready?" Mike asked Chris.

"More than ready." He stood up awkwardly and followed her out into the hall, where they spoke to the chief inspector.

By the time Mike had put her washbag and clothes back into the suitcase in the boot of the car, Callum and Harper were through the front door and down the steps. Jay was already next to the big Mercedes. There was a round of perfunctory handshakes, and the brothers slid onto the rear seats.

For a brief moment, the last two people left standing outside the vehicles were Jay and Mike who exchanged looks that conveyed so much. The Mercedes sped off first.

CHAPTER THIRTY-TWO

Mike and Chris hadn't said a word and were barely a mile from the villa when a blue Audi pulled across the road in front of them, screeching to a halt.

It happened so fast that she had only enough time to brake and hope for the best. Apart from some suppressed screams, there was silence. Two men dressed in black jeans and bomber jackets jumped out. If Mike had read the manuals, she might have recognised them as the men who had been on their flight from Doha. Chris had read the manuals and should have spotted them earlier in the airport. In that unhurried but efficient way that only professionals can adopt, they motioned for Chris to get out of the car. He looked quickly at Mike, but his face was displaying no emotion; if anything, it was frozen.

Leaning forwards slightly, Mike sat gripping the steering wheel.

The two men approached the car and opened the front passenger door. Chris fell out of the car, half pulled and half pushed onto the tarmac. One of the men slammed the passenger door shut, shouting and waving at Mike to drive off. With the heightened emotions of the moment, there was no time for a calm and logical analysis, so she simply obeyed. By reversing six feet, she could then swing out around the Audi and drive down the hill towards the junction with the cement works and port access road.

For a minute or so, she drove with most of her attention on her rear-view mirror. In truth, whatever was taking place behind her was happening in the dark and wasn't that easily discernible. All around her, there was a general lack of noise and an emptiness that didn't reflect the chaos and confusion. Completely disorientated, she pulled into a passing bay and got out of the car, looking back up the slope.

She was just in time to see Chris's limp body, illuminated by the headlights of the Audi, being carried to the barrier and flung over and to hear it cascade down the rocky slope, bouncing and somersaulting into the sea. Afterwards, there was an eerie silence, apart from a low background hum from the works and the gentle crash of waves on the shingle shore.

Distraught and breathing heavily, she got back into the car, trying to make sense of everything. Her heart would not slow down, and in her mind, she was replaying the last few weeks, for which everything was in desperate need of reinterpretation. Why had she not spotted the clues earlier?

With a casual disregard for just about everything, including her own health, she drove as fast as she could around the bends through the foothills until the gradients lessened and she joined other vehicles making their way across the coastal plain.

After one and half hours, as the signs for Ras Al Khaimah airport appeared, she still hadn't stopped shaking completely.

When she finally arrived at the counter where she had rented the Volvo, she paid no attention to the tall girl in the uniform whose English hadn't been improved by repeating the same few sentences every day at speed. Not even concentrating on the paperwork, Mike signed where directed and handed over the keys of the car. Unaware of either her surroundings or the handful of passengers at that time of night, she pushed her luggage on a trolley into the terminal.

With enough material to fuel her nightmares for a lifetime, she caught the last flight to Doha.

———

Over breakfast at her hotel the next day, she was still replaying the events over and over again. It was a beautiful Saturday morning, and a taxi was going to come at 9.00am to take her to the British Embassy. Sleep had been hard to find, with constant images in her mind of a body bouncing down a rockface into the moonlit Persian Gulf; each time, the details were embellished.

What had just happened? A numbness had spread through her, and she could no longer feel any emotion. Perhaps this was self-protection?

She was on automatic pilot as the hotel staff loaded her suitcases into the taxi and she instructed the driver to take her to the British Embassy on Al Shabab Street. The journey passed in a blur.

It transpired that turning up at the embassy entrance with two suitcases tested the system to the limit as there was a lack of storage space and she had to have both of them searched, scanned and swabbed before she could be escorted, for the third time, across to the main block and up the stairs. At his office door, Kevin was standing waiting to greet her, the sleeves of his white shirt rolled up and his striped tie loosened. He gave her a warm hug that she, rather out of character, both needed and enjoyed. She was feeling very alone in the world.

In his office was a woman in a thin, mauve trouser suit who was introduced as Yolanda, Kevin's boss.

"He's dead," is all Mike said, once she had accepted the offer to take a seat.

"What?" Yolanda and Kevin spoke in unison.

"When I left the villa, driving the hire car, we'd only travelled a mile when a car blocked our way. Two men got out, dragged Chris out of the car onto the tarmac and told me to drive off. I stopped at the bottom of that part of the hill to see what happened, and" – she stopped as she ran it through her mind for the umpteenth time – "they threw him down the rockface into the sea."

"Oh, that's awful." Yolanda was probably incapable of sounding completely sympathetic, but it was a good attempt.

"Have you any idea who they were?" Kevin asked, looking at her inquisitively through his tortoiseshell glasses.

"No, they looked like Arabs in Western dress. I can't remember any distinguishing features. It was dark."

They stopped while drinks were brought in and resumed with Kevin asking her to tell them what happened from when she had locked herself in the panic room. She described crawling out through the tunnel, the frustration of crawling back inside and the relief of clambering back out again. Mike said how annoyed she was at not trying the word 'DUPLICATE' as the code word, given that it was on the label attached to the key, for heaven's sake.

Kevin interrupted to ask what BlueStar had said when she had given her intermediary the key originally.

"Chris was the intermediary; it was him who found her and visited her. It was him who she gave the key to and, I'm guessing, gave the password to. Of course, he never told me it; he just said that he had been given a key. I'm sorry I never told you about him, but ... well, I didn't know at that stage whether I could trust you."

"He needed you to get him into the villa because he wanted you to find Habib's records and files. You do know that he would have killed you and destroyed all trace of the stuff in the safe?" Yolanda said. "He guessed that he was mentioned that material somewhere."

"When I saw his name in the notebook, I was so scared. I couldn't believe it. He was such a good actor."

"You were mad to get in the hire car with him," Yolanda stated, only voicing what Mike knew to be true.

"But he didn't know I'd found it. I kept that from everyone. It was just that I didn't know if I could trust anybody: The police? Mohammed? The Murchisons? My world had just been turned upside down."

"You did brilliantly." Kevin's dimples had reappeared, and his voice was at its most reassuring.

"Who was he working for?" Mike was still unsure.

"The Iranians, as you will have guessed. They had identified Habib as a Western source and were about to take him out," Kevin explained, "and when I say 'Western source', I mean Leonard's source. Habib was getting nervous and wanted to give the safe key and code to BlueStar in case anything happened to him. That's why he flew to Doha personally to hand them over. He had called Leonard out to the villa to give him the files and notebook – again, personally – as he couldn't risk transferring them by any other means because he knew he was compromised and there was probably a rotten apple in the basket somewhere."

"Why didn't they kill me when they killed Chris?"

"Chris wasn't killed by the Iranians who were worried that his cover had been blown; it was the Assyrian network," Kevin clarified.

"How did they know Chris was the 'bad apple', as you call him?"

"Because I told BlueStar once you'd messaged me from the track near the listening post. Of course, I didn't know that Chris had actually accompanied you to the villa. Fortunately, Shamiram had those two men watching the place – or at least nearby. They were there if necessary to try to get the files themselves or from anyone who retrieved them."

Here, Kevin was slightly awry as he didn't realise that Blue-Star was suspicious that Chris had been part of the explosion at her optician's shop and was having him followed by two colleagues on the same flight to Ras Al Khaimah as Mike and Chris.

"So, it was Chris who instigated the bombing of the optician's?"

"Yes, of course, and once he had the key and code word, she was a prime target to be removed. The Iranians must have been thrilled that he had found her and had his hands on the key and code. The Assyrians are a pain in the backside of Tehran," Kevin said.

He took a sip and continued, "The files and notebook have been retrieved overnight by my colleagues in Oman; they'll be here soon. They've looked at them, and the files will be of interest to the Assyrians and to all of us in Five Eyes. They give us shedloads of information on the Iranian navy and their ship/armament designs and plans. The notebook, as you grasped from your quick look, covers the spying network that Iran has in the west. Of course, your eyes fell on Chris Crippen's name."

"Was the Murchison boys' crypto farm a target?"

"We're checking that out," Yolanda said, "but I suspect it was organised crime rather than the Iranians, but it's possible."

"By the way," Kevin said, "I checked up on Leonard; his operation was successful, and he's back in London."

"What? London? That man! I could ..."

The look that appeared on Mike's face, framed by the bright-red wig, made Yolanda rock back on her heels.

———

It was a glorious September day in rural Oxfordshire. Columns of midges rose and fell in the shafts of sunshine and a red kite flopped lazily in the thermals above the coniferous woodland, having gorged itself at the local landfill site.

In her cabin, Mike was playing with the two brass keys attached to their identical tags and thinking what might have been if only she had known that the first one had come from Habib. Life really is all about timing.

The rural idyll was disturbed by the sound of a vehicle outside; she didn't get visitors. It was three weeks after her return to England, and the noise of a large delivery van below her cabin broke the peace and quiet of the pine forest.

Two men opened the back doors and called up to Mike as she stepped outside onto the landing, wondering what was happening: "Michaela Kingdom, Forester's Lodge?"

"Yes," she replied, as if there were another property that could be confused with hers.

They began to carry a wooden crate up the external stairs. It was clearly heavy, and the man leading had to lean over and walk up backwards, puffing and panting.

They deposited it in her room, obtained the necessary signature and took the obligatory photograph. She was left staring at what she hoped wasn't a Trojan horse. As she stepped back outside, the van was still manoeuvring so it could drive back down the track. They both waved at her, but she was preoccupied with finding her jemmy and screwdrivers. These were to be located in her toolbox behind the tractor under the cabin. The van was disappearing from view as she climbed back up to her front door. Her excitement was building. After the removal of six large screws, she levered the wooden lid open to reveal a mass of shredded paper in which was a bubble-wrapped object.

It was the statue of *The Running Man*.

She stood it in the centre of the room and burst into tears.

A note from Callum and Harper thanked her for all her hard work trying to save them and to further their father's clandestine objectives. When she had taken a call from their PA, who had phoned a week earlier to ask for an address so the brothers might send her a small gift, she had no idea what this might be. She had worried it might be a case of wine, which she didn't drink.

Small gift? It was worth more than her cabin, the nearby cottage and half of the houses in the next hamlet.

For the rest of the day, she looked at it, touched it, moved it, researched it on the net, and generally forgot about her life and the traumas it inevitably seemed to contain.

———

Seven days later, her phone had rung while she was transferring her wigs to three new metal stands; the polystyrene heads had been consigned to the bin. Clotho, Lachesis and Atropos had been, quite obviously, a mistake. You really, really should not tempt the Fates. Once was too often.

"Hello, Tom! It's lovely to hear from you." Mike was eternally grateful for everything he had done, all beyond the call of duty. The conversation had ended with, "Yes, I would love to meet you for lunch."

And now, here she was, on an early September's day, in a lovely bistro in Chiswick on the western edge of London that she had frequented years ago while at Five Eyes. It was a blonde-wig day, a new beginning perhaps, and she had a smile on her face. The trauma of her recent trip around the UAE, Qatar and Oman was fading, and it was gradually being replaced by happier thoughts. The street's trees were still a deep green and casting a dappled shade on the pedestrians outside the restaurant window.

Tom arrived and they hugged for a long time, removing the

need to say a thousand words about what they had both been through and how dependent they had been on each other's support.

"S-So pleased you're s-safe," Tom began. He wasn't privy to most of what happened, but he seemed to have the general picture.

"I'm home and happy. How are you? How is your new boss?"

"S-She's great. S-She took over a difficult s-situation. We're b-back to normal."

"Was it ever normal under Leonard?"

Tom didn't answer, instead a voice sounded behind her.

"Mind if I join you?" A middle-aged man wearing a clean but unironed white shirt pulled out a chair and sat down.

Tom mouthed the word 'sorry'.

"What?" Mike was dumbfounded, "I thought you were going to be suspended across the Pond?"

"Nah, false alarm, and don't blame Tom; I asked him to arrange lunch. I knew you wouldn't come if I called you."

"Run out of dubious anagrams? But, honestly, if I'd known, I would have brought your suitcase. I've lugged the damn thing halfway around the Middle East."

He relaxed into his chair, having been initially nervous about the encounter. "So that's where it went. I'm sure that Señor de Valderi will be most grateful. He's running out of pants."

"Has anybody asked you whether you spend your life working out anagrams of your name?"

"No, not all the time ... only when I'm hallucinating from anaesthetics or lack of food."

"If that was for sympathy, you failed ... but you have lost a lot of surplus fat, I have to say."

Tom was pleased to have prime seats at the equivalent of the Wimbledon final, but he had no intention of taking part.

"They took out most of my insides in Germany."

She shook her head. "They threw away the wrong bits."

He ignored her. "And they tell me I have to eat little and often."

"As opposed to a lot and often?"

They broke off to read the menus and to order salads for Tom and Mike, a steak and kidney pie and chips for Leonard, a bottle of red wine from Cahors, and some bread and olives. Fortunately, the tables near them were all empty, apart from a couple of old ladies who were already seated when they had arrived. They felt they could talk relatively freely.

"Was pretending to be ill part of your plan?" Mike asked.

"Was it hell! Why didn't you answer my call in my hour of need?"

Mike's relatively calm demeanour was disappearing fast. "What? You—"

"When you didn't answer, I could only think of Kevin. I couldn't call any of our guys because I wasn't meant to be there. I was supposed to be on my way to Washington to face the music. They had worked out that the leaks had come from my office over the previous five years."

"At The Greedy Pelican, did you know or suspect that it was Chris?"

"Of course; he was one of the many possibilities. I wanted you to check him out."

"*What?* I nearly died."

"You nearly died? I nearly died. Join the club." He had what might pass for a smile on his face. "You would never have gone out to the Middle East otherwise. Chris was going out there anyway."

She was shaking her head while inwardly conceding that he had played her yet again. "Going to see Habib wasn't part of the plan, though, was it?"

"No, he called me just after we met at The Greedy Pelican."

He paused while a waiter uncorked the wine and asked Leonard to taste it. The waiter poured a glass for Leonard while Tom and Mike declined. The waiter left. "No, that was the worst timing of my life. Cam and Mary were unbelievable ... as was BlueStar, but I never knew her. Hopefully, she and her friends will reappear once the dust has settled."

"Are Langley still after your ass?"

"No, why would they be? I sorted it all out, and I got them all the stuff in the blue files and notebook. They were impressed. I put in a good word for you, by the way." He took a big swig of wine and popped two olives in his mouth.

"You? You got them all the stuff? Jesus Christ!"

"Hey, I just said that I put in a good word for you. They were wondering if you would like to come back full time here in London, working for me."

"What? What, are you mad? No."

"I bet that, by the time I've eaten my pie, you say yes."

"No."

"It hasn't arrived yet. Boy, the service is slow here. Tom, why did you pick this place?"

"I can p-pronounce its name."

"Fair enough. I should give The Greedy Pelican a miss, if I were you."

Mike glared at him intensely and was about to say something.

"What? *What?* I meant because the food is crap. Ah, here comes my pie. Made up your mind yet?"

ACKNOWLEDGMENTS

I would like to begin by declaring my debt to the late Gerald Pollinger who, with his father, was agent to Graham Greene among others. He represented me in the late 1990s and his support and advice were invaluable, particularly as I began to write the Mike Kingdom series; he never lived to see *The Tip of the Iceberg* completed.

Further thanks go to my wife, Natasha, and my sister, Angela, who have shouldered the burden of reading my first drafts.

All three of the Mike Kingdom thrillers have been edited by Lindsay Corten and she still has not changed her name and moved abroad. I hear her voice in my ear even as I write this. She has been the most wonderful critical friend.

Jem Butcher has produced the stunning covers for the series picking up on all of the subtleties as only a gifted designer can.

My thanks go to Adrian Hobart and Rebecca Collins at Hobeck Books whose advice, support and friendship are what every writer needs. It only took me twenty-nine years to find them.

Finally, a big thank you to the reviewers and bloggers who have all been so generous and who have, unwittingly, given me the strength to follow Mike Kingdom wherever she takes me.

DAVID JARVIS

ABOUT THE AUTHOR

David Jarvis went to art college, and then ran his design and planning practice for forty years, working all over the world. He ended up planning countries. His canvases just got bigger and bigger.

HOBECK BOOKS – THE HOME OF GREAT STORIES

We hope you've enjoyed reading this novel by David Jarvis. To keep up to date on David's fiction writing please do follow him on Twitter/X, BlueSky or Instagram.

Hobeck Books offers a number of short stories and novellas, free for subscribers in the compilation *Crime Bites*.

- *Echo Rock* by Robert Daws
- *Old Dogs, Old Tricks* by AB Morgan
- *The Silence of the Rabbit* by Wendy Turbin
- *Never Mind the Baubles: An Anthology of Twisted Winter Tales* by the Hobeck Team (including many of the Hobeck authors and Hobeck's two publishers)
- *The Clarice Cliff Vase* by Linda Huber
- *Here She Lies* by Kerena Swan
- *The Macnab Principle* by R.D. Nixon
- *Fatal Beginnings* by Brian Price
- *A Defining Moment* by Lin Le Versha
- *Saviour* by Jennie Ensor
- *You Can't Trust Anyone These Days* by Maureen Myant

Also please visit the Hobeck Books website for details of our other superb authors and their books, and if you would like to get in touch, we would love to hear from you.

Hobeck Books also presents a weekly podcast, the Hobcast, where founders Adrian Hobart and Rebecca Collins discuss all things book related, key issues from each week, including the ups and downs of running a creative business. Each episode includes an interview with one of the people who make Hobeck possible: the editors, the authors, the cover designers. These are the people who help Hobeck bring great stories to life. Without them, Hobeck wouldn't exist. The Hobcast can be listened to from all the usual platforms but it can also be found on the Hobeck website: **www.hobeck.net/hobcast**.

ALSO BY DAVID JARVIS

The Mike Kingdom Thrillers
The Tip of the Iceberg
This Is Not a Pipe
The Violin and Candlestick

The Collation Unit